CARIBBEAN RESCUE

COASTAL FURY BOOK 16

MATT LINCOLN

PROLOGUE

IT WAS the height of summer in Miami, and the *Rolling Thunder* was packed. The beaches were crowded with families that had descended upon Miami in droves as soon as school had let out, and even my own bar, usually frequented only by older professionals and retirees, was bustling with new faces. Among them were more than a few haggard-looking dads who had likely slipped away to have a drink and a few minutes of peace, at least according to Mike.

"What do you think?" Mike asked me as he nodded toward a man sitting at the other end of the bar, steadily draining a pint of strong beer. "That safari hat he's wearing screams 'dad,' don't you think? Only people with like four kids wear stuff like that."

"Don't you have anything better to do?" I asked, as I moved to refill his own pint. "Why are you always here? Shouldn't you be off golfing or doing whatever it is that retired people do?"

Mike was the former owner of the *Rolling Thunder,* though back when it was under his control, it was a tacky, tiki-themed shack known as *Mike's Tropical Tango Hut.* Nevertheless, even after selling it to me, it felt like he was still here all the time.

"I could ask you the same thing," he countered as he took a sip of his beer. "Rhoda and Nadia handle everything here pretty well. You retired from MBLIS, and yet here you are every day."

"This is my bar," I retorted as I took a look around the place I'd lovingly transformed from a kitschy dive into a place people might actually enjoy drinking at. "But yeah, I guess you're right."

MBLIS, or the Military Border Liaison Investigative Services, was the name of the government agency that I had spent most of my life working for. It had already been a few years since I'd retired and taken over the bar, but I'd have been lying if I said I didn't miss those days sometimes, especially when my favorite group of kids stopped by to hassle me for a story about the good old days. Even after I'd retired, the idea of spending all of my time lounging around just didn't appeal to me. I'd always been drawn to action and adrenaline, and though the bar wasn't exactly the most high-energy place, it was certainly better than spending all of my time lazing around.

"'Course I'm right," Mike replied. "And besides, it's fun trying to people-read, don't you think? Now, look at that guy and tell me he didn't come to Miami with his wife and four kids."

I rolled my eyes at his antics, but looked over at the man, anyway. He was wearing one of those wide-brimmed hats with the flap that comes down the back to protect your neck from getting sunburned. He was also wearing a pair of khaki shorts and a painfully ugly blue and yellow tropical-patterned button-down over a plain white t-shirt. His outfit definitely screamed tourist, but it was the wedding band on his finger and the fanny pack strapped around his waist that made me think that Mike's assessment might be right.

"Yeah, I could see that." I shrugged as I poured myself a pint of my own. If I was going to play this silly game with Mike, I might as well enjoy it. "I don't know, though. He might just be married."

"Nah." Mike shook his head confidently. "New-lywed guys don't dress like that. That right there is a man who has changed diapers."

"How would you know?" I laughed before taking a sip of my beer.

"I ran a bar for *decades,*" Mike replied confidently. "You see all kinds working this kind of job. At this point, I can tell about a hundred things about a person with a single glance. Just give it a few years running this place, you'll be able to read people with just a look, too."

"Whatever you say, Mike." I smiled at him as I took another sip of my beer.

Even though it was busy, most of the crowd tonight was on the older side and relatively calm. It was nothing like some of the trendier places along the beach, which would no doubt be filled with college students and kids from the nearby base. It was calm enough that I could humor Mike for a little while longer while he pointed out which customers were *definitely* fathers because of some minuscule detail about their clothing or appearance.

"You ever wish you'd given it a try?" Mike asked me a little wistfully.

"What?" I snorted. "Entertaining myself by

making up wild backstories for random strangers? Can't say I have."

"No," he scoffed as he drained the last of his current pint. "You know, the easy life. Actual retirement. Vacations that don't involve getting into gunfights with international crime lords."

"I think you might be going senile in your old age," I deadpanned. Honestly, I didn't think I'd ever be the kind of guy to just... do nothing.

"You're a smart-ass," Mike snorted.

"I learned from the best," I countered as I moved to refill his pint again.

We continued with our antics through several pints, until the sun was starting to go down, and by then, it was getting late enough that the bar was starting to dwindle down to my regulars.

"Where's your fan club today?" Mike asked, as he lifted the glass to his lips.

"The kids from the base?" I clarified. "Haven't seen them in a few days."

"Huh," Mike remarked with surprise. "Seems like they're always here. At least, any time I happen to stop by. Feels a lot quieter without them around."

As if on cue, the door to the bar burst open, and Ty's boisterous voice filled the bar.

"Spoke too soon," Mike chuckled as he turned to look at the group.

Ty, Charlie, Jeff, and Mac were all laughing and chatting animatedly as they walked through the bar to their usual booth. They were all decked out in swimwear, and judging by their wet hair and sandy clothes, I assumed they'd just come back from the beach.

"Hey, kids," I greeted as I approached them with a tray of drinks. I knew all of their usual orders by heart now, they were here so often. "Looks like you had a fun day."

"Yeah." Jeff grinned. "We had the day off, all of us. It's the first time in a while all of us had off on the same day, so we decided to hit the beach while it was nice out."

"I'm glad to hear you had a good time," I replied as I distributed the drinks. "And that you didn't run straight here. You guys should have some fun on your days off instead of hanging around this place all day."

"Aw, you know you love us." Mac smirked before taking a sip of her drink.

I'd be lying if I said I didn't. I definitely had a soft spot for this group of kids, and I really enjoyed having an audience to tell my stories to.

"Hey, where's your drink?" Charlie as me as I finished passing around their orders.

"What?" I raised a confused eyebrow at him.

"Come on." He flashed me a lopsided smile. "You have to tell us the next part of the story!"

I smiled back as I realized what he was getting at.

"And don't try to give us any excuses about being busy!" Ty chimed in. "We saw you chatting with Mike at the bar just now."

"Alright, hold your horses." I lifted a hand to stop him. "I didn't say no. Just give me a minute to get myself a drink."

"Yes!" Charlie exclaimed excitedly.

Honestly, it was a pretty nice stroke to my ego to have these kids so excited to hear about my stories. It had gotten to the point that I actually looked forward to their visits.

"I'm glad it's so chill in here," Mac remarked as I sat down at their booth with my own drink. "The beach was fun, but during the summer, the number of tourists around can get a little overwhelming, especially all the kids."

"What's wrong with kids?" Ty asked as he took a sip of his beer.

"Nothing, really," Mac shrugged. "I mean, I like kids fine. I've babysat my niece a few times, but I'm not so thrilled when there are hundreds of them running around screaming."

"Yeah, the beach was really crowded," Jeff agreed with a nod. "It's nice to be able to relax in here."

"Well, I'm glad my bar is useful to you," I chuckled.

"Anyway," Charlie interjected impatiently. "About that story? You had just wrapped up the case with the Hollands, right? And you found out that they had just been messing with you about all the *Dragon's Rogue* stuff?"

I raised my eyebrows at him, a little impressed. I could always count on Charlie to catch everyone up with where the story had left off. The kid had some memory.

"Speaking of the *Dragon's Rogue*," Jeff cut in, "You said you were going to tell us about the anchor."

"That's right!" Ty exclaimed as he turned to look at the large anchor mounted on the wall just to the right of where we were sitting. "You told us last time that this is the anchor from the *Dragon's Rogue*, right? So you found it? What happened?"

"And the *chest!*" Jeff chimed in. "That one that you found in the sunken pirate ship. You didn't tell us what was in there!"

"Slow down," I replied, unable to hide my smile

at the eager looks on their faces. "Yes, I did find the anchor pretty soon after we closed the Holland case, but it was still a while before I found the ship itself."

"Wait, but... how?" Charlie sighed with frustration. "How does an anchor just become disconnected from its ship?"

"We'll get to it," I assured him. "To be honest, it was a while yet before I found the ship, though the search did end up ramping up in part due to what I found inside the chest."

"Okay," Jeff replied anxiously as he sat up straighter. "So, what happened next?

"Well, first there was the anchor," I answered as I thought about the best point to start the story from. "To explain how I got my hands on it, I first need to tell you about how we ended up getting involved in a twenty-year-old cold case."

"Whoa," Mac muttered. "How'd that happen?"

"Well," I began as I took a long sip of my drink in preparation, "it all started with a little boy that was found wandering alone on the beach."

1

THE SUN WAS SHINING bright and hot above her as she made her way quickly across the beach. The sand felt warm and soft beneath her feet. She wasn't wearing any shoes. She'd jumped into action the moment an opportunity had presented itself, so she hadn't had time to put any on before leaving.

All around her, people were enjoying their time on the beach. Her heart pounded forcefully as she passed them by, unable to shake the feeling that they were all watching her. It was the height of tourist season, so the shore was packed. Couples stretched out along beach towels, overpriced drinks clutched in their hands. Families played near the edge of the water, anxious parents careful not to let their small children drift too far away.

Her own fist tightened around the tiny hand clenched in hers. She looked down at the little boy at her side, stumbling across the uneven sand as quickly as his little legs would let him. He was shorter than he should have been at this age, and she felt intense sorrow over that fact. She'd do better by him, though. As soon as they were free, she'd make sure he got the life she'd never had a chance at.

"Picture? Picture?" She flinched as a tall man holding a camera suddenly approached her, his white teeth bared in a friendly smile.

He must have thought she was a tourist. She certainly looked like one, with her blond hair and blue eyes. Her son, too, though his own skin was several shades darker, was sporting a mop of gorgeous yellow ringlets. Anyone who saw them here, walking barefoot along the beach, would have immediately assumed they were just another pair of tourists enjoying a nice day out.

"No, thank you." She smiled stiffly before scooping her son up into her arms and walking briskly away from the man. She was certain that she'd seen him around before, selling photos to tourists. If she recognized him, then there was a good chance he might recognize her, and she absolutely could not let that happen.

She realized suddenly, as she made her way further down the beach, that she actually didn't know what to do now. The moment she'd noticed that the usual guard was busy fooling around with Joanie, she'd grabbed Eddy out of bed and booked it. Now that she was out here, though, she wasn't sure what to do next.

She didn't have any money. Hell, she'd left without even getting any shoes. And it wasn't as though she could ask anyone for help. This entire area was *their* turf, so there was no telling who she could trust.

Before she could decide, she heard a shout tear across the beach.

"Where the hell are you?!" a gruff voice screamed from behind her.

A chill ran through her as every muscle in her body tensed at the call. She hugged Eddy tighter against her chest as she chanced a look backward. It only took her a moment to spot the guard, Antonio, standing at the edge of the boardwalk. He was scowling, his face twisted into a vicious snarl as he quickly scanned the area, looking for her.

She turned around before he could spot her and took off in a random direction. She didn't know where she was going, but she couldn't let Antonio catch her. She couldn't go back, not after she'd finally summoned the courage to leave. There was no telling what they would do to her if they managed to drag her back, or worse, what they might do to Eddy.

The crowd was thicker here, and the faces of the people around her all seemed to blur together as she shoved her way through.

"Where do you think you're going?" Antonio's voice roared again, now just inches behind her.

She yelped as a thick set of fingers curled around her arm. He gripped her hard enough that she was certain it would leave bruises.

She snapped her head around to look at him. How had he caught up to her? He'd been on the other end of the beach just seconds ago, hadn't he?

She noticed that several people around them had stopped what they were doing and were now staring in their direction.

"Stop!" she screamed as she attempted to twist her arm out of his grip. She looked around at the crowd pleadingly. Maybe one of them would help her. "Let me go!"

"Shut your mouth," Antonio sneered as he tightened his grip.

She winced in pain. It felt as though her bones were about to snap.

"Hey, man," a blond, broad-shouldered stranger barked as he approached them. "What's the problem?"

She looked up at the newcomer, a mixture of shock and relief blooming in her eyes.

"Mind your own business," Antonio growled as he attempted to yank her away by the arm.

"You're making it my business," the blond man replied as he shoved Antonio away from her. He had an American accent and stood about a head taller than Antonio. "The lady told you to let her go, didn't she?"

"Hey, what's going on here?" a different man interjected as he stepped between Antonio and the woman. By now, more people had turned to watch the confrontation, and for the first time in a long time, she felt as though someone was actually on her side.

"Get out of my way!" Antonio snapped as he attempted to push past the men.

"Yo, you need to chill," the second man replied.

"She's holding a kid, man. What do you think you're doing?"

"Yeah!" another voice chimed in, female this time.

More and more people began to come to her defense, and for just a moment, she felt as though she might actually make it out of there.

Then she spotted the other men approaching, and the moment ended.

She couldn't stay there. As well-meaning as these people might be, they had no idea what they were up against. She made a split-second decision and fled while Antonio was distracted.

She sprinted now, tearing across the beach as fast as she could. The muscles in her legs ached, but she couldn't slow down. She wouldn't get another opportunity like this.

She looked frantically around as she ran, desperately searching for some place to hide. There was nothing, though. Just a long stretch of open beach, interrupted only by the occasional stall or hut selling local street food or tacky souvenirs.

Then she saw her chance.

A couple of tourists were stepping unsteadily off a small fishing boat, wide smiles spread across their faces. Helping them back onto the dock was a handsome young man with tanned skin and dark, curly hair. She recognized him. She'd seen him giving tourists rides in his boats before, and sometimes he rented them out too.

Before she even registered what she was doing, she began to walk toward the dock.

"So, how much for the day?" She heard the tourist couple ask the boat-owner as they finally made it off of the boat and onto the dock.

"Well, normally, my prices are fixed," the handsome boat owner replied. "But for such a darling couple such as yourselves, I'll give you a good discount."

They were still laughing as she slunk her way quickly past them. She clambered onto the boat as quickly as she could, before anyone could stop her.

"Oh, um, excuse me," the boat owner muttered, clearly confused by her actions.

She ignored him and set Eddy down before moving toward the helm.

"Don't move, okay?" she called quietly over her shoulder to him. He didn't respond to her, just sat still where she'd left him, which wasn't unusual. He was a quiet child. Too quiet, to be honest, and it broke her heart that he had grown up to be like this. It was okay, though. They'd be gone from here soon to somewhere far away where he could grow up like a normal little boy.

She gave him a small smile before turning to examine the boat controls. The key was still in the ignition switch.

She'd ridden on a boat like this once, a long, long time ago. Her own parents had rented one, just like the nice couple behind her had intended to do. She'd sat on her father's lap, and he'd let her push the throttle. She could still remember the joy she'd felt as they'd zoomed across the water that day. The last day she ever saw her parents.

"Hey, stop!" the boat owner yelled as she pushed the throttle all the way forward, the same way she'd done back then. He ran down the dock toward the boat, but it was already accelerating away.

She gasped as the boat took off at an alarming speed. She held the steering wheel nervously. She'd never even driven a car before. As if there was a chance the men would have let her.

A split second later, a loud bang resonated through the air, and Eddy screamed.

She let go of the wheel and turned around. The first thing she saw was Antonio standing on the edge of the dock and aiming his gun up at her.

"Eddy!" she screamed as she crouched down to

examine him. He was crying, but to her relief, it seemed as though he was uninjured. He must have just been frightened by the loud noise. There was a small hole in the hull of the boat just a few inches away from him, and she shuddered at the thought that he'd come that close to being hit.

She peered back up over the edge of the boat. Antonio was just a small dot in the distance now, and growing smaller by the second.

"Just lie down for a little while, okay?" she crooned as she kissed the top of the boy's head and gently eased him onto the floor of the boat. She wished now that she'd at least thought to bring a blanket or something for him. The weather was clear and hot right now, but it would start getting dark in just a few hours.

He did as she said without offering any resistance, and she felt a pang of frustration at how obedient he was. She'd seen other children his age on the beach before. They were always rowdy, running around and screaming and pitching fits when their parents tried to drag them away from their fun. Eddy wasn't like that at all.

As she got back up to return to the helm, she told herself that it would be okay. Once they were somewhere safe, Eddy would have the chance to do all of those things, too. They just had to wait a little while longer.

For a few minutes, it didn't seem real. It wasn't until she looked back and realized that the entire island was nothing but a black spot in the distance that she allowed herself to relax, a bubble of broken laughter rising out of her.

She'd done it. She'd really done it. After years of suffering in that living hell, she'd finally escaped.

They were free.

2

OLIVIA

SPECIAL AGENT OLIVIA HASTINGS sighed as she made her way down the long hallway, the heels of her shoes clicking against the linoleum flooring as she moved. As a senior agent for the Special Victims department of the FBI's Miami Division, she was unfortunately all too familiar with these types of crimes. It never got any easier to deal with child victims, though. It was always extra heartbreaking when an innocent child suffered as a result of someone else's actions, and Olivia was certain there was an especially painful place in Hell for the kind of people that hurt kids.

Once again, she'd been called in to assist in a case involving a child. What was peculiar about this case was that no one seemed to be sure exactly what kind of crime had been committed. Something had obviously happened since, according to the preliminary report she'd received, the boy had been found malnourished, filthy, and covered with burns. At best, it was a case of severe neglect, and at worst, well, Olivia supposed that it was up to her to find out.

The weather in Miramar, Florida, was both hot and humid that day, and Olivia found herself regretting the choice to wear a jacket that morning the moment she stepped outside. They were called the Miami division, but really they were located about half an hour north of the oceanside paradise most people envisioned when they pictured Miami. Miramar was far enough inland that they ended up with all the uncomfortable mugginess of Florida without any of the pretty scenery.

Weather like this always made her feel sluggish and grumpy, so she hurried across the parking lot to her car. She wasted no time in turning the AC on the moment she got inside, and she let out a sigh of relief as soon as the ice-cold air hit her.

She spent the drive over to the police station taking slow, calming breaths. She'd been doing this job for nearly a decade now, and she was damned good at it, but she'd have been lying if she'd said that the cases didn't sometimes get to her. How could they not, when so many of them involved innocent, helpless, vulnerable people experiencing things no one should ever have to go through? It was important to know how to remain calm and collected. She owed that much to the victims that relied on her.

The report that her boss had given her had been frustratingly vague.

"They don't have a lot to go on yet," her director had told her. "But since the victim is an unaccompanied minor who appears to have been abused, it falls under our jurisdiction."

Now that she was here, she was really hoping that someone would be able to clue her in a little.

"Agent Hastings?" a nervous-looking man with wiry hair and thick glasses called out to her as soon as she stepped through the doors of the station.

"That's me," she replied with a nod.

"Hi." The man smiled awkwardly. "I'm Detective Levi Brownstone. I spoke with your director on the phone earlier."

"I see," Olivia replied as she reached out to shake the man's hand. "I don't suppose you could fill me in a little about the case? The details you gave us over the phone were pretty scarce."

"Ah, yes, sorry," the detective mumbled. "That's

the thing. I don't really have many more details to give."

"What do you mean?" Olivia asked.

"Well, we can't find anything." Levi shrugged as he led Olivia further into the station. "And I mean *anything.* After getting him checked out at the hospital... he's fine by the way, other than the sunburns... we took footprints, fingerprints, dental scans, and even a DNA sample, but everything came back negative so far."

"Everything?" Olivia raised an eyebrow at him. It wasn't all that unusual, she supposed, considering a kid would be less likely to have any kind of government record. Kids don't have driver's licenses, jobs, passports, or criminal records, so it wasn't too unusual that nothing came up. Still, in today's world of social media and digital technology, it was weird for there to be absolutely nothing.

"We even ran a facial scan." Levi shrugged. "Though, to be honest, that kind of technology is still pretty experimental. We weren't able to find any birth or school records either, and when we input his suspected age and physical description into the missing person's database, we didn't get a result there either."

"That's... strange." Olivia frowned.

"Yeah, it really is." Levi nodded. "It's like he just popped out of nowhere. As for the kid's medical condition, it's all over the place."

"How do you mean?" Olivia asked as they came to a stop in front of a door.

"Well, you know how I said 'suspected' age?" he replied. "Well, the doc that examined him says it's difficult to tell, but that he thinks the kid is around five or six years old. They thought he was younger at first, though, because he's barely three feet tall, and apparently, his bone growth is pretty stunted."

"So it's evident this is a case of long-term neglect," Olivia muttered coldly.

"Seems that way." Levi nodded. "What's more, the kid barely talks. I thought he was a toddler the first time I spoke to him since he just talks in one-word sentences."

"What about the people that called the police?" Olivia asked. "I heard it was a young couple."

"Yeah, a couple of teenagers," Levi confirmed. "I guess they were out on a date when the kid just walked right up to them."

"Any reason to suspect them?" Olivia asked, though she doubted a pair of kids were involved.

"Nah," Levi sighed. "I thought that too, til I saw the two of them. If the kid is really five, like the doctor thinks, then I seriously doubt he's theirs. The girl seemed pretty shaken up too."

"Alright." Olivia nodded. "Let me talk to him."

Levi opened the door and led her inside. She was relieved to see that it wasn't an interrogation room, but rather something that looked like a small break room. The boys in blue could be a little dense when it came to handing special victims, and she'd been genuinely concerned that they might have stuffed the poor kid into a tiny interrogation chamber while they waited for her.

Instead, he was sitting on the floor, dragging a bright purple crayon across several sheets of paper at once.

"Wow, that looks beautiful!" the woman sitting on the floor beside him praised him.

The kid looked up and gave her a small, lopsided smile before returning to his drawing.

"Mrs. Abernathy," Levi announced as he cleared his throat. "This is Agent Hastings. She's from the FBI Special Victims unit."

"It's nice to meet you, Mrs. Abernathy," Olivia said as she leaned down to shake the woman's hand.

"Likewise." The woman smiled up at her.

"Mrs. Abernathy is the social worker assigned to the boy's case," Levi explained. "I'll leave you guys to it. Don't want to crowd the kid, make him feel nervous or anything."

"I think that would be a good idea." Mrs. Abernathy smiled warmly at him.

He nodded once before turning to take his leave.

"He's a charming one," she chuckled as soon as the detective was gone. "Reminds me a little of my oldest. Do you have children, Agent Hastings?"

"I'm afraid not," Olivia replied. "I'm married to my work."

"Aren't we all?" Mrs. Abernathy smiled ruefully before looking down at the kid. "Eddy? This nice lady wants to talk to you. Do you think that would be okay?"

"Eddy?" Olivia whispered as the boy put his crayons down and turned his big blue eyes up at her.

"Just got it out of him a minute before you came in," Mrs. Abernathy whispered back. "He seems to be responding to it."

"Hello, Eddy." Olivia smiled down at the child in front of her.

"Hi," he replied quietly, though she noted that he wasn't making eye contact with her.

"My name's Olivia," she offered as she eased herself down to sit on the floor next to him. "You can call me 'Ollie' if you want, though. That's what my friends call me."

"Okay," Eddy replied. He still wasn't looking at her, but the tensity in his small shoulders seemed to ease a little.

"Is there something special that your friends call you?" Olivia prodded gently. Asking about his friends and interests would be more likely to get him to open up than asking directly about what had happened to him.

"No," he replied flatly before picking up a crayon and turning it over in his fingers. That was interesting. It seemed as though he had no trouble with small motor functions, which would indicate that his developmental issues were more cognitive than they were physical. Still, it was odd given how short and skinny he was for his age. How was it that he was so behind in some areas, but not others?

"Well, that's okay." Olivia smiled. "What kinds of games do you like to play with your friends?"

"I don't have friends," Eddy murmured. "I not allowed."

Olivia exchanged a perturbed look with Mrs. Abernathy. That was a pretty blatant red flag.

"Well, how about you be my friend?" Olivia asked. "I sure would love to have a new friend."

The crayon went still in his hand as he looked up at her. He stared at her for a long moment, and Olivia was momentarily stunned by how blue his eyes were.

"Okay." He nodded after mulling it over for a while. He started to rock gently back and forth, which could have either been a sign of distress or of happiness. Olivia hadn't spent enough time with him to figure out which it was.

"Really?" She grinned as convincingly as she could, despite how awful the situation made her feel. "That makes me so happy!"

She spent another hour much in the same way, slowly building up a rapport with the boy. She alternated between asking him increasingly meaningful questions and just playing with him, careful not to do anything that might upset or overwhelm him. It was important to have both patience and an abundance of calm when dealing with vulnerable kids, and Olivia had both in spades.

"So, what are your thoughts?" Olivia quietly asked Mrs. Abernathy a little while later, once Eddy had returned to his art. They had moved to sit at a nearby table where they could speak without being overheard while still being able to keep an eye on him. Even though he wasn't talking much, it did seem like Eddy was listening when they spoke since he always responded to what they asked, even if it was in one-word answers.

"There are pretty obvious signs of neglect," she replied seriously. "He should be speaking a lot more by this age, and even if we were to just assume that he's shy, it's still obvious that he has issues expressing his feelings. What's more concerning is that usually, kids will lash out and act aggressively when they're unable to communicate, but he does the exact opposite. He just shuts down and stops talking entirely."

"I agree." Olivia pursed her lips. "Do you think he might be on the spectrum?"

"I had my suspicions at first," Mrs. Abernathy replied. "But I don't think so. I think a lot of the habits we observed are likely closer to coping mechanisms and a result of lack of social interaction."

"You think he was isolated?" Olivia asked.

"Well, he did say he wasn't allowed to have any friends," Mrs. Abernathy sighed sadly. "Social interaction is extremely important for young children. It could certainly explain the communication issues and his inability to maintain eye contact."

"That's—" Olivia cut herself off, unable to find a

term that was adequate to describe just how appalling she found the situation.

Their conversation was interrupted by a knocking at the door, and a moment later, Levi poked his head into the room.

"Uh, sorry to interrupt," he began nervously. "I need to speak with you, Agent Hastings."

"We were just about finished," Olivia replied before turning to Mrs. Abernathy.

"Thank you for speaking with me." She smiled at the social worker. "And for allowing me to speak with Eddy."

"Of course," Ms. Abernathy replied. "Whatever I can do to help this little man."

She looked fondly down at Eddy, and Olivia felt glad that he was in the care of someone who genuinely seemed to care about him.

She followed Levi out into the hallway. "What's going on?"

"We just got a call from your director," he explained. "The DNA samples we sent out to your lab are back."

"Oh, right," Olivia replied abashedly. "I turned my phone off so my interview with the victim wouldn't be interrupted. Sorry about that."

"No, it's fine," Levi muttered. "Um, anyway, it looks like we might have a match."

"A match?" Olivia repeated, unsure at first what he was talking about. "Wait, a match for the victim? How? Everything came back negative when the police ran a preliminary search. Is it attached to a sealed case or something?"

If the DNA was part of a case that wasn't public knowledge, it would make sense that it hadn't come up on a regular police search. The FBI had more than a few cases that required certain levels of security clearance to access.

"Not exactly," Levi replied. "It actually wasn't from a police or federal database."

"Well, where did you find it, then?" Olivia asked, thoroughly confused at this point.

"Maybe you should just look over the details yourself," he muttered. "I've got everything pulled up in my office now."

"Alright," Olivia replied. "Lead the way, then."

3

ETHAN

I DID my best not to snicker as Holm hauled the massive cork board onto my boat. We'd decided to spend the afternoon going over every clue and detail we'd managed to dig up about the *Dragon's Rogue*, and I'd been a little confused when he'd insisted on heading home to pick something up before coming over.

"What the hell is that?" I asked as he propped the bulky thing up on the back of the couch so it could lean against the wall.

"I took the liberty of charting everything we've discovered so far," he replied proudly as he stood back to let me admire his work.

It was funny how suddenly my search for the *Dragon's Rogue* had suddenly become our search. I'd been on the hunt for the old pirate ship ever since my grandfather, who'd been just as obsessed with finding it, had passed the torch onto me. In all fairness, Holm had played a pretty big part in finding a lot of the clues so far, so I supposed it was only fair that he felt it was his quest now too. In any case, it was nice having my best friend along for the journey.

Still, the cork board was so over the top that I couldn't help but smile. It was covered in sheets of paper, photos, and post-it notes, all interconnected by bits of different colored string. It looked like one of those old-fashioned detective boards.

"You've been really bored the past few days, huh?" I teased.

"Painfully so," he replied without missing a beat. "But it's still cool, right?"

He looked so proud of his work that I didn't have the heart to bring him down. And it actually was pretty cool, now that I got a closer look at it. It wasn't anything we didn't already know, but at least now, everything was all summarized in one place.

"Yeah," I chuckled. "It's not bad, actually. What do the different string colors represent, though?"

"Oh, nothing really," Holm replied as he walked over to my fridge to pull out a beer. "I just thought it looked cooler that way. You weren't wrong when you'd accused me of being bored the past few days."

The truth was that things have been incredibly slow around the office as of late. Just a few weeks ago, we'd finally managed to capture the Hollands, the drug-kingpin couple that had been eluding us for months and who had gone out of their way to screw with me and my quest to track down the *Dragon's Rogue*. It had been an amazing accomplishment, and one that we'd been extremely proud of.

However, cases had basically dried up since then. It was a good thing since it meant people weren't out committing crimes, but without anything to investigate and no drug lords to hunt down, the MBLIS office had become unsettlingly quiet, especially now that the FBI had cleared out. It had been a relief at first to have our office all to ourselves again, but these days, with nothing important to do, I found myself almost missing them.

Our finances were finally starting to improve, so it wasn't like we were at risk of losing our jobs anymore, but now, instead of being sent home because there wasn't enough pay to go around, it was because there just weren't any cases. There wasn't much point in having us just sit around at the office doing nothing.

It had been a welcome respite at first, a sort of mini-vacation after all the stress we'd been through. It didn't take us that long to grow tired of it, though.

We were federal agents, after all, and former SEALS. Action and adventure were in our blood, and neither Holm nor I were happy with spending every afternoon just sitting around. I couldn't blame him for trying to alleviate some of that monotony with a little arts and crafts project.

"Hey," I called as I pulled my own beer from the fridge. "Why don't you finally take that fishing trip? We're basically on vacation right now anyway, and you're always talking about how you're going to do it."

"Nah," Holm grumbled as he fell onto the couch before taking a sip of his beer. "It's the middle of summer. Too many tourists out on the water. Plus, with my luck, we'd land a huge case the moment I left."

"Can't argue with that." I shrugged as I popped my beer open and took a swig. "Have you talked with Mariah lately?"

I smirked as Holm sputtered and choked on his beer.

"Yeah." He cleared his throat clumsily. "We talk every now and again."

"That's nice," I replied, half teasing and half genuine. I really was happy for him, but that didn't mean that I wasn't going to joke around at his expense.

"Yeah, it is," he replied grumpily. "How are things with you? Talked with any of your ten girlfriends lately?"

"I don't have any girlfriends," I retorted immediately. "Sure as hell not ten of them."

"Uh-huh," he scoffed. "At this point, you've got so many I'm not surprised you've lost count."

I grabbed the nearest cushion off the couch and launched it at his head. I guessed I couldn't be too mad, though, since I'd started it.

"Seriously, though," he snickered as he tossed the pillow back at me. "Has Tessa gotten back to you yet? Wasn't she going to help you find someone who could open the chest?"

He was, of course, talking about the antique pirate's chest we'd found hidden inside an old shipwreck during our last mission. As usual, I'd been quick to share all the details of our most recent find with Tessa, a friend who was almost as invested in the search for the *Dragon's Rogue* as I was. Since she had more connections than I did, at least when it came to the field of archeology and restoration, I had the chest shipped to her after she'd promised she'd find someone who could safely open it.

Because it had been underwater for such a long time, just exposing it to open-air or harsh light could be enough to irreparably damage it and whatever might be inside. It would take an expert to be able to open it.

"No," I sighed with disappointment as I dropped onto the other end of the couch. "She hasn't gotten back to me since I sent it out to her."

"That sucks." Holm frowned before taking a sip of his beer. "I was hoping we could spend the day talking about the stuff we'd found in Scotland since it's not like we have anything else to do right now."

"Well, I did get some information about the earring and the coin we found," I replied.

"What?" Holm snapped. "Since when? And you didn't tell me?"

"It kind of slipped my mind?" I replied sheepishly. "And I didn't realize you were this invested, honestly."

"Seriously?" Holm frowned indignantly. "After everything we've gone through to find all this stuff? We almost died several times looking for this dang ship!"

"You're right. I'm sorry," I replied placatingly.

"Anyway, yeah, I took the stuff down to Coins and Things. Apparently, the coin isn't actually a coin at all. It was a charm."

"Like, for good luck?" Holm asked.

"Exactly like that." I nodded. "Apparently, those kinds of charms were believed to bring good luck during long voyages. Same with the earring, actually. Gold hoop earrings were considered good luck."

"Obviously didn't do the dead guy any good," Holm remarked.

"Yeah, I guess not," I muttered. "This is just a theory, but Tessa thinks they might have been gifts from Grendel."

"Why does she think that?" he asked.

"Well, Grendel's journal did mention something about helping a 'friend' plan for a trip to Scotland, right?" I explained. "We can't be sure since the entry was pretty vague, but it would make sense if part of his preparations had included giving the dead guy the charm and the earrings. It would have meant that he wished his friend a good voyage, and it would explain why the guy was keeping the charm safe inside the satchel and why we found that envelope with Grendel's seal on it."

"That does sound plausible," Holm replied thoughtfully as he took another sip of his beer.

"Right?" I replied. "It's all speculation, though, since we don't even know if the dead guy was the 'friend' that Grendel was referring to."

"If it was," Holm replied, "then Grendel must have been pretty pissed off about his friend's death."

That was true. The skeleton we'd found had a bullet hole straight through his forehead, which meant that someone had executed the poor sucker. Based on what we currently knew about Grendel, I could only imagine that his reaction to his friend's death would have been bloody.

Just the thought of it got my blood pumping, and I felt a renewed determination to get to the bottom of whatever had really happened on board that sunken ship.

4

OLIVIA

AGENT HASTINGS BIT her lip nervously as she prepared to contact the person their forensics team had managed to track down. This entire case was so unusual that it was setting her on edge. She preferred to always have a solid plan before she acted, as well as several contingencies in mind for whatever might happen. That just wasn't possible in this case, though.

They'd managed to track the woman down by cross-referencing the kid's DNA against a database owned by one of those ancestry tracking companies. Olivia had never been interested in that kind of stuff, so she'd never given it much thought. She had no idea that those companies stored their clients' information even after they'd sent out the results or that they would hand it over to the FBI so easily.

Of course, she was glad they had since this bit of information was going to make locating Eddy's family significantly easier. Still, she couldn't shake the unsettling way the whole thing made her feel. Did the people who sent their DNA off to these companies realize that they were basically giving them permission to do whatever they wanted with it afterward? Personally, she didn't much like the idea of some company handing her genetic information out like that, but this wasn't the time or place to ruminate on that.

The match was only partial, distinct enough that it might not actually be a relative, but close enough that it was better than anything they'd managed to dig up so far. What was peculiar was that the woman's address was listed as being in Pennsylvania, several states away from Miami. If she was related to the kid, it meant that the boy had made quite the journey in getting here.

She dialed the number they had on file, once again feeling chills at how easily the company had handed all the woman's personal information over, even if it did benefit her.

"Hello?" a confused-sounding voice answered after a few rings.

"Hello," Olivia began calmly. "My name is Olivia Hastings. I'm a federal agent with the Special Victims Miami Division of the FBI. Is this Christina Newark?"

"Um, yes," the woman replied stiltedly. "Wait, did you say FBI? Are you serious? Is this some kind of joke or something?"

"I'm afraid not," Olivia replied. She really hated doing this in such a sloppy manner, but this was the only lead they had so far. "Is it true that you submitted an ancestry search a few months ago?"

"Umm... yeah?" the woman answered nervously. "Why? Am I related to a serial killer or something?"

"It's nothing like that," Olivia assured her. "The fact is that we're attempting to locate the relatives of the lost child. The DNA you submitted came up as a match for him."

"Whoa, really?" Christina asked. "Is he okay? I mean, do you think he's like my cousin or something?"

"It's possible," Olivia replied vaguely. If this woman, Christina, was the boy's mother, then the DNA would have been a closer match. As it was, a cousin would make a lot more sense.

"Wow, that's crazy," Christina sighed. "So, like, what did you want from me, exactly?"

"Well, to be honest, I was hoping you could tell me more about him," Olivia replied. Unfortunately, it sounded as though Christina was completely clueless about the boy. "As it is, we have no idea who he is or where he came from."

"Aw, that's so sad," Christina responded. "I don't really know anything about a kid, though. I mean, no one in my family's ever mentioned a—"

She suddenly cut herself off with a gasp.

"Ms. Newark?" Olivia called. "Is everything okay?"

"Oh, crap," Christina muttered. "Maybe my mom knows something about it."

"Why do you say that?" Olivia asked a little impatiently. She just didn't have the same calm demeanor with adults that she could maintain when speaking with kids.

"Well, I don't really know," Christina answered. "The thing is, I'm pretty sure my mom had another kid at some point. I found some old baby stuff in our attic a few years ago. I thought it was mine, but when I brought it down to show my parents, my mom freaked out. Like, completely lost it."

"Is that right?" Olivia muttered. That was certainly noteworthy.

"Yeah," Christina continued. "My dad ended up calming her down, and then he told me never to ask about it or bring it up again, and he took the box of stuff. I figured I must have had a brother or sister who died or something. I never brought it up again, like my dad said, but like, maybe he was actually just missing this whole time?"

It was a pretty far-fetched theory, but it made about as much sense as anything else had so far.

"How long ago was this?" Olivia asked.

"Well, I think I was about fifteen," Christina replied. "So about four or five years ago?"

Olivia's heart rate began to climb at that. It definitely matched the child's estimated age. Maybe Christina was wrong about the exact circumstances of what had happened, but it definitely seemed like they were onto something.

"Ms. Newark," Olivia replied, "could you please give me your mother's contact information?"

"Yeah, yeah, for sure," Christina replied.

Olivia could hear her fumbling around on the other end of the line for a moment before she rattled off her mother's name, number, and address.

"Thank you, Christina," Olivia told her once she

finished taking all the information down. "You've been a huge help. Please don't hesitate to call if you have any other comments or concerns."

After passing her contact information along to Christina, she ended the call and wasted no time in calling one of her contacts back at the department, Xavier. Agent Xavier Mills was a brilliant information tech who Olivia often turned to when she needed information fast.

"Hello?" he answered immediately. "How's my favorite crime-fighter?"

"Hey, I need you to do a background search on someone," Olivia replied.

"Ooh, you're in a hurry, huh?" he asked, his tone instantly several degrees more serious. "Alright, I got you. What do you need?"

"Her name is Barbara Newark," Olivia explained before giving him her address. "She might have given birth and/or given a child up for adoption around five years ago."

"Oof, that's kind of a tall order." Xavier hummed. "You know that stuff is super confidential. It might take me a minute."

"Okay," Olivia sighed with disappointment. "Just let me know whenever you get something."

"Will do," Xavier replied. "I'll call you back as

soon as I find anything. You better spend that time thinking of how you're going to repay me for doing you such a huge favor."

"Really?" Olivia whined. "I thought we were friends."

"We are," Xavier replied simply. "But I don't barter in friendship. Cover the first round next time we go drinking, and I'll call it good."

"Ugh, you're so stingy," Olivia grumbled, though she was smiling as she spoke. "Fine, first round's on me."

"Excellent," Xavier replied. Olivia could tell that he was grinning just from the sound of his voice. "Catch you later."

"Bye," Olivia answered just before he ended the call.

Olivia set her phone down while she thought about what to do next. She was sorely tempted to call the woman herself right now, but she knew that would be foolhardy. Until she had more solid information to work with, it would be better if she just waited.

She was about to get up and see if this station had any vending machines anywhere when her phone suddenly went off.

"I thought you said it would take a minute," she

scoffed as she answered Xavier's call.

"Don't get too excited now," Xavier responded. "I don't really have good news for you."

"What do you mean?" Olivia asked warily.

"Well, I found her," Xavier replied. "She's pretty active in her kid's PTA chapter, and she volunteers at their town's church, so she's all over social media. I didn't find anything about a kid, though."

"Nothing?" Olivia asked disbelievingly.

"Zilch," Xavier replied. "Didn't have to try to crack any adoption records open because there are no adoption records to crack. No hospital stays, no mention of a pregnancy or baby anywhere that I can see."

"How is that possible?" Olivia grumbled. Everything had seemed to match up, so what were they missing?

"I dunno," Xavier shrugged. "Lady seems like your average small-town soccer mom, to be honest. Was that all you needed?"

"For now, yeah," Olivia replied, unable to keep the frustration out of her voice. "Thanks, Xavier."

"Anytime," he replied before ending the call.

As soon as he did, Olivia dialed the woman's number into her phone. She guessed there was no other option now.

"Hello?" a cheerful-sounding woman answered right away. "Is this Anne? I know Tammy said she was going to give you my number. I'm afraid the lemon squares aren't quite ready yet."

"Mrs. Newark, my name is Olivia Hastings," Olivia cut her off smoothly. "I'm a federal agent with the Special Victims Unit of the FBI's Miami division."

"Oh!" the woman yelped, surprise evident in her voice. "What's going on? Is Christina okay? Has something happened?"

"She's fine," Olivia answered quickly. "I'm calling because we think you might have information about a missing child we currently have in our custody."

For a moment, the call went silent, and Olivia actually thought that the woman might have hung up on her.

"What did you say?" she mumbled after a few long moments of tense quiet, all the earlier cheerfulness gone.

"I actually spoke with your daughter Christina earlier," Olivia explained. "She submitted an ancestry kit a few months ago. When we cross-referenced the DNA of the child in our custody, it came up as a match for hers." Better to keep it vague and let her do the talking, as opposed to outright asking if she knew who the child was.

Barbara Newark made a sound that was halfway between a gasp and a sob.

"Are you serious?" she croaked. "Did you really find my baby?"

It felt as though every nerve in Olivia's body was set on fire as she heard that. It seemed like they had been on the right track after all.

"We might have," Olivia answered. "He's here in Miami right now. Could I—"

"*He?*" Barbara cut her off with a gasp. "What do you mean he?"

For a moment, Olivia was uncertain how to respond.

"The child we have in our custody is a boy," she replied. "Around five years old."

"Is this some kind of sick joke?" Barbara screamed so hard that Olivia had to pull the phone away from her ear. "My daughter disappeared nearly twenty years ago! What kind of morons do you have working at the FBI?!"

"Ma'am, I don't—"

"Go to hell!" Barbara yelled before hanging up.

Olivia was left clutching her phone to her ear, more confused now than before she'd made the call.

5

ETHAN

I T WAS A GORGEOUS, sunny day out, and I clung to the thin hope that Diane might actually have something for us to do that day.

I'd barely made it two steps into the office before the curly-haired ball of energy that was our lab tech, Bonnie, intercepted me.

"Ethan!" she exclaimed as she hooked one of her arms around mine. "I've got a surprise for you."

"Really?" I smiled as she half-dragged me down toward the forensics lab.

"Yep," she replied, a Cheshire cat grin stretched across her face. "Remember that skeleton bone you gave me?"

"No way," I gasped as I finally realized what she was talking about.

"Yes way," she replied smugly as we walked through the doors of the lab. "It took a while since I had to get a historian buddy of mine to consult on it. Ancient remains are a tad trickier to root through than modern ones, especially when they've been sitting underwater for a few centuries. We managed to get something, though."

"What is it?" I asked eagerly as she led me over to one of the computers. "You know who he is?"

"We've got a pretty good guess." She nodded happily. "Of course, we can't be sure one-hundred percent since it's almost impossible to fully trace DNA that far back with such an incomplete database to pull from. Given the circumstances, though, there's a pretty big chance this is our guy unless there just happens to be *another* eighteenth-century pirate with suspiciously similar DNA patterns."

"The suspense is killing me, Bonnie," I groaned dramatically. "Who is it?"

"This guy, right here," she declared as she opened one of the windows on the computer with a theatrical flourish. "Captain Abraham Leycester, also known as the *Blue Demon*."

"Pretty intense name," I remarked. "I've never heard of him, though."

"I'm not surprised." Bonnie shrugged. "He was a

fairly small-time pirate for most of his life. It wasn't until 1708 that he really started making a name for himself, but then he suddenly disappeared without a trace."

"Yeah," I scoffed, "because someone shot him in the head and sank his ship."

"Again, not surprised," Bonnie replied. "He made himself a lot of enemies by constantly attacking British cargo ships. There's not a whole lot of information available about him, but from what I managed to dig up, it seems like he was a bit ahead of his time."

"How do you mean?" I asked as I peered down at the computer screen. On it was an old painting of a mean-looking man with a long black beard, wearing a bright blue coat.

"He was kind of an American patriot before America was even a thing," she explained with an almost giddy smile, her hands moving animatedly as she spoke. "Back when the colonies were still just that, he was one of the first to speak out and demand more rights for the people living there. Of course, the American Revolution wouldn't be for almost a hundred more years, so when his words fell on deaf ears, it seems like he decided to take matters into his own hands. The few records that still exist of him describe him as being generous with the things he plundered. He'd steal from British ships and distribute what he got back to the colonies."

"Sounds pretty decent of him, actually," I muttered as I stepped away from the computer screen. "And similar to Grendel's own 'Robin Hood' persona. It would make sense that the two were friends."

"Yeah," Bonnie replied wistfully. "If only he wasn't also a ruthless murderer, then maybe I could actually get behind the guy. Apparently, the reason he was called the *Blue Demon* was because of his penchant for going on ship-wide massacres every time he attacked a boat. One report from a survivor who hid inside a barrel of rum described him as being completely insane. According to him, Leycester was smiling and laughing the entire time he was killing people, screaming about vengeance and justice."

"They can't ever just be cool, can they?" I sighed as I folded my arms over my chest. "There's always gotta be some little detail that ruins the whole story."

"I dunno, I still think he's pretty cool," Bonnie remarked with a shrug. "I mean, he was a pirate, after all. Can't be too surprised that he had a tendency to do bad things."

"Yeah," I conceded with a shrug. "I just wish I knew more about how he was related to Grendel and the *Dragon's Rogue*. I mean, we found that envelope with Grendel's seal on it, so they had some kind of relationship. As cool as this is, unless we figure out how they're connected, I won't get any closer to finding the *Dragon's Rogue*."

"Have you heard back about what was inside that chest you and Holm dredged up?" she asked.

"Holm was just asking about that yesterday," I replied. "And no, I haven't. I'm still waiting to hear back from Tessa about it."

"Well, maybe my guy could help," Bonnie suggested with a shrug. "I mean, he's a historian, so he must have colleagues who know about artifact restoration."

"Really?" I asked. I was getting excited just at the prospect of it. "Let me call Tessa right now, then."

I had just pulled my phone from my pocket when Holm walked through the door.

"There you are," he said as he spotted Bonnie and me. "I didn't even see you come in. What are you doing down here?"

"I was just telling him about the results we got off that finger," Bonnie declared happily.

"Finger?" Holm furrowed his eyebrows at us before it clicked. "Wait, the skeleton we found in that wreck? You were talking about it without me? Wait, what did you find? No, crap, never mind that now, Diane needs to see us."

"Really? I asked, genuinely surprised to hear that.

"Yeah." He nodded. "She's got a case for us. Apparently, it's a weird one and also urgent since there's a kid involved."

"Oh, no," Bonnie murmured behind me. I could understand her feelings. It was always especially bad whenever kids were involved.

"Alright," I replied, just slightly disappointed. Of course, as soon as I started to actually get somewhere with my search for the *Dragon's Rogue*, we'd immediately get a new case. I wasn't too upset, though, since I'd been itching for some action for almost two weeks now.

Diane had a serious expression on her face when we stepped into her office a minute later.

"What's going on?" I asked.

"I need you two to head down to the police

station," she explained right away. "We've got a bit of a mess on our hands with this one."

"What kind of mess?" Holm asked warily.

"Take your pick," Diane deadpanned. "I've got the FBI fighting with us over jurisdiction, and I just spent an hour convincing an overprotective Social Services agent to allow us to speak with the child involved."

"Wait, what exactly happened?" I asked.

"Sorry," Diane grumbled as she massaged the bridge of her nose. "I've spent all morning on the phone dealing with everything, and it's got me all scrambled up. Three days ago, a five-year-old boy was found wandering around, alone, on a beach here in Miami. He was malnourished, severely dehydrated, and extremely sunburned. For the past three days, the police and FBI have been scrambling to locate the child's relatives and figure out what happened to him. Then, yesterday, there was an unusual development in the case. They now believe that the child came here, with his mother, from Turks and Caicos."

"Turks and Caicos?" I repeated. "So that's why we're being called in now?"

"I don't understand, though," Holm interjected. "If they found the kid's mom, then what's the issue?"

"The issue is that they *haven't* found her," Diane replied. "What's more, she's our main victim here."

"What?" Holm and I both asked in unison, twin looks of confusion etched across our faces.

"I told you," she muttered bitterly. "It's a mess."

6

OLIVIA

OLIVIA WOKE up early the next day, intent on speaking with Eddy once again. Speaking with Barbara Newark yesterday had been a bust, and until they could find another lead to follow, the only thing she could do was try to pull whatever information she could from the boy. Mrs. Abernathy had given Olivia her contact information and the address of the home where Eddy would be staying for the time being, and Olivia wanted to do right by him as quickly as she possibly could.

She had just finished getting dressed when her phone rang. She frowned when she saw it was her director calling.

"Hello?" she answered.

"Agent Hastings," Director Evans greeted her. "There's someone here to see you. A Ms. Christina Newark. She says she might have information about the missing child case."

Olivia felt as though her heart had just skipped a beat. Had she heard him correctly? The woman she'd spoken to on the phone had really come to Miami all the way from Pennsylvania?

"I'll be right there," she replied before ending the call.

With her earlier plans abandoned, she rushed down to the FBI office.

Olivia had known that something wasn't adding up yesterday after her disastrous phone call with Barbara Newark. The fact that her daughter Christina had come all the way here proved that there was more to the story.

She headed straight to her boss's office the moment she made it in. Even before she made it to the door, she could see the young woman sitting inside.

"Director Evans," Olivia greeted her boss with a nod as she strode into his office.

"Agent Hastings." He nodded back before turning to look at the young woman sitting on the couch pressed against the far wall of the office. "This is Christina Newark."

The first thing Olivia noticed was the girl's eyes. They were the exact stunning shade of icy blue that Eddy's had been. There wasn't a doubt in her mind that the two were somehow related.

"I spoke to you on the phone yesterday," Olivia stated as she reached down to shake the girl's hand.

"Yeah, I remember," she muttered shyly.

"I appreciate you coming all this way," Olivia said as she sat down in one of the chairs adjacent to the couch. "May I ask why you wanted to see me?"

"Oh, it wasn't all that far." Christina shrugged. "I go to Jacksonville State, so it was only a few hours' drive. And I just couldn't stop thinking about what happened yesterday."

"You mean our talk?" Olivia prompted.

"Yeah, that," Christina replied. "But also my mom. About an hour after we talked, she called me screaming. She was completely hysterical, crying and yelling and asking me if it was true that I had spoken to you. It was all so crazy that I just wanted to come and talk to you."

"Well, I'm glad you did," Olivia replied. "Did your mother say anything else about the boy?"

"No." Christina shook her head. "Or, if she did, I didn't manage to catch it. It was hard to understand what she was saying, to be honest. Ever since my dad died, and I left for college, it seems like the smallest things send her over the edge."

Olivia felt a little bad now. She hadn't intended to upset the poor woman, but she had to do what she had to do to get to the bottom of this case.

"Anyway," Christina mumbled nervously. "You said this kid was, like, related to me, right?"

"Yes, we think so." Olivia nodded slowly. "Why?"

"Well, can I meet him?" she muttered meekly. "I mean, I dunno what my mom's deal is or why she's lying since she's obviously hiding something and this kid apparently is related to us, but, like, if he's my family, I wanna meet him."

Olivia turned to look at her boss. Honestly, she wasn't sure if she had the authority to make that call.

"Social Service's ultimate goal is almost always to reunite children with blood family." Director Evans shrugged. "I'll make a call and see what they say."

"Really?" Christina exclaimed, her eyes going wide. "Yes, please do that. Thank you so much."

He smiled at her before picking up his desk phone to make the call.

"You seem really excited about meeting him," Olivia remarked quietly to her. She could hear the director speaking on the phone. She didn't want to speak loudly enough to disturb him, but she didn't want to make the girl sit in silence, either.

"I just couldn't stop thinking about him all night," she confessed. "I was an only child growing up, and I got lonely sometimes. At least I had my mom and dad, though. But then I imagined him all alone, a little kid with no one around him in a big scary police station. It just didn't feel right to just forget about it when he might actually be my long-lost cousin or something, you know?"

"You're a sweet girl." Olivia smiled warmly at her.

"Okay," Director Evans declared a few moments later as he hung up the phone. "I've spoken with Mrs. Abernathy. She's waiting for both of you now."

Christina made a sound like an excited yelp and shot up off the couch.

"Let's go," she said, a wide grin spread across her face.

"Alright," Olivia agreed as she stood up after her. "Let's go."

Olivia could feel the excitement radiating off of Christina on the drive over to the group home. It was cute, seeing how excited she was to meet Eddy, but it was also a bit concerning. If the kid turned out not to be related to her, then it would only hurt more if she got her hopes up.

"We're here," Olivia announced as they pulled up to the unassuming house.

These days, rather than large austere buildings packed to the brim with displaced children, an effort was made to provide temporary homes that were as normal and welcoming as possible.

The door opened wide as they were walking up the driveway, and Mrs. Abernathy stepped out to greet them.

"Good to see you again, Agent Hastings," she greeted Olivia. "And you must be Christina."

Olivia noted how her eyes immediately went wide as she took in Christina's appearance. She must have noticed the similarity as well.

"That's me," the young woman replied shyly.

"Well, come on in." Mrs. Abernathy gestured for them to walk through the door. "Oh, but take your shoes off before you step into the den, won't you? The little ones tend to crawl around, so I try to keep the floor as clean as possible."

"Oh, of course." Christina hurried to slip her sandals off.

"Right this way." Mrs. Abernathy beckoned us further into the house and into the living room. I spotted the curly mop of blond ringlets right away.

"Eddy," she called softly. "You've got a visitor."

"Oh my—" Christina gasped as the boy sitting on the couch turned to look in our direction.

It was evident that Mrs. Abernathy had put a lot of love into getting Eddy cleaned up. The rat's nest he'd been sporting the last time Olivia had seen him was gone, replaced with long, bouncy curls blonder than she'd realized. He'd been so covered in filth that it had looked almost brown.

"Mommy?" Eddy mumbled as he looked up at Christina, the expression on his face just as shocked as hers.

Olivia and Mrs. Abernathy exchanged an alarmed look as Eddy clambered off the couch and waddled toward the girl.

"He looks just like me," she muttered as she crouched down to get closer to the boy's eye level.

She was right. Their hair and eye colors were identical. The only big difference was that Eddy's skin tone was several shades darker and currently mottled red by the burns.

"Mommy," he mumbled again as he looked up at her, though this time he sounded less sure.

"Oh, honey," Christina muttered as she looked down at him. She sounded as though she was about to start crying. "I'm not your mom."

Eddy stared at her for a long moment before lifting his arms up at her. Christina reacted right away and wrapped her arms around him.

Olivia exchanged another concerned glance with the social worker. It was a touching scene, and though there was no doubt in Olivia's mind that the two were related, it was still a tenuous situation.

"Why don't we all have a seat on the couch?" Mrs. Abernathy suggested kindly.

"Good idea." Christina sniffed as she wiped a tear from her eye. She stood up straight and took Eddy's hand as she moved over to the corduroy-upholstered couch. He clung to her every step of the way.

"He opened up to you quite fast," Mrs. Abernathy noted a few minutes later after the four of them had spent some time talking. Though it would have been more accurate to say that Agent Olivia and Mrs. Abernathy mostly watched while Christina and Eddy talked. He was still answering in stilted, one-word sentences, but at least he was answering.

"That's good, right?" Christina smiled as she ran a hand through Eddy's locks.

"It is." Mrs. Abernathy nodded cautiously. "Are you absolutely certain there isn't anything else you can tell us about him? Anything your parents might have mentioned over the years?"

"No." Christina shook her head helplessly. "I mean, I always suspected there was something my mom was hiding. And then, after the way she freaked out yesterday, I knew something was up, you know? I just can't imagine why she would hide him from me."

She looked down at Eddy with absolute adoration.

"Wait," she suddenly snapped her head up to look at us, her eyes wide with fright. "What's going to happen to him now? Will he be put up for adoption?"

"Well, it's still too early to decide anything," Mrs. Abernathy replied gently.

"I can take him," she blurted out. "I mean, I can drop out. I'll get a job. I'll figure out whatever my mom's issue is and get her to come around."

"Slow down for a moment," Mrs. Abernathy cut her off, though not unkindly. "We're getting way ahead of ourselves. There's still a lot that needs to be done, including a criminal investigation. We're still not entirely sure how he's even related to you."

"But he is related to me, right?" she countered. "I mean, look at him."

She made a great point. Olivia thought that if someone had told her that the pair were actually siblings, she wouldn't have questioned it.

"I'm going to talk to my mom," she suddenly declared, the conviction in her voice palpable. "I'm not going to let him just go into the system. I'll talk to her."

The rest of the afternoon flew by in a flash, and Christina seemed extremely reluctant to leave as the sun began to set.

"Okay," she murmured as she leaned down to give Eddy one last hug. "I've gotta go now, okay, cutie? I'm going to be back really soon, though. I promise."

Eddy looked more upset than Olivia had seen him since she'd met the kid. So far, he'd barely shown any sign of emotion at all, but right then, his lips were downturned into a clear frown, and his eyes were watery. He still didn't cry, however, only nodded his head before turning to play with his toys.

"I'll talk to my mom," Christina reiterated her promise as she stood back up to look at Olivia. "I'll figure out a way to get her to see reason. She might not be too happy with me after, but I'll get it done."

There was a fierce look of determination in her eyes. Olivia wasn't sure what she was planning, but she sincerely hoped that she'd be able to get through to her.

They left the house after that, and Olivia dropped her off back at the FBI office before heading home. It had been a long and emotional day, and she was ready to get some sleep.

It felt as though she had barely closed her eyes when she suddenly heard her phone go off beside her in bed. She could see light streaming through her windows, though, which meant that she'd slept through the night.

She groaned as she reached over to pluck the phone from her nightstand.

"Hello?" she grumbled sourly into the phone, determined to go back to sleep as soon as she finished this call.

"Agent Hastings," her boss replied, "I just got off the phone with Christina Newark. Her mother is on her way to Miami now."

"What?!" Olivia exclaimed, all traces of sleep gone instantly.

"Apparently, she's on a plane to Florida," he continued without missing a beat. "They'll be meeting you at the group home. And just so you're prepared, Ms. Newark warned me that her mother was not in the best mood."

"Awesome," Olivia quipped sarcastically. "Okay. I'll get everything ready and head down there."

She ended the call and then took a moment to process what had just happened. Honestly, she was a little impressed. Christina obviously hadn't been messing around when she'd declared that she would convince her mother to change her mind about speaking with us.

"Well, better prepare myself for battle," Olivia muttered to herself as she got out of bed.

After getting dressed, she decided to head down to Mrs. Abernathy's place early. This would give them time to get on the same page, and it would also give Olivia an opportunity to chat with Eddy without any other distractions present. To her dismay, though, he didn't seem all that interested in talking that morning, so in the end, she spent the following three hours chatting and having coffee with Mrs. Abernathy.

"That must be them." Mrs. Abernathy stood when the doorbell suddenly rang. Olivia watched as she shuffled over to the door to answer it.

For some reason, Olivia felt nervous, though she wasn't entirely sure why. Maybe she was just hoping that everything would turn out well for Eddy, who was the one who really mattered here.

"Hi," Christina greeted her cheerfully as she walked through the door and into the house. Olivia stood up to greet her and was surprised when the young woman actually pulled her into a tight hug.

"It's nice to see you again," Olivia replied.

"Where is he?" Christina asked eagerly as she looked over Olivia's shoulder.

"He's right—" she was just about to respond when she suddenly caught sight of a woman standing just behind Christina.

She had the same shade of curly blond hair, though hers was streaked with gray and pulled into a messy bun atop her head. Her eyes, too, were the same icy blue, flanked by fine lines and set into a cold, steely gaze.

"Why don't I go get him?" Mrs. Abernathy replied softly. "Please, have a seat."

Christina sat down in exactly the same spot she'd sat yesterday. Her mother took a moment longer and was uncomfortably stiff and rigid as she sat down.

"You must be Barbara," Olivia greeted her politely. "I'm—"

"I know who you are," the woman spat bitterly.

"Mom," Christina snapped quietly.

Barbara opened her mouth as though she wanted to say something more but shut it with a click of her teeth just a moment later. The air between them was extremely tense, and Olivia wondered just what had transpired between them in the past twenty-four hours.

"Okay, we're coming," Mrs. Abernathy called as she slowly walked back down the hallway. Olivia knew that she was making the announcement as much for Eddy's sake as for Christina's and Barbara's. The meeting was sure to be an emotional shock for all three of them.

Olivia watched Barbara Newark closely. Even if she maintained her silence, just the way she reacted might tell them a lot.

She stood up the moment Mrs. Abernathy and Eddy rounded the corner out of the hallway and into the living room, only to fall right back down, directly onto her knees.

"Oh!" she let out a noise that was somewhere between a scream and a sob.

"Mom!" Christina gasped as she knelt down to check on her mother, who was now openly sobbing on the ground.

"Mrs. Newark." Olivia leaned down to address her. "What's wrong?"

"What is this?" Barbara gasped between sobs. "Is this some kind of trick? Why is this happening?"

"Mom, what the hell are you talking about?" Christina gaped at her.

"He looks just like her," Barbara cried as she snatched her handbag off the coffee table with shaking hands. She rummaged through it for a moment before pulling out her wallet and slipping a picture from behind her driver's license. "He looks just like my Allie."

She held the picture out to Olivia, who took it from her gently. Her eyes went wide as she looked down at it.

It was obviously an old photograph from the age of printed film that had long since been faded by time. The child in the picture, however, was uncannily similar to the little boy standing before her now. It looked as though someone had taken a picture of Eddy himself.

"That's my little girl, Allison," Barbara explained as fat tears rolled down her face. "She disappeared almost twenty years ago. Why? Why does he look like her?"

A cold silence fell over the room as the woman finally revealed her dark secret. Olivia looked back and forth between her, the photograph, and the boy.

She had no idea how she was supposed to answer the woman's question.

7

ETHAN

HOLM and I headed out to the group home the kid was staying in as soon as Diane had finished briefing us over the details of the case. Well, as many details as she could give us, anyway. Apparently, between the FBI not wanting to hand over the case and the details being so confusing, to begin with, it wasn't totally clear just what exactly was going on.

"Just when we'd gotten rid of the FBI, too," Holm muttered from the passenger seat. "Not that some of them hadn't turned out to be cool, in the end. It was nice not having to play nice and worry about juris-diction, though."

"I hear you," I sighed.

"Maybe the mom was involved in drug trafficking," Holm mused aloud. "Got spooked and split when it seemed like things were going wrong?"

"And she just left her kid behind?" I responded incredulously. "Why would she have him with her in the first place if she was running drugs?"

"I dunno." Holm shrugged. "Why did the Hollands build a whole-ass ship and create a fake journal just to mess with you? People do dumb stuff, especially criminals, and especially when they're panicking."

"You're not wrong," I replied. It was a bizarre case, and I was itching to get to the scene and figure things out.

"That's definitely the place," Holm snickered as we pulled up to the house. Two sleek, black cars with dark tinted windows that just screamed FED were sitting in the driveway.

"No subtlety as usual," I snorted as I parked and got out. Unlike the FBI, MBLIS preferred to keep a low profile. Very few people had ever even heard of our organization, and we preferred to keep it that way. It made it easier for us to move around and strike undetected.

"Although," Holm hummed, "there is something kind of respectable about just blatantly announcing your presence like that. Kills any element of surprise, but it's one hell of a power move."

"Don't go joining the FBI on me now, Holm," I teased as we walked up to the door.

"Wouldn't dream of it," he replied easily as I knocked.

The door opened almost immediately, and a talk, wiry-haired woman wearing thick glasses greeted us.

"Hi." I smiled politely at her. "I'm Agent Marston, and this is Agent Holm. We're with MBLIS."

"Of course," she replied as she opened the door wider for us. "I'm Mrs. Abernathy. I was expecting you. Come on in, join the party."

I could hear voices talking as we stepped inside. Mrs. Abernathy closed the door behind us before leading us further into the small house.

My first impression of the home was that it seemed cozy. The furniture was a little mismatched and worn, but in a way that seemed lived-in rather than trashed. There were also photographs and picture frames hung all over the walls. I assumed, judging by the wide range of ages and ethnicities present, that they must be pictures of all the children that had come through here.

Even more evidence indicating the presence of kids were the toys that covered every part of the room. Stuffed animals sat on the couches in place of throw pillows. The bookshelves along one wall, aside from housing a colorful array of books, were also home to various dolls and figurines. Even the floor hadn't escaped unscathed, as there was a large pile of toys in the center of the living room, all, apparently, for the little boy currently sitting on the floor examining a plastic toy truck.

Aside from the kid, there were four adults sitting in the den. Two of them, judging by their clothes, must have been the FBI agents. I couldn't immediately discern who the other two might be until I spotted the child sitting between them.

The kid had a dreamy, faraway look in his eyes, and his skin was raw and red. I figured he must be the victim then. The two women flanking him both had the exact same hair and eye color, which meant that they must be some kind of family to him.

"Agent Hastings, Director Evans," Mrs. Abernathy's voice broke through the group's chatter. "These are Agents Marston and Holm. Agents, this is Agent Olivia Hastings. She's been handling the case up until now. And this is Christina Newark and her mother, Barbara Newark."

She huffed for breath as she finished the lengthy introduction.

"Nice to meet everyone," I responded. I noted immediately that the female agent, Olivia, appeared to be glaring daggers at me. She had dark brown hair and eyes that were set into an unimpressed glare. It was an intimidating look, and I wondered if she was the reason MBLIS was squabbling with the FBI over jurisdiction.

"Nice to meet you," the director said as he stood to shake my and Holm's hands. "I was the one who got in contact with your director. When I heard the details of the case, well, it became evident that this might be more complex than we initially thought."

"Right," Holm replied. "We heard that you think the kid came here from Turks and Caicos. That would put it under MBLIS jurisdiction."

I noted as Holm spoke that one of the women, the older one, Barbara, seemed to flinch at his words. That was peculiar.

"Not necessarily," Agent Hastings spoke up. "As it currently stands, only one of the cases falls within your jurisdiction."

"Huh?" Holm raised an eyebrow at her. "What do you mean, one of the cases?"

"Why don't we start from the beginning?" Director Evans suggested. "It would be good to get everyone on the same page before we decide anything."

"I agree." I nodded.

"I'll make some coffee for everyone," Mrs. Abernathy declared before bustling off to the kitchen.

"I'll take the floor," Holm declared before suddenly plopping himself down on the shaggy carpet. I was confused as to what he was doing until I looked up and realized that the only spot free was on the couch, directly next to the hostile Agent Olivia.

She shot me a cold glare, and I silently cursed Holm as I moved forward to take a seat next to her.

She didn't even try to hide her disdain as she turned to glare at me. I felt goosebumps rise along my arm at her stare. Still, I couldn't help but notice how nice her perfume smelled, like cotton and vanilla.

"Alright," Mrs. Abernathy sighed as she handed out an assortment of mismatched mugs before taking a seat on an ottoman in front of one of the armchairs. "Mrs. Newark, I know we've already been through this a few times, but would you mind explaining everything one more time to the two gentlemen?"

"I think she's feeling a little stressed right now,"

the younger of the two women immediately piped up.

"No, it's okay," the older woman replied softly.

"Mom, don't push yourself," the younger one, Christina urged her.

"It's alright." Mrs. Newark smiled warmly at her daughter. "They're here to help. All these years, I've hoped for a miracle, and now it seems like it's finally happening."

"Okay…" Christina muttered though she seemed reluctant to let her mother continue.

Mrs. Newark took a long, deep breath before continuing.

"Nineteen years ago, my daughter disappeared," she began quietly. "My husband and I didn't have a lot of money when we got married. We were young, and I was pregnant, and we decided that we should focus on our daughter, so we never had a honeymoon. Then, the year that she turned five, we got a big promotion at work, so we—"

She stuttered to a halt and bit her lip.

"Mom, it's okay if you want to stop." Christina gently rubbed her mother's back.

"No!" Mrs. Newark croaked as she furiously rubbed tears from her eyes. "No. It's alright. Just give me a moment."

The entire room was silent as we waited for her to continue. I could tell, just by looking at her, that remembering this and talking about it was causing her a great deal of pain, and I didn't want to interrupt.

"We decided we'd finally take a little vacation," she continued after clearing her throat. "It was the honeymoon we never got to have, except this was even better because we'd have our little girl with us. We spent a few days researching vacation destinations before we settled on Turks and Caicos."

I exchanged a silent look with Holm but didn't say anything.

"We bought tickets and flew out the next day." She smiled bitterly. "It was all so last minute and rushed. If only we'd... Anyway, we were on vacation. It was the fourth night, and Allison had fallen asleep. She was only five, she couldn't stay up very late, especially after spending all day playing at the beach. My husband and I decided to head down to the hotel bar to have a few drinks."

Her voice had become more distant and robotic as she continued her story, as though she was trying to disassociate herself from what she was saying.

"She was right upstairs in the hotel room," she muttered weakly. "We... We didn't even leave the hotel. We were right downstairs in the lobby. The door was locked. I don't— I don't understand."

It didn't take a genius to figure out what must have happened then. It was clear by the tone of her voice and the way she was struggling to even continue speaking.

"When we went back upstairs, she was gone," she said flatly. "I thought we'd come into the wrong room at first because she wasn't in bed where we'd left her. But all our luggage was there. Our money was there. The stupid little souvenirs we'd bought were still there. But she—"

She finally broke down, unable to hold back her tears any longer.

"We spent months looking for her," she sobbed. "I didn't want to come back to the US without her. But then we started having issues with our visas, and I found out that I was pregnant with Chris. I didn't want to give birth there. I couldn't stand the idea of having a child of mine anywhere near that place. So we came back without her."

"I'm so sorry, Mrs. Newark," I muttered, unsure what else I could possibly say after hearing such a horrific story.

"But now, Eddy's here!" she rasped as she ran her fingers through the child's hair before looking up at me with pleading eyes. "He said that he came here with his mom, on a boat. Turks and Caicos aren't that far from Miami. He's her spitting image, and Agent Olivia said they ran DNA tests! He's related to us, s-so, that means she must be here too, right?"

Suddenly, everything began to fall into place, and I understood why Olivia had mentioned that there were two cases here. We were dealing not only with a lost child but a missing woman as well. One who had been kidnapped as a child and as an American citizen while she was on foreign soil. No wonder the FBI was squabbling with us over jurisdiction.

"Please." She clasped her hands together as she stared at me. "You have to find her. My little Allie is here somewhere. I know she is."

I took a deep breath as I looked back at her.

"I'm going to do everything I can," I promised.

8

ETHAN

"I MISS when it was just drugs," Holm muttered as we stepped into the kitchen to discuss everything we'd just heard. Mrs. Abernathy was in the living room consoling Mrs. Newark, who was currently crying. The FBI agents, as well as Holm and I, had taken the opportunity to excuse ourselves, give them a moment of privacy, as well as talk details.

"Yeah, I know how you feel, brother," I sighed as Mrs. Newark's anguished face flashed across my mind. I'd take fistfights with no good drug-lords over broken-hearted mothers any day.

"So, you can see now why we thought we might benefit from MBLIS's cooperation on this one," Director Evans remarked.

"Cooperation?" I asked. "What is that supposed to mean?"

"It means," Agent Olivia huffed, "that we'll be working together on this one, fellas."

She turned her icy glare onto me once more. She looked like she was in her mid to late thirties, with sharp, regal features that gave her a commanding look. The freckles that dotted her nose and cheeks gave her a youthful appearance, though, and her warm brown eyes were alluring even when they were set into that steely gaze.

"As it stands, we have two separate victims," Director Evans explained. "The mother, who would very obviously be your victim, and the child—"

"Who is under my supervision," Olivia interjected. "He's a traumatized, highly vulnerable, five-year-old boy. That makes him a special victim, which places him solidly within my jurisdiction."

I wasn't sure if I agreed with that entirely, and honestly, I might have been able to make a case against it. However, the determined look in her eyes was so fierce and, frankly, sexy that I honestly didn't think I'd mind spending the next few days working with her.

"I'm not sure that's—" Holm attempted to say

before I shot my arm out blindly to elbow him in the side.

"Of course, we understand entirely." I smiled at them. "I'm looking forward to working with you."

Olivia raised a perplexed eyebrow at us before turning and walking back into the den.

"Well, for now, I think we should divide our efforts and focus on the two victims separately," Director Evans continued. "I currently have my lab running a more conclusive test to determine whether Mrs. Newark is indeed the child's maternal grandmother. In the meantime, I could give you the information we currently have regarding the circumstances under which the boy was found. It's possible that there might be some sign as to the mother's whereabouts in that area."

"Okay." I agreed. "We can head there now and take a look."

"I'll have everything forwarded to you, then," he confirmed before heading off after Olivia.

"What the heck was that?" Holm hissed as soon as he was gone.

"Sorry," I chuckled. "I didn't mean to hit you that hard. I wasn't looking."

"Why did you elbow me at all?" he grumbled. "I

would have thought that you of all people—Wait. Are you serious?"

"What?" I asked as innocently as I could manage.

"Honestly, Marston?" he deadpanned. "With that ice queen? She looked like she wanted to punch you the moment you sat down next to her."

"I don't know what you're talking about." I shrugged.

"Are you even capable of ignoring a pretty woman?" He sighed dramatically. "She's an FBI agent out for our blood because she thinks we're trying to steal her case, and you're still getting all gooey-eyed over her?"

"Come on. We should get down to the beach." I pointedly ignored his accusation. "Need to go search for clues and whatnot."

I snickered as he followed behind me, grumbling something about girlfriends and life being unfair.

It felt good to step out of the house and into the warm summer sun. Things had gotten so heavy in there. It was always just a bit more painful when a case involved kids.

As soon as we got into the car, I rolled the windows down. It was nice out, and a little fresh air would be good while we made the drive down to the beach where the kid had been found. The beach itself wasn't too far away, but the real issue would be figuring out exactly where the kid had come from. The beach was massive, after all.

"Wow, it's packed today," Holm remarked as I pulled the car into one of the parking lots near the beach. He was right. Even from here, I could tell that the tourists were out in full force today.

It wasn't surprising. It was the height of summer, after all. Miami was in prime tourism season, and the beaches were ripe for families, couples, and party-goers.

Of course, this meant that any evidence that might have been left behind was long gone, either washed away by the tide or stomped into oblivion by hundreds of bare feet as they traipsed across the sand.

"What exactly are we looking for?" Holm yelled over the road of the crowd as we made our way down along the shore.

"I don't know, to be honest," I replied. "According to the report that Evans gave me, the two teenagers who called the police found the kid here, right in front of that ice cream place."

"Well, there's gotta be some sign of... something." He shrugged. "The kid didn't just pop out of nowhere, and I doubt he walked too far, right? Let's keep looking."

We continued down the length of the beach, past the area that was crowded with tourists, long past where the boardwalk ended. We stopped when we reached the point where sand gave way to grass and rock. By this point, there were basically no tourists around. There weren't even that many buildings around since the only thing out this way was a steep, rocky cliff. It was a popular spot for young couples to sneak away to, though it seemed to be unoccupied right now.

"Maybe we walked the wrong way," Holm huffed as he wiped the sweat off his forehead. A walk along the beach wasn't exactly tiring for us, but the intense heat made even a light stroll feel strenuous. "I mean, I didn't see any sign of a boat on the way here. And this far out, any boat that tried to come close would be completely wrecked on the rocks."

"Maybe that's why we didn't see anything on the way here," I muttered as I glanced down over the side of the cliff. "If the boat was destroyed, then there wouldn't be one to find."

"You don't think...?" Holm turned to look at me.

"One way to find out," I sighed as I began to step carefully down over the side of the cliff. The rocks there were loose and uneven, so it was a slow and risky process.

"I really hope we don't die here," Holm scoffed as we made our way slowly down the side of the cliff. "Can you imagine that? After everything we've survived, dead from tripping over a rock."

"Don't trip then," I retorted just as my foot slipped against a piece of loose rock. I hissed as my ankle jerked in an unnatural direction as I attempted to keep my balance.

I heard Holm snicker behind me, and I had to resist the temptation to turn around. I might have actually fallen if I tried.

"Seriously," Holm huffed tensely as we got closer to the base of the cliff. "I don't think that— Dammit."

I looked up to see what he was reacting to and noticed it immediately. Just a few yards away from the base of the cliff, half-hidden behind a large chunk of jagged rock, was a piece of something smooth and white. Even broken and in pieces, I instantly recognized the hull of what was once a boat.

My heart sank. Even from this distance, I could tell that the thing was wrecked, which wasn't a good sign.

It took an agonizingly long time for us to finally make it back onto level ground at the base of the cliff. The moment I'd made it down, I raced over to where the boat was stuck. The water was up to about my ankles here, but I ignored it as I hurried to inspect the damage.

It looked like a small bowrider, though it was difficult to tell from this angle. The boat had crashed onto the rocks in such a way that its bow was facing straight up, making it impossible to see the deck or cockpit from where I was standing. A large portion of the side was also caved in, as though it had struck first on that side before finally getting stuck like this.

I wasn't sure how stable the thing was, but I needed to have a closer look, so I circled around to the other side of the boat and began to climb up. As I hauled myself up, I nearly gasped at the sight I came face to face with.

Lying on the floor of the boat was the body of a woman, badly sunburned and unnaturally still. I cursed as I clambered beside her to check for a heartbeat, but I could tell by the stench even before I'd checked for a pulse that she was already gone, probably for some time now.

"She's dead," I informed Holm as he climbed up into the boat beside me.

"Damn..." he muttered as he stared down at the body.

Though it was matted and covered in dirt, I could tell that the woman's hair was the same shade of bright blond as Eddy's.

"Wait, so the kid climbed up the cliff and walked all the way down to the crowded part of the beach?!" he exclaimed as he looked up at the cliff we'd just cautiously scaled down. "That was like a mile of beach!"

"Kids are tougher than you think," I replied. "Resilient, too. Little guy kept walking until he found someone to help him."

"She did right by him," he murmured as he looked back down at the woman's body. "After everything she went through, she sailed from Turks and Caicos to Miami in this little rickety thing?"

"She saved her child," I said through gritted teeth. "I'm going to make sure she gets justice."

9
ETHAN

I GRIMACED as I watched Agent Olivia deliver the bad news to Mrs. Newark from Mrs. Abernathy's kitchen. She was speaking quietly enough that I couldn't quite make out what she was saying, but there was no way I could miss the intense grief that flashed across her expression as she let out an agonized wail and fell to the ground.

"This sucks," Holm muttered beside me.

"Yeah." I frowned. I couldn't imagine how awful it must feel to finally get a glimmer of hope that your kid might be alive, only to have it crushed almost immediately.

After we'd discovered the body, we'd called to report what we'd found. Forensics had been dispatched to deal with the body and the scene, and

Diane was currently attempting to trace where the boat had come from. We already suspected, based on Barbara Newark's story, that they might have come from Turks and Caicos, but there was no telling what Allison Newark had gone through in the past two decades. Until we knew exactly where the boat had come from, we couldn't proceed with the case.

Agent Hastings sighed as she walked into the kitchen a moment later, likely to give the woman a little space to process the news.

"Sorry you had to do that," I said as she leaned against one of the countertops.

"Don't be," she replied, all the earlier venom in her voice now completely absent. "Unfortunately, conversations like this aren't all that unusual for the Special Victims Department. I'm used to giving people bad news. Besides, I seriously doubt there was anything you could have done if that's what you're worried about. According to the police report, Eddy had mentioned something about his mom 'sleeping' on the boat to the kids that found him. She was probably already dead when they got to Miami."

There was an undeniable edge of sadness in her voice, but how calm and collected she was overall impressed me. She spoke matter-of-factly and exuded confidence, and I was certain she'd be a pleasure to work alongside.

"Ahem," Holm cleared his throat exaggeratedly.

He was shooting me a smug grin, and I flushed as I realized I'd started staring at her while lost in thought. I had to resist the urge to elbow him again.

Agent Hastings furrowed her eyebrows at us and threw us an unimpressed look before speaking again.

"I think we should try to talk to Eddy again," she said as she crossed her arms across her chest. "You haven't spoken to him yet, right? You need to get caught up to speed anyway, and he seems to be opening up more now that Barbara and Christina are here."

"That's a good idea," I murmured as I peered out of the kitchen and toward the living room.

Mrs. Newark was fussing with her grandson's hair, her hands trembling as she gently pushed the curls out of his face.

The three of us filed back out into the living room. I noticed for the first time that Director Evans was no longer there.

"Barbara," Agent Hastings addressed her quietly. "The MBLIS agents would like to talk with Eddy for a little while."

"Oh," she muttered weakly, her eyes still shiny with tears. "Alright, b-but, I can stay here with him, right?"

There was a note of desperation in her voice, and my heart broke for the poor woman. After receiving news of her daughter's death, I could understand why she wouldn't want her grandson out of her sight for an instant.

"Of course you can," Agent Hastings replied kindly. "We can talk right here in the living room if you want."

"Well, why don't Agent Hastings and Agent Marston stay then?" Mrs. Abernathy suddenly suggested. "The rest of us can go have a chat in the other room. I wouldn't want to overstimulate Eddy, especially since it's already been such an eventful day."

She was tactful with her wording, but it was obvious that she was telling everyone aside from Agent Hastings and me to get lost for the sake of not spooking the kid.

"She's right." Christina nodded as she stood up off of the couch. "You stay here with him, Mom."

"I'll leave it to you then." Holm turned to me and shot me another pointed look before glancing surreptitiously at Olivia.

I made a mental note to get back at him later as he followed Christina out of the room.

Mrs. Abernathy ushered them into the kitchen, though I could see her hanging back and monitoring the conversation from afar. Of course, as Eddy's social worker, she'd be making sure she was nearby to intervene if necessary.

Eddy had slipped away from his grandmother and onto the floor in the meantime. He was holding a dinosaur toy in each hand and crashing them together in a fierce battle, sound effects, and everything.

"Hey, Eddy," I said softly as I slid off the couch and onto the ground next to him. "My name is Ethan. What have you got there?"

"Dinosaw," he replied immediately.

"That's pretty cool." I smiled at him. "Are they having a fight?"

"Fighting, fighting!" he parroted before emitting a dramatic growl and having one dinosaur bite at the other's neck.

"Ouch, that's rough," I remarked as I watched him play. "I wonder which one is going to win?"

"Stegasawas," he replied seriously before holding one of the toys out to me.

It surprised me to see that it really was a

stegosaurus, but even more surprised that the kid even knew that word, considering how developmentally delayed he seemed in other areas. I glanced up at Mrs. Abernathy, who had drifted a little closer from the kitchen and was now staring intently at him as well.

"Wow," I replied over-enthusiastically. "You know the name of this dinosaur? You're pretty smart, Eddy."

"Tank you," he replied. "Danny teach me."

I could feel the tension shift in the air as soon as those words left his mouth. There was a look of confusion on Mrs. Newark's face behind him, and I lifted a hand to stop her before she could say anything.

"Oh, really?" I asked. "Is Danny a friend of yours?"

"Yeah," he mumbled as he turned the dinosaur toy over in his hands. "She lives with me and Mommy."

Mrs. Newark let out a strained, high-pitched choking noise behind him. There was a look of horror on her face.

Agent Hastings eased herself onto the ground next to us but didn't say anything.

"She lived with you?" I repeated. "Where was that? Where did you all live together?"

Of course, I didn't have high hopes that the kid would be able to confirm that he'd come here from Turks and Caicos, but maybe he could give us details that would enable us to narrow it down.

"In da big house," he replied before abandoning the dinosaurs and moving on to a coloring book.

"Did anyone else live in the big house with you?" I prompted gently.

"Yeah," he replied as he dragged a crayon haphazardly across the page.

"Who else lived with you?" I asked when he didn't offer anything more.

"Da ladies," he answered before picking up a different colored crayon. "Nina. Daisy. Jojo. Webecca…"

It took me a moment to realize that he was drawing a different blob on the paper with every name he listed.

"Is that them?" I asked as I watched him continue to add multicolored blobs to the drawing.

"Yeah," he replied before pointing to a smaller blob in the center. "Dat me."

Mrs. Newark was silently crying now, tears

streaming down her face as she watched our interaction.

"Wow, you and your mommy sure had a lot of friends," I remarked as I looked at the drawing. I counted at least ten blobs around the little one. "Were the ladies nice to you?"

"Yeah." Eddy nodded. "Dey play with me when Mommy gone, and we play hide and seek from the bad guys."

"Uh-oh," I replied. "Who are the bad guys?"

"Dey mean," Eddy mumbled. He was rocking back and forth more intensely now, and his chin was tucked into his chest. I'd noticed that the kid hadn't been making eye contact with me the entire time we'd been talking, but I'd assumed it might just be a result of his developmental issues. Now that he'd brought up "bad guys," I wondered if there might be more to it.

"They were mean to you?" I frowned. "I'm very sorry to hear that, Eddy."

I wanted to ask him for more details on what he meant by mean, but I was worried that it might just upset him. He already seemed like he was in distress.

"Eddy," Agent Hastings chimed in.

He looked at her right away, which confirmed my

suspicion that it was *me*, specifically, that the kid was unable to look in the eye. My stomach churned at the thought of what he might have experienced to have that kind of reaction to men as opposed to women.

"You want to know something cool about my friend Ethan?" she asked him as she placed a hand on my shoulder. I might have laughed at the idea of her calling me her "friend" when she'd been practically murdering me with her eyes earlier if it hadn't been for the kid. "He's got a super cool power. See, Ethan is a good guy. His special power is beating up bad guys, just like that stegosaurus beat up that mean T-Rex."

Eddy glanced over at me for just a second, his eyes wide and sparkling with a mix of awe and skepticism.

"Isn't that right, Ethan?" Olivia muttered pointedly.

"Yep." I grinned at Eddy. "I'm gonna find those bad guys and beat them up for being mean to my friend, Eddy."

A long moment of silence passed before Eddy replied.

"Okay," he mumbled. He was looking away from

me again, but I could see the ghost of a smile on his lips.

"Eddy, could you tell us more about what happened with the men?" Olivia asked.

I held my breath as I waited for the kid to answer. Out of the corner of my eye, I could see that Mrs. Abernathy was hovering nearby, likely ready to step in the moment the kid got too stressed.

"Dey were mean," Eddy repeated his earlier statement. "Dey got mad and hit. Hitting not nice."

"You're right," I agreed as I attempted to maintain my cool. "That isn't nice at all."

"Did they hit you, Eddy?" Olivia asked directly.

"No," he mumbled to my intense relief. "When dey get mad, Danny play hide and seek wit me."

"So they would only hit the ladies?" I asked as the picture started to become clearer.

"Yeah," he replied. "But no face."

"What?" I asked.

"No face," he repeated. "No hitting face, or no money."

"Oh my word," Mrs. Newark cried suddenly, her face ashen white.

Honestly, I couldn't blame her. I could barely believe the words that had just come out of his mouth. It was obvious he was just parroting what he'd heard someone else say, but still, it was obvious what the implication was.

"Why don't we stop here for now?" Mrs. Abernathy suggested as she strode back into the room. "Mrs. Newark, can I get you some water?"

"That's actually a good idea," Agent Hastings replied before looking straight at Eddy. "You've been a super big help, buddy."

She stood up and indicated for me to follow with a quick flick of her head. I got up and followed her into the kitchen, passing Christina as she made her way back into the living room.

"Well, as horrified as I am, I can't say I'm surprised," Olivia sighed as we stepped into the kitchen. "I mean, Allison was missing for twenty years and suddenly reappears with a kid?"

"How much of that did you manage to catch?" I turned to look at Holm.

"All of it, pretty much," he replied, his face twisted into a disturbed sneer. "Ugh, that poor kid."

"Well, we've got a pretty good idea of what the situation is, right?" Olivia looked between the two of us. "Judging from the circumstances of her disappearance and Eddy's description, it's likely that Allison was being trafficked. She must have gotten pregnant at some point and had Eddy."

"And... they just let her keep him?" Holm asked incredulously. "I mean, don't get me wrong, I'm glad they did, but surely it would have been easier and safer to just get rid of him, right? I feel like the last thing a pimp's going to want around is a screaming baby."

"You're not wrong," Olivia muttered. "It is strange. Regardless, that's what we have to work with right now."

Before either of us could respond, Holm's phone went off.

"It's the office," he informed us. "Just a second."

He stepped out of the kitchen to take the call, leaving Olivia and me alone.

She was staring off into space, an unsettled look in her eyes.

"You okay?" I asked.

She blinked at me in surprise before smiling ruefully.

"Yeah," she chuckled. "It just never gets easier, you know? Kids, I mean."

I knew exactly what she meant. I'd thought the same thing myself several times just today. It was always worse when kids were involved.

"I hear you," I sighed.

"You were great in there, by the way." She smiled

at me. "With Eddy, I mean. A lot of people freeze up or put their feet in their mouths when it comes to interacting with kids. You managed to connect with him, though. I'm impressed."

"Well, I'm glad I surpassed your expectations." I smiled back at her. She had an adorable, toothy smile and a little dimple on her cheek when she did.

"Well, I wouldn't go *that* far," she scoffed playfully. "I could definitely use a drink after that, though. Are you—"

"That was Diane." Holm returned at just the wrong time. "She said that they managed to track down the owner of the boat."

"Already?" I asked. "That was fast."

"Well, they didn't have to do much digging," Holm replied, "since it was apparently reported stolen about a week ago. It popped right up. Guess where the owner lives?"

"Turks and Caicos," Olivia and I both answered at once.

"Bingo," Holm confirmed. "Diane wants us back at the office. She wants us to fly out tomorrow."

"Guess I'll take a raincheck on that drink then." Olivia smiled at me a little sadly before leaving the kitchen.

Holm watched her leave with a wide-eyed look of disbelief on his face.

"No," he balked as he snapped back around to look at me. "No. How? When? She was ready to kick your ass like an hour ago. How are you already flirting and making plans to go out for drinks?"

"I'm just a likable guy." I smirked at him.

"Yeah, right," he deadpanned. "Anyway, come on, let's get back to the office to get briefed. I want to head home and pack before it gets too late."

I snickered as he continued to grumble all the way out of the house, my blood already pumping at the thought of a new adventure.

10

ETHAN

THE NEXT FEW hours passed by in a whirlwind. Diane had come to an agreement regarding jurisdiction with the FBI. As we'd previously discussed, MBLIS would take over the Allison Newark case, while Eddy's case would remain with the FBI. Specifically, it would remain under the authority of Agent Hastings, who would travel to Turks and Caicos with us. Not that I minded that particular detail.

As I was packing, I spotted Grendel's journal sitting on the coffee table where I'd left it the previous day, after going through everything with Holm. I felt just a twinge of regret at the timing of the case. After spending days wishing we'd land a new case, we'd finally gotten one right as I was beginning to get excited about delving back into my search for the *Dragon's Rogue*.

After thinking it over for a moment, I plucked the journal off the table and tucked it into my carry-on bag. I'd already looked through every page of the journal at least once, but I still carried it around everywhere I went.

Even though I'd already looked through the entire thing, it felt as though I discovered something new every time I leafed through the pages. Some of the entries were so disjointed and full of Grendel's paranoid ramblings that it often took a second, or even a third or fourth reading before I understood what he was trying to say. If nothing else, it would give me something to do on the flight down there.

After a quick final check to make sure I had everything I might need, I left my boat and headed over to my car. I tossed the single duffle bag into the trunk of my car before getting inside to head to the airport.

Really, I didn't need much. My years in the SEALS had taught me to pack quickly and efficiently. A few changes of clothes and the journal were all I really needed, and it was better to travel light, in my opinion. I never knew when I might suddenly have to move, so it was better not to be burdened down.

I rolled the windows down again as I headed to the airport. I honestly loved Miami. The ever-present sun, the sea breeze that you could smell from anywhere in the city... with my job being as crazy as it was, there was something calming about going for a drive with all the windows down, even if it was just for a few minutes.

Holm and Olivia were both waiting for me by the main entrance when I got to the airport.

"There you are." Olivia smiled as I approached them. "We both got here at the same time and happened to run into each other. We were wondering what was taking you so long."

"You didn't have to wait for me," I replied as the three of us headed toward security. "There was a lot of traffic."

"That would have been rude." Olivia shrugged. "Might as well stick together if we're going to be working the case together."

We were flying commercial again, but considering the flight was less than two hours long, I didn't really care.

"Dibs on the window seat," Holm called as the three of us boarded the plane.

"I call the aisle then," Olivia replied without missing a beat, much to my dismay. We actually hadn't planned to book our seats right next to each other. Looking at how crowded the plane was, though, it was likely they might have been some of the only seats available.

"My legs are longer than yours," I protested as she began to stow her bag in the overhead compartment.

"And that's my problem, how?" she teased before plopping down into the aisle seat.

I was a pretty tall guy, so the idea of sitting in the cramped middle seat for two hours actually wasn't very pleasant, but then again, it *was* only two hours. Compared to some of the international flights Holm and I had been on, it was nothing.

"Fine, but I get the aisle coming back," I grumbled.

"We'll see." She shrugged before flashing me an impish grin.

The next two hours passed by in a flash as Olivia and I chatted and traded barbs back and forth.

"So, they were actually looking for the exact same ship?" she asked. "Not just to mess with you, but honest to goodness trying to find it as well?"

I had just finished telling her about my search

for the *Dragon's Rogue*, as well as our hunt for the Holland's and how they'd been wrapped up in everything.

"Yeah." I nodded. "Well, at first, it was honestly just a coincidence, but then they deliberately started going for it after they found out I was searching for it, too. They even went as far as to create a fake journal just to throw me off."

"That's... bizarre," she scoffed. "Some people really have too much time on their hands."

"You're telling me," I muttered.

"So, why are you so invested in this?" she asked, genuinely curious. "I mean, I can tell just by the way that you talk about it that it really means a lot to you."

"It was my grandfather's dream first," I explained. "The ship actually belonged to our ancestor, and he spent his life looking for it. He passed the torch onto me before he died."

"That's really lovely." She smiled at me. "It's nice to see someone pursuing their passion like that. You don't see it often nowadays. People just go through the motions and do the bare minimum."

"Thanks." I grinned at her. "Most people just look at me like I'm a weirdo for being obsessed with pirate ships."

"Well, those people are boring," she retorted. "People shouldn't worry so much about what others think. We only have one life, you know? Better spend it doing what makes us happy."

"I like that," I replied as I churned her words over in my head.

She opened her mouth as if to say something to me, but before she could, the plane's intercom system crackled to life as the captain announced our imminent descent into Turks and Caicos.

"What did he say?" Holm asked as he pulled his headphones off of his ears. "Are we landing?"

"Yeah," I replied, unable to keep the disappointment completely out of my voice. It seemed as though every time Olivia and I started to get somewhere, we were interrupted.

I'd just have to carve some time out for us while we were on the island.

11

ETHAN

MY FIRST IMPRESSION of Turks and Caicos was that it wasn't unlike Miami. It was hot, it was crowded, and I could smell the salt in the air.

The beaches definitely seemed cleaner, though. That wasn't to say that Miami's beaches were ugly or anything, but it honestly wasn't all that uncommon to stumble across a broken beer bottle, or a pile of trash left behind by careless tourists. The sand along the shore here seemed uniformly pristine and almost spotless, despite the large number of people milling around. The water, too, was stunningly bright and clear, even from a distance.

We'd landed at Providenciales International Airport on the Western Island. Providenciales, commonly referred to as Pravo by the locals, comprised the Western, Northern, and Eastern Caicos islands. Southern Caicos was home to the large, densely populated Cockburn Town, but since the boat owner was located on the Western island, we'd decided to center our investigation there for now. For that reason, our first destination was the police station in Kew Town, in Western Caicos.

"We should drop off our stuff first," Olivia hummed as she looked around the pickup area. Dozens of tour guides and taxi drivers lined up outside the exit, offering their services to people as they left the airport. "Unless we want to start chasing bad guys with all of our luggage in tow."

"That's a good idea," I replied. "How far is it?"

"Not far at all," Olivia answered. "Actually, the island is so small that nothing is all that far from anything else. According to the GPS, we could *walk* from one end of the island to the other in less than six hours. The hotel's only about ten minutes from here."

"Let's go then," I replied as I slung my bag over my shoulder.

The scenery was beautiful as we made the short trek over to the hotel. I could see the ocean from the street we were on, which was lined with palm trees and bright green plants with enormous leaves.

Though most of the houses were painted in shades of white, every once in a while, we'd pass one that was a bright shade of banana yellow or canary blue. Everything on the island seemed extremely colorful and fresh.

"This is it," Olivia announced as we came to a stop in front of a large green building. I'd been so absorbed in the scenery that I'd barely noticed the time pass.

As we stepped into the hotel, a blast of cool air from the AC hit me. The inside of the hotel looked a little like the lobby of an apartment building, and I wondered if it had been converted from one.

"Why don't we meet back here in fifteen?" I proposed. "That'll give us time to put our stuff down and freshen up."

"Good idea," Olivia replied as we stepped onto the elevator. We'd all gotten rooms on the same floor. Unlike the plane seats, that had been deliberate, as it would be safer for all of us to be close by just in case anything went wrong during the case.

We got off of the elevator and headed into our rooms, which were side by side on one side of the hall. Holm had the room to my right, while Olivia had the one to my left.

I didn't have enough time to shower, so I settled

for splashing some water on my face. Though the weather here felt similar to Miami's, it was definitely hotter on the island, and even the short walk from the airport to the hotel had left me sweating.

After doing one last check to make sure I had all the essentials, namely my gun, my badge, and a few sets of handcuffs, I headed downstairs to meet up with Holm and Olivia.

"Last one to the party again, Marston," Olivia teased when she saw me. She and Holm had already made it down.

"It hasn't even been fifteen minutes," I countered.

"Well, I can't sit still," she replied. "Come on, let's get to the station already."

The three of us headed out of the hotel and back onto the street. The difference between the cool interior of the hotel and the sun-baked street was palpable.

"The police station is right over here," Olivia muttered as she looked up the directions on her phone. "Let's just hurry and get this over with."

"What do you mean?" I asked as we approached the large, two-story building. It looked a little like a motel, with an exterior staircase that led up to a walkway on the second floor. The only thing that indicated it was a police station was a small banner pasted to the front that read "Kew Town Police Station" in bold red letters.

"I mean that I don't have time for stupid formalities," she huffed. "The quicker we touch base with the locals and establish that we've got this under control, the quicker we can get down to actually investigating."

It was becoming alarmingly evident that Olivia very much fit with the stereotype of the territorial FBI agent that didn't play well with others. Not that I didn't see her point, though she could do a little better about not making it so obvious.

The interior of the station didn't look much different from any of the other rural stations I'd visited during my travels. The main entrance opened to a modestly decorated lobby. A single police officer was manning the main desk. Just beyond him, I could see a corridor that led into the rest of the building. There weren't any glass partitions or intense security measures in place that I could see. Kew Town must have been a relatively safe place.

"Hello," Olivia greeted the man sitting at the front desk coolly. "I'm Agent Olivia Hastings with the FBI. These are Agents Holm and Marston with MBLIS. We're here to speak with Captain Turner."

She spoke quickly and clearly, in an authoritative voice that left no room for argument.

"Of course," the man replied as he stood up. "I'll take you back to his office."

We followed him further into the police station, down a narrow hallway, and toward an elevator. We got off on the second floor, and he led us through a bullpen area similar to the one back home in our own office.

The officer knocked twice on a closed door at the end of the large room before heading inside.

"Agents here to see you, sir," he said before stepping aside to let us in.

The man sitting behind the desk looked to be in his fifties, with a rich, deep skin tone and a smoothly shaved head. He had a wide, unsettling grin on his face, like the most exaggerated caricature of a customer service smile I could imagine. All fake.

His office, too, made me feel unsettled. Aside from a large wooden desk, a few chairs, and a row of filing cabinets against the back wall, there was no furniture in the room. Honestly, it seemed more like a prison cell than an office.

"Welcome to Turks and Caicos, Agents." He smiled at us before standing to shake each of our hands. "Though I wish you were here under more pleasant circumstances."

"So do we," Olivia replied curtly. "To get straight down to business, I assume you know why we're here? I'm certain you received a briefing from my director prior to our arrival."

"Of course," he replied. "Please, rest assured that we are ready to do everything we can to assist you in your investigation. An officer will accompany you during your time here on the island."

Olivia clenched her jaw. It was obvious that idea did not please her. Honestly, something about the guy seemed kind of off to me as well. He was a little too cheerful for my taste.

"That's not to say that we don't trust the FBI," he continued, though that was definitely what it sounded like if the tone of his voice was anything to go by. "It's just that as the crime occurred here in our country, it is only appropriate that a member of our law enforcement be involved as well."

"Of course, we understand," I replied quickly when it seemed like Olivia was about to snap.

"Excellent." He smiled morosely. "Well, let's not waste any more time then. I'll go get Officer Keys now."

He stood and left the office.

"We've already got two separate entities covering this case," Olivia muttered. "Why not add one more?"

"Not like we have much choice," Holm pointed out. "That's the fun part of international criminal investigation, having to hash through every country's laws and policies. As long as we're here, we have to play by their rules, at least to some extent. We're used to it."

"I just hope they don't stick us with some hot-headed jerk," Olivia muttered grumpily.

Fortunately, she got her wish, as the officer that Captain Turner returned with was all smiles and relaxed posture.

"Hey, what's up, guys?" He grinned at us. "My name is Walter Carson. I'll be assisting you with your case, then."

"Carson?" Olivia raised an eyebrow at him before turning to look at Captain Turner. "I thought you said—"

"Unfortunately, Officer Keys is on leave right now," the captain grumbled.

"Yeah, if that's what you want to call it," Officer Carson snickered.

The captain shot him an angry look, but Carson seemed unfazed. He was tall, and his hair was braided into neat rows atop his head and gathered at the base of his neck in a small ponytail.

"Officer Carson will accompany you," he muttered.

"Yeah, 'cause don't no one else want to do it," Officer Carson interrupted him again.

"Carson!" the captain barked, one of the veins in his neck standing out so much that it looked painful.

"Yeah, yeah, alright," Carson sighed almost disinterestedly. It was kind of amazing watching him just casually brush off his boss like that. "Come on then, let's not waste any more time here. You agents ready to go or what?"

"You don't have to ask me twice," Olivia replied.

The police captain looked like he'd just bitten into a sour lemon. I was curious as to what had just happened for his demeanor to have changed so suddenly, and I tucked the thought aside as I followed Olivia out of the office.

"Thank you for your cooperation," I heard Holm tell the captain behind me before following me out.

"He sure seemed friendly," Olivia muttered once the door was closed, and we were out of earshot.

"You noticed that too, huh?" I replied quietly as we made our way out of the station.

"How could I not?" she scoffed. "That guy's smile

was creepy. And what was up with how he suddenly came back all mad?"

"The captain doesn't like it when things don't go his way," Carson laughed as we stepped out onto the street.

Olivia's face flushed as she realized that he'd heard our exchange, despite the fact that we'd been whispering.

"Sorry." He smiled sheepishly as he noted the embarrassed look on her face. "Didn't mean to eavesdrop on ye. Don't worry, though. I'm not gonna tell the captain what ye said! Anyway, now that we're outta that stuffy old office, why don't we introduce ourselves properly? I'm Officer Walter Carson, but you folks can just call me Walter."

Unlike the captain, Walter's smile seemed genuine, and I didn't get the impression that he was putting on a show or hiding anything from us.

"Good to meet you, Walter." Olivia moved forward to shake his hand firmly. "I'm Agent Olivia Hastings. This is Agent Ethan Marston and Agent Robbie Holm."

"Nice to meet you," he responded as he shook each of our hands. "Are ye all FBI, then?"

"No, actually," I replied. "Agent Hastings is, but

Holm and I belong to an organization called MBLIS."

"Embolis?" Walter cocked his head at us, his brows furrowed in confusion.

"M-B-L-I-S," Holm spelled the acronym out for him. "It stands for Military Border Liaison Investigative Service. We handle crimes that cross borders or that involve multiple countries, or that take place out in international waters, stuff like that."

"Ah, I see." Walter nodded thoughtfully. "That explains why you're here in Turks & Caicos, then, right? I understand now. The office has been all abuzz since we heard that we'd be getting a visit from FBI agents."

"Yeah, you mentioned something about that," Olivia muttered. "You said that no one else wanted to be assigned to work with us. Why is that?"

"They don't want trouble." Walter shrugged. "I heard the details of the case earlier. Ye all found some girl dead, right? Be perfectly honest with you, no one around here wants to go anywhere near a case involving a dead American girl."

"So why did you volunteer?" I asked.

"Cause, unlike them, I actually take my job seriously," he retorted before giving me a grin. "And because I knew it would piss off old Turner. Only reason he wanted Keys on the case with you is that Keys is a brown-nosing little snitch who would have reported everything you did back to the boss."

"I'm shocked," Olivia deadpanned.

"Yeah, well, lucky for you," Walter chuckled, "Keys is on a*dministrative leave* right now. And by that, I mean he was arrested last night up in Grace Bay. Guess he got a little too carried away with the cocaine this time! Ah, you shoulda seen the look on the captain's face when he marched into the main office to ask where Keys was. It surprised me he hadn't heard since gossip's been going around all morning."

"Your captain didn't know that one of his officers is in jail right now?" I asked, struck with disbelief at his words.

"Man, the captain doesn't know *nothing,*" Walter laughed.

Walter seemed positively gleeful about that, and I wondered just what went on behind the closed doors of that police station. Nevertheless, I was glad we had someone like Walter working the case with us.

"Let's go speak to the owner of the boat," I suggested after checking the time. We'd dropped our bags off at the hotel earlier, and there was still plenty of daylight left for us to begin our investigation. "According to the information we managed to dig up, he runs a boat rental shop on the beach near here."

"Let's go then," Olivia agreed. "He might have seen something. He might even recognize her if he's a local."

Our destination was the beach located at the northernmost part of the city. As we started walking, I realized that Olivia's earlier statement about nothing really being far away on the island was true, since it would only take us about ten minutes to walk there.

"It's so pretty," Olivia remarked as we walked past the brightly colored buildings, flanked on either side by massive palm trees. On the streets, I could see locals and tourists alike walking around, admiring the scenery at a leisurely pace. It didn't seem like anyone was in a rush to get anywhere, and I imagined that it would be an amazing place to actually have a vacation. If only we weren't here for such a tragic reason.

"You know exactly where the place is?" Walter asked us a few minutes later as we stepped onto the beach.

"No," I replied as I looked out along the coastline. It was stunning, coated in sand so pure and even that it almost looked white. "His address is near here, though. I figured since it's the middle of the day, in the middle of tourist season, that he'd be out on the beach right now. We can check his home next if we can't manage to find him."

"Sounds like a plan to me," Walter hummed as he led us down the busy boardwalk. Shops and stalls lined the wide pedestrian boardwalk, and I couldn't help but have a glance as we passed by. One particular stall caught my attention, not because of the way it looked, but because of the way it *smelled.*

The plump woman running the little place was deep-frying something inside of a large vat of oil before placing it onto a thick bun and piling it high with lettuce, tomato, and some kind of sauce I couldn't readily identify.

"Ah, shark caught your eye, huh?" Walter called as he turned to see what I was looking at.

"What?" I asked, a little embarrassed at having been caught staring.

"The shark." He nodded toward the stall. "Kinda thing you can only find here. Mama Rosie makes the best ones on the Western Island, too. Wanna stop and have some?"

"It's alright," I replied a little reluctantly. "It

smells amazing, and I'm always up for trying a new and exciting local dish, but we really should try to get some investigating done before we take a break."

"We can come back closer to dinner time," Olivia suggested. "There's a lot of stuff here I'd like to try out too. We can have a look around after we finish up for the day."

"That sounds good." I smiled at her.

As we continued down the boardwalk, I couldn't keep my eyes from drifting over to the shops and restaurants lining the walkway. One, in particular, caught my eye, a hip-looking bar that was crowded with tourists. I wasn't certain at first what about it had drawn my attention since it didn't look any different from any other tourist-trap bar.

Then I realized what it was. A young woman was standing near the main entrance. She didn't look all that different from the rest of the tourists, but her behavior was strange. She was standing almost unnaturally still, and something about her posture was setting off alarm bells in my head.

"Hey, Ethan!" Olivia's voice broke me out of my thoughts. I looked up, and it surprised me to discover that I'd lagged behind the rest of the group. "Hurry up!"

"Sorry," I called back distractedly as I looked back at the bar.

The girl was gone.

I blinked and wondered If I'd just imagined it. It was odd, and part of me wanted to go investigate, if only to ensure that I hadn't been seeing things. I had to focus on the case now, though, so I pushed the thought to the back of my mind.

"Oh, I see boats," Olivia remarked a few minutes later. Sure enough, a few yards away, just off of the beach, was a small docking area lined with boats of various sizes.

"This is where all the boats on this part of the beach dock," Walter informed us. "The man we are looking for is most likely working somewhere around here."

The area was dotted with signs advertising fishing trips, boat rentals, and even scuba lessons, so I knew that Walter must be right about this being the spot.

We stepped off the boardwalk and onto the sand toward the water where the boats were docked. There were markedly fewer tourists on this part of the beach. Most of the people walking around appeared to be fishermen and boat workers, though there were a few tourists milling around, most likely in search of a boat rental.

I kept stumbling as I made my way across the beach. The sand was so fine and smooth here that it shifted and gave way easily as I stepped over it, and I just knew I was going to end up with sand in my shoes by the end of this.

"Excuse me," I called to one of the men standing on the boat nearest to us. "We're looking for a Kenneth Johnson. He rents boats out here."

"Kenny?" the man asked as he stepped off the boat to come to speak with us. "Yeah, he works down on the other end of the docks. But uh, just between you and me, my service is a lot better, you know? Faster boat and cheaper price, too."

"Thanks," I replied. "But we aren't actually trying to rent a boat."

"You need a guide?" the man asked immediately. "Maybe some fishing equipment? I can tell you right now, you won't find anything better than what we offer here at Jacob's Boats."

"We actually need to question him with regard to a criminal matter," Olivia interjected.

The man glanced up at her and then seemed to suddenly notice Walter for the first time. The smile fell from his face the moment he spotted the police uniform.

"Ah, I see," he mumbled awkwardly before pointing down toward the end of the dock. "Well, uh, Kenny's over there. Down by the pier, you can't miss it."

"Thanks," I replied, but the man had already turned around and was getting back onto the boat.

"You know that guy?" Holm asked Walter as we started down toward the pier at the edge of the dock. "He got all quiet the moment he saw you."

"Nah." Walter shrugged. "Probably just didn't want to talk to a cop. Turks & Caicos is a beautiful place, full of friendly people, but that doesn't mean there's no crime here. The thing is, though, people here are a close-knit bunch, especially these fisherman types. They aren't going to want to talk ill of one of their own, even if they do know something."

"Great," Holm grumbled. "Just what we need on a case where we already have almost no clues."

We made our way down the line of boats. Finally, we made it to the wooden pier that the other man had directed us toward. Two boats were docked right beside it, one a little speedboat, and the other a larger fishing boat similar to the one we'd found Allison's body in. A large hand-painted sign was jammed into the ground just in front of the boats, advertising various services such as guided fishing and boat rentals.

"Hello!" a young man with curly hair and deeply tanned skin called from one of the boats as he spotted us approaching. He jumped nimbly off and walked toward us. "How can I help you folks? Interested in a boat rental?"

"Are you Kenneth Johnson?" I asked him.

"Yeah, why?" he replied, the smile slipping off his face just a little as he eyed us warily.

"I'm Agent Marston with MBLIS," I introduced myself as I pulled my credentials out of my pocket to show him. "This is my partner Agent Holm, and this is Agent Hastings with the FBI. We need to speak to you about the person who stole your boat a few days ago."

"Oh, that," he snapped, his face twisting into an annoyed pout. "So you finally caught that girl, huh? Crazy cow. Just jumped into my boat, *with a kid* no less, and took off at full speed! Took a third of my business with her. I'm trying to make a living here, and this girl just takes off with one of my three boats!"

"So you actually witnessed her taking it?" Olivia jumped in.

"Of course I did!" Kenneth scowled. "I was just about to rent it to this nice British couple when she jumped right in and stole it! So, what, was she trafficking drugs or something? Why's the FBI involved in some stolen property case? I knew that girl was into something bad."

"We're involved," I replied curtly, "because that girl was a trafficking victim, and we believe that she stole your boat while attempting to flee from her captors."

Kenneth's face went white at my words, and he stuttered for a moment before speaking again.

"I-I didn't, wow. That's crazy," he stammered quietly.

"What did you mean when you said she was into something bad?" Olivia asked.

"Huh?" he replied dumbly.

"You just said 'I knew that girl was into something bad,'" Olivia clarified. "What made you think that?"

"Oh, well..." he muttered as he shifted his eyes down toward the ground. "Something weird happened right after she took it."

"What do you mean by weird?" I asked.

He looked up at Walter before flitting his gaze back down to the ground.

"Look, I don't want to get in trouble," he mumbled.

"Why would you get in trouble?" I asked. "Did you do something wrong?"

"No!" he replied vehemently. "Well, not really. It's just... I didn't mention this to the police when I first reported the boat stolen."

He was carefully keeping his gaze away from Walter as he spoke.

"That doesn't matter," I insisted. "Just tell us now. This girl was a victim for years. Whatever you saw might help us get her some justice."

"There was some guy after her," he finally revealed.

"What do you mean?" Olivia snapped, probably more angrily than she'd meant to. "You saw someone trying to hurt her?"

"Yeah," Kenneth mumbled, unable to look her in the eye. "Right after she took off, this psycho came running up and started shooting at her."

"Shooting?!" I exclaimed, alarmed at the idea of someone opening fire in the middle of a crowded beach like this.

"Did you see what he looked like?" Olivia asked.

"No." Kenneth shook his head. "He just came out

of nowhere and started shooting. I got on the ground, and when I looked up again, he was gone."

"And it didn't occur to you to mention any of this to the police?" I asked him incredulously.

He swallowed and glanced over at Walter again before answering.

"I didn't want to get involved in anything shady," he replied nervously. "I figured that girl must have been deep in drugs or something if someone was trying to gun her down in broad daylight. Why else would she steal someone's boat like that if she wasn't up to no good?"

"Maybe because she was trying to escape the people who were trafficking her!" Olivia growled.

"Look, I didn't know, okay?" Kenneth retorted. "You have to understand, though, around here…"

He looked around nervously, as though checking to see if anyone was listening.

"What is it?" I prompted.

"Look, to be completely honest, I'm not really surprised," he revealed. "It's awful, what happened to that girl, but it's not exactly a rare sight around here."

"Prostitution, you mean?" Olivia asked.

"Yeah." Kenneth nodded, still glancing around hesitantly. "And the people in charge of those girls, the ones who run the bars and brothels? They've got eyes and ears everywhere."

I suddenly realized why he was acting so skittish.

"You think they're around right now?" I asked.

"Oh, I *know* they are," he replied as he took a backward step away from me. "Look, like I said, I'm sorry about what happened to that girl, but it's not really any of my business. Just forget about the boat."

"Wait!" I called as I took a step toward him.

"I don't want to end up like that girl," he snapped back at me, his eyes wide and frantic.

"I get that," I replied. "But we can make sure that doesn't happen. We'll get you somewhere safe until we can figure out who's behind this."

"I don't know..." Kenneth muttered.

"Her son's name is Eddy," Olivia suddenly chimed in. "She gave her life to get him to safety. He's all alone now. All we want is to get some justice for him and his mother."

"What, she's dead?" Kenneth gaped.

"Yeah, she is," I added somberly. It had been smart of Olivia to go for an emotional appeal. It had really seemed like we were about to lose him. "She didn't survive the boat journey. Right now, you're the only one who might know anything about who's responsible for this."

"Come on, man, you can't put that responsibility on me," Kenneth grumbled. "Okay, fine. I'll tell you about what I know. But look, you need to promise—"

I saw the red mist first, so suddenly and unexpectedly that my brain didn't immediately understand what it was. I was so focused on hearing what Kenneth was about to say that I didn't even realize at first that he'd stopped talking.

It hit me then, just a split second later, that the red mist was coming from Kenneth. It was his face, exploding into a burst of blood and mangled flesh.

Someone had just shot him, I realized at the exact moment that I registered that the loud bang I heard was the sound of a gunshot.

I'd just watched our primary witness get shot to death right in front of me.

For a long, surreal moment, it felt as though time stood completely still. Then everything began moving again, violently and all too quickly.

"Get down!" Walter shouted as he drew his gun from the holster at his hip.

A second later, panic broke out all over the beach.

12

ETHAN

I DREW my own gun and spun around to find the source of the gunfire. It felt like time had stopped for just a moment right after the shot, but now it seemed like everyone on the beach had realized what had happened. Some people dropped to the ground, covering their own heads or attempting to shelter children and loved ones. Others frantically ran in every direction, stumbling over the sand and falling to the ground, only to be trampled by others attempting to get away.

"There!" I heard Walter yell as he lifted his gun toward the boardwalk. I followed his line of sight and found what he was looking at. Three men were standing just about a hundred yards away by the boardwalk, their own guns held aloft and pointed directly at us.

"Get down!" I yelled the moment I recognized the murderous intent in their eyes. I managed to throw myself onto the sand just as one of them pulled the trigger again. A woman who just happened to run into the path of the bullet let out a short, surprised yelp of pain before falling to the ground.

"Cover me," Olivia suddenly yelled before slipping into the crowd.

"What?" I called, but she was already gone.

I rolled into a crouch and lifted my own gun, but there were too many people between us for me to get a good shot.

Walter, on the other hand, didn't seem to share my concerns. He fired off two shots at the men, narrowly missing a young couple who happened to be running by them as he did.

"What are you doing?" I roared at him. "You're going to hit a civilian!"

"What am I supposed to do?" he yelled back. "We're sitting ducks!"

He wasn't wrong. There was nothing around for us to take cover behind, and the men obviously didn't have any qualms about killing any of the random bystanders who happened to be running by. Holm stood just to my left, his gun clutched in his hand. It looked like he was also struggling to find an opening to shoot.

I was just about to suggest that we run, if only to lead the men away from the innocent crowd, when I realized I'd lost my visual on Olivia.

I looked around for her frantically, horrified at the idea that she might have been shot in the few seconds my focus had been elsewhere. Then I suddenly spotted her, quickly weaving her way through the crowd as she circled around to catch the men from behind.

"Get ready!" I muttered to Holm, who was still taking cover on the ground. "I think Olivia's about to give us an opening."

Just as I finished speaking, one of the men fell forward with a pained grunt. Standing just behind him was Olivia, her gun pointed straight at where the fallen man had just been standing.

The two other men turned toward their fallen comrade in shock, and I took the opportunity to move in. I sprinted straight for the second man, who turned around just as I made it within punching distance of him. He moved to lift his gun, but he was too late, and my fist smashed into his nose with a satisfying crunch.

Holm had already moved in on the first man who had fallen to the ground, and Walter was going after the third. As for the man I was currently fighting with, he had dropped his gun when I'd punched him, and he was currently attempting to hit me back.

I raised my arm to block his blow, but he surprised me when he suddenly switched tack and hit me in the side instead. This guy clearly knew a thing or two about fighting, then.

Nevertheless, I could tell that his movements were unpolished and sloppy.

He was definitely strong, though. I could tell that much just from the force behind his punches. He was fast too, and it was all I could do to block his punches as he continued to rain them down on me.

Still, I was a former SEAL. I had years of martial arts and close-combat training under my belt. Regardless of how strong this guy was, it would be embarrassing if I lost to a street fighter who didn't know how to pace himself.

Just as I'd suspected, after just a minute or so of launching non-stop punches at me at full force, his blows became weaker. This was my chance.

I dodged his punch and hit him hard in the stomach. He wheezed as the blow knocked the wind out of him. I didn't give him a chance to recover and quickly swept his legs out from under him with a harsh kick to the back of his knees.

He yelped as he suddenly fell backward onto the concrete boardwalk.

He groaned as his head struck the ground, and I wasted no time shoving him onto his stomach and twisting his arms behind his back.

I made quick work of getting him cuffed and then turned to see how my partner was faring. Holm was bent over the guy that Olivia had shot and was taking his pulse. The guy was completely still, and the surrounding sand was quickly staining red. I could tell even from this distance that Holm wasn't about to get a pulse off of him.

Just as I was about the check on Walter, I heard another gunshot.

I snapped my head around to find the source of the sound, just in time to catch sight of Walter falling to the ground, the man he'd been grappling with taking off at a sprint away from the beach and toward the town.

"Dammit!" I yelled as I got to my feet and

hurried to Walter's side as quickly as I could manage on the uneven sand.

"I'll call for help!" Olivia yelled somewhere behind me.

"I'm sorry," Walter huffed as I fell to a crouch beside him. He had one hand pressed tightly against his side, and he was struggling to draw breath. "I disarmed him, but he had another gun. Rookie mistake. Didn't even realize it until he'd already shot me."

"Just take it easy," I cautioned him. "Olivia's calling for help now. We're going to get you some help."

He looked ashen, and his hands were beginning to tremble, so I helped him keep pressure on the wound by placing my own hands over his.

Now that I wasn't hyper-focused on my own fight, I took a moment to glance around at the beach as well. Two people were lying nearby, in similar states as Walter. Several others were scattered along the beach, nursing minor injuries. They'd probably gotten hurt during the chaos as everyone scattered and trampled over one another to get away.

Then, of course, there was Kenneth. He was still lying where he'd fallen, half-submerged in the water, his blood staining the bubbly sea foam a repulsive pink.

I gritted my teeth in anger as I surveyed all the chaos around us, all of these innocent people hurt because of him and his ilk. I was going to make sure he paid for everything he had done.

13

ETHAN

I RAN a hand through my hair as I leaned against the back of the bench where Holm, Olivia, and I were sitting. The Cheshire Hall Medical Center was located far enough inland that I actually couldn't see the ocean from here, though that didn't make the view any less lovely. Massive, bright green palm trees lined the front of the building, though I couldn't bring myself to relax enough to enjoy them.

Four hours had passed since the attack on the beach, and we were still dealing with the aftermath. Our primary source of information had been shot dead right in front of us. The police officer who'd been escorting us had been shot in the side and was currently in the hospital. One of the three men who had shot at us was dead, and another had escaped and was currently at large. Worst of all, three bystanders had been killed as a result of the chaos. Two had been shot in the crossfire, and a third, an elderly man on vacation with his wife, had suddenly collapsed with a heart attack during the panic. That was to say nothing of all the minor injuries that had been incurred as people ran and struggled to get away.

"Well, it looks like we won't be getting another escort," Holm informed Olivia and me as he finished his call with Diane at the main office and tucked his phone back into his pocket. He'd just given her a rundown of everything that had happened.

"Captain Smiley didn't want to cooperate?" I guessed.

"He did not," Holm confirmed. "Actually, he insisted that we 'get the hell out of Turks & Caicos,' according to Diane. Apparently, he's telling everyone who'll listen that it's our fault that Walter got hurt and that we need to vacate the country as quickly as possible. That's not happening, obviously. She'd already spoken with the consulate, and we have permission to be here, so that's not an issue. It does look like we'll be flying solo, though, since the local PD is refusing to cooperate."

"Fine by me," Olivia scoffed. "Too many cooks

spoil the broth, as they say. I liked Walter fine, but having four people and three different law enforcement agencies on a single case is a little too crowded for my tastes."

"Don't hold back," I teased. "Tell us how you really feel about it."

She smirked and rolled her eyes at me.

"I am glad Walter's going to be okay, though," she continued. "I was so shocked when he stumbled back looking like that."

"I am too." I nodded before turning to look at her. "That was quick thinking on your part, by the way. We would have been screwed if you hadn't distracted them."

"Thanks." She smiled shyly at me. "I didn't even think about it, to be honest. The moment people started running, I took off too. It was easy to blend into the crowd and circle around behind them. I just wish I'd managed to take him down before anyone else got hurt."

It had certainly been a rough way to start our first day here, and it was only about to get more stressful.

"So, you guys ready to go interview the one man we managed to arrest?" I sighed as I stood up off the bench.

"That's still happening?" Olivia blinked at me in surprise. "After the police captain basically tried to kick us out of the country? You really think he's going to let us?"

"I wasn't planning on asking his permission." I shrugged. "We have jurisdiction here. This is our case, and that is our suspect. If he doesn't want his officers working with us, that's his business, but I'm not about to let him keep us away from the guy who shot at us."

"Yeah, I guess you're right," Olivia sighed. "I just don't want to go back there again, to be honest. That guy gave me the creeps."

The hospital was actually far enough away from the station to warrant getting a taxi unless we wanted to make a thirty-minute trek up to the station.

Ultimately, though, we ended up having to call for an Uber since we weren't able to find a taxi even after walking ten minutes from the hospital. It really seemed as though most people around here just walked, as I'd seen very few cars at all on the roads, aside from the taxis that had been lined up outside the airport.

As we rode back to the station, I wondered if we should look into getting a rental car. Turks and

Caicos weren't particularly big, so getting around by walking was manageable for the most part, though it did become inconvenient in times like these where we happened to be just a bit too far from our destination. As we pulled up to the station, I made a mental note to discuss it with Holm and Olivia that night at the hotel.

We'd barely made it two steps inside before the officer manning the front desk stood up and motioned for us to stop.

"I don't think you should be here," he warned us nervously.

"What?" I retorted.

"What the hell are you doing here?!" A voice boomed from further inside the station. Captain Turner was marching straight toward us, his jaw clenched, and his hands balled into fists. "You have a lot of nerve, showing your faces here after the condition you left my officer in!"

"*We* didn't do anything to him," I bit back. "We're here to interrogate the man who did."

"Oh, no, you're not," he sneered. "You're not taking another step forward. Get out!"

"Yeah, that's not happening," I scoffed. "That man is a suspect in a federal investigation. You can't block us from speaking to him."

"You Americans," he snarled. "Always thinking you can just go wherever you want, do whatever you want. You might bully everyone else, but you won't bully me!"

"Maybe you'd be a little more receptive to the MI5?" Olivia interrupted.

It seemed she'd struck a nerve because Turner's face actually went pale at that.

"The Turks and Caicos Islands are a British territory," she continued. "If the FBI doesn't scare you, then maybe they will. I can assure you, though, that they're going to be on our side. We're going to speak with that man one way or another. How stupid you wind up looking to British Security Service once that happens is all up to you."

His face twisted into an ugly grimace as she finished speaking. He was glaring daggers at all three of us, and I was certain he was shooting us murderous thoughts.

"Take them back," he spat at the officer behind the desk before storming back off.

"Sorry about him," the officer muttered once he was out of earshot.

"Is he always like that?" Olivia huffed.

"Well, sometimes he's..." the man trailed off. "Yes, pretty much. You get used to it, though."

"I feel for you," Holm murmured.

The man just smiled awkwardly in response.

"I'll take you back to the interrogation room, then." He smiled awkwardly before leading us further into the station. "His name is Frank Phillips. He has a few prior arrests for drug distribution, as well as one for domestic assault. Oh, but don't tell the captain I told you."

"Not a chance," I assured him. "Hopefully, we won't see him again for the rest of our stay here."

The officer smiled gratefully. I felt bad for the man. He seemed like a good guy just trying to do his job. It must be awful having such a piece of crap boss. It made me want to do something nice for Diane whenever we made it back home.

"The interrogation room is right in here," the officer said as we came to a stop in front of a door. I could see the man through the little square window in the door, sitting at a table. "I'll go and get Frank if you'll just wait here a moment. One of you should stay out here, too. You need to push this button for the door to open. I would, but I need to get back to the front."

"I'll wait outside," Holm offered. "That way, Olivia can be involved too."

He made it sound like he was doing it for purely

practical reasons since this way there would be both an MBLIS and FBI representative in the room, but I could have sworn I heard him snicker something about a "third wheel."

"We have a monitoring room you can watch from," the helpful officer informed us. "I can take you there as soon as I'm done fetching Frank."

"Thanks," Holm replied gratefully.

The officer left then, presumably to get Frank from his holding cell. For just a second, I was hit with the terrifying thought that the nice guy act might all be a ruse and that he might be letting Frank escape now while we waited here unawares.

However, my fears were proven to be unfounded just a moment later when he suddenly rounded the corner, his arm firm on Frank's elbow as he guided him down the hallway.

Frank sneered at us viciously as the officer led him past us and into the interrogation room.

"Alright," he announced a moment later as he reemerged from the room. "He's ready now. I'll show you to the monitoring room, then."

I watched as he and Holm stepped into an adjacent room before I stepped into the interrogation room with Olivia.

Frank looked up at us as we walked inside, his face set into an unfriendly scowl.

"Hello, Frank," I greeted him casually as I moved to take a seat opposite him at the table. He squared his shoulders and puffed out his chest, doing his absolute best to give off the best "tough guy" impression he could. In my experience, though, the more intimidating a guy tried to look, the more of a pathetic coward he was. Maybe scaring him into talking would be the best angle to approach him from.

He ignored me completely and instead turned to look at Olivia. Just as I'd suspected. This guy was so big and tough that, of course, he would immediately go for the smaller female target than the man who had just spoken to him.

"You're the one who shot my buddy," he snarled at her, baring his teeth like a rabid dog.

"Yeah, that was me," she replied impassively, clearly unimpressed with his "menacing" display. "That's what happens when you open fire on a beach full of innocent people."

"You're a coward," he spat at her. "Shooting a man in the back is the lowest of the low."

"Funny you should talk about cowards," I hummed. "Tell me, how much courage does it take to shoot an unarmed woman? Or, how about we talk about your other friend? The one who took off as soon as things started going south and hid behind a young girl so that the police officer pursuing him wouldn't shoot?"

His mouth twisted into a puckered frown as though he'd just bitten into a lemon.

"Now you have nothing to say, of course." Olivia nodded.

"Of course, I have nothing to say to a couple of pigs!" he sneered. "I'm no rat. I'm not going to snitch on my own brothers."

"Well, *that's* a mistake," I scoffed. "Because I can assure you, they won't show you the same loyalty."

"What do you know of loyalty?" he asked, his deep voice gravelly with anger.

"I know that criminals like you and your 'brothers' always turn on each other in the end," I replied. "You know it too, don't you? Eventually, someone's going to panic to spill the information we want. And once those floodgates open, that's it for the rest of you."

I was bluffing since we didn't even have anyone else in custody, but Frank here didn't need to know that. It seemed like the bluff was working, too, as he suddenly swallowed heavily and looked down at the table.

"What was the total casualty count?" Olivia asked me casually. She tossed me a look out of the corner of her eye, and I knew she'd caught on to what I was doing. "Was it three dead and seven injured?"

"Four dead, if you count Frank's buddy," I replied as I turned to look Frank directly in the eye.

"Yikes." Olivia grimaced. "That's a lot of victims. A lot of damage for one single person to be saddled with."

"W-what do you mean by that?" Frank stammered, his jaw going slack.

"Exactly what it sounds like." I shrugged. "We've got a beach full of dead and injured people and only one perp in custody. One of your friends is dead, and the other hightailed it out of there as soon as the going got tough. Do you really think *he* won't turn on you if he gets the chance? I mean, he left you behind to deal with the consequences all by yourself. I'd sure hate to be the one to go down for all those crimes on my own."

"I wonder what kind of prison time we're looking at," Olivia mused out loud. "Ten years per victim, at least, don't you think?"

"Definitely," I agreed, though I actually had no idea. "Not to mention a harsher sentence once the judge finds out how uncooperative he was during the investigation."

"Alright."

"Yep, can't forget about that." Olivia nodded. "I wonder how soon we could get the extradition process started."

"I said alright."

"I can call my director right now and ask," I said as I pointedly ignored Frank to pull my phone out of my pocket.

"Listen to me!" the man roared as he slammed his fist down onto the table.

"Okay." I smirked as I slipped my phone back into place. "We're listening, now talk."

"I don't know where Thomas is," he grumbled. "That's the other man who was with us. We're not exactly friends, you know? We go where we're told and do what the boss tells us to do."

"And who is this 'boss' of yours?" Olivia raised an eyebrow at him.

"I don't know his name," Frank replied.

"Convenient," Olivia deadpanned.

"I'm telling the truth!" Frank hissed. "He's paranoid about anyone finding out his identity. It's not a good idea to call attention to ourselves in our line of work."

"That line of work being prostitution," I countered.

"That's right," he replied. "Anyway, I don't know his name, but I know how you can get in contact with him. There's an old guy that runs an antique store over in Grace Bay. He knows how to get in touch with the boss."

"And you know this how?" Olivia asked.

"He's the one who gives us our assignments," Frank explained. "He's an old geezer who sits on his store's porch all day, so he's the perfect cover."

"You're a real charmer, you know that?" Olivia snarled at him.

He flashed her a malicious, yellow-toothed grin before continuing.

"Go there and tell him that 'Simon' sent you," he told us.

"Simon?" I repeated. "Why would I say that, Frank?"

"You think we use our real names?" he snapped at me angrily. "I just got finished telling you that I don't even know my boss's name. Use your head! I thought you feds were supposed to be smart."

"Settle down," Olivia warned him before pulling

her phone out of her bag. She glanced at me side-
ways, a look of suspicion on her face. I could tell she
wasn't entirely buying what Frank was telling us, and
I couldn't blame her. Something about it seemed off
to me, too.

"Alright," he muttered as she pulled up a GPS
app on her phone. "Tell us the address."

14

ETHAN

HOLM MET up with Olivia and me outside the interrogation room just moments after we wrapped
everything up.

"Well, that guy was *definitely* hiding something,"
he scoffed right away.

"Why do you say that?" I asked.

Before Holm could answer, Captain Turner's
grating, fake-nice voice came booming down the
hallway.

"Agents!" he bellowed cheerfully, all of his earlier
hostility gone. Or, at least, well hidden beneath a
thick veneer of false friendliness. "I'm glad I caught
you. I have good news. I've found someone to
replace Walter as your escort."

"Oh, for goodness' sake," Olivia muttered as the

captain stepped confidently toward us, a lanky, nervous-looking officer hot on his heels.

"This is Officer Jackson," the captain introduced the new officer with a strong clap on the back. "He'll be accompanying you for the rest of your time here on the island."

"Yeah, no. I don't think so," Olivia retorted immediately before I could reply. I was about to indicate the same, though maybe not quite as bluntly.

"I'm afraid I'll have to insist," the captain pressed on, his frightening smile cracking just a bit. "It's only proper that you be accompanied by a member of the local authority while you are here in *our* country."

"It is." She shrugged. "But you kind of forced our hand earlier with that little tantrum you threw, so we went ahead and got permission to continue the investigation on our own. Amazing what the *FBI* can do, huh? Turns out the greater government of Turks & Caicos isn't fond of the idea of American children being kidnapped while visiting their islands. So thank you, but no thank you."

Turner had been getting redder and redder as Olivia spoke, and by the time she was finished, he looked about ready to blow. His jaw was clenched, and his eyes looked like they were about to bug out of his head.

"Well, we'll just get going then," I said as I did my best to stifle the laughter that was threatening to burst out. As entertaining as it was to watch Olivia give the captain a verbal beatdown, I figured we probably shouldn't push our luck.

As we hurried down the hall and toward the exit, I noticed that the lanky officer Turner had dragged with him looked immensely more relaxed, as if he was relieved that Olivia had refused. I could only imagine what he'd asked the officer to do. Probably spy on our investigation for him as he'd intended with Keys.

"I'll have my director call and see what he can do about having him transported somewhere else," Olivia sighed as we stepped outside. The sun was beginning to set, and the island air was a lot cooler now. "I'd rather not have to deal with that idiot Turner the next time we have to speak with him, and I have a feeling getting a call from the FBI will scare him more than a call from an agency no one's ever heard of. No offense."

"None taken," Holm replied. "We prefer to keep a low profile, anyway."

"You think we'll need to interrogate him again?" I asked.

"I don't know," she muttered in response. "I think

Holm was right about him hiding something. Plus, I just don't trust Turner not to lose him. He seemed awfully eager to keep us away from him, don't you think?"

"You think he's in league with the traffickers?" I asked, genuinely curious to hear her thoughts.

"Maybe." She shrugged. "Or maybe he just wants to avoid pissing off the wrong people, the same way that Kenneth did. Either way, I'd rather not leave our suspect in his inept hands for any longer than we have to."

"Can't argue with that," I chuckled. "Anyway, it's getting late. Why don't we hold off on the antique store owner until tomorrow? You said you wanted to try some of the local food, right?"

"Yes, I do!" Olivia's eyes suddenly went wide with excitement. "I'm starving. I haven't had anything to eat since this morning."

"Yeah, I could eat too," I remarked as I suddenly realized just how hungry I was.

"Let me just make that phone call real quick," she muttered as she stepped away from us.

"You in too?" I turned to look at Holm.

"Eh, I think I'm going to sit this one out." Holm snickered. "I'm not so keen on the idea of being a third wheel for the rest of the night. You two have been making eyes at each other since we were on the airplane. It's almost nauseating, to be honest."

"Shut up," I said as I punched him lightly on the shoulder, though I was secretly grateful he was choosing to duck out.

"Don't have too much fun, though," he teased. "We've still got work tomorrow."

"Weren't you leaving?" I asked him.

"I'm gone, I'm gone," he snorted with laughter as he turned to head back to the hotel on his own.

"Where's he going?" Olivia asked as she returned.

"He wasn't feeling up to walking around," I lied smoothly. "I think he was tired after the crazy day we've had."

"Aw, that's too bad," she replied. I was pleased to hear that she didn't sound disappointed about it at all. "Should we head back to that shark place? I'm curious about what it'll taste like."

"Sounds good to me." I smiled as we began to head back toward the part of the beach where we'd first spotted the woman selling fried shark. Now that we weren't on our way to speak to a witness, I could actually take the time to enjoy the scenery better. It looked nice even as the sun was going down, maybe even better, as now everything seemed to glow as the sunset cast long, golden rays across the town.

It surprised me to find that the beach was still fairly crowded, despite the shooting that had taken place earlier. It seemed as though everything was back to business as usual. It was a little unnerving, but I decided to shelve the issue for another time. Right now, I wanted to enjoy my time with Olivia.

"Shoot, looks like it's gone," Olivia sighed as we reached the spot where the woman had been set up earlier. The stand was gone, and in its place was a completely different cart. The man working the spot now appeared to be selling what looked like some kind of fish sandwiches. They looked good, but it wasn't nearly as exciting or novel.

"That's a shame," I replied, honestly a little disappointed. "It's not every day you get a chance to eat shark."

"Well, let's just keep looking," she suggested. "It looks like a lot of other stuff is available, too."

All along the boardwalk were restaurants, bars, pop-up stands, and little carts manned by people selling not only food but little trinkets and souvenirs as well.

"I wonder what a 'conch fritter' is," I mumbled

out loud as I read the name off a large sign affixed to the top of a permanent outdoor eatery.

"Let's find out," Olivia replied before hooking her arm around mine and leading me toward the small restaurant. The building itself was small, with a large window set into the wall facing the street. All around the building were tables and chairs where patrons could eat after putting their order in at the window.

"What'll you have?" the man standing at the order window asked us with a toothy grin.

Whatever conch fritters were, we'd be in for a treat if they tasted half as amazing as the smells wafting out of this place. I could see people cooking on large stoves just behind the man at the window. Steam was rising up from the hot surfaces with an enticing sizzle, and I could feel the heat as it billowed through the window onto us in deliciously scented waves.

"We'll have some conch fritters," Olivia answered before looking back up at the sign posted above the window. "Oh, and some grilled lobster, please."

"Coming right up!" the man replied before yelling something back into the kitchen. He turned back to us after someone yelled something back. "That will be twenty-five dollars even."

Olivia reached down as if to pull something from her bag, but I intercepted her before she could.

"I've got it." I smiled at her before pulling several bills from my wallet and handing them to the man.

"Should be ready in about fifteen minutes," he informed us before moving on to help the next customer.

"Looks like all the tables are full." She frowned as she looked around at the patio around the outside of the building. That was an understatement, as people were sitting on the curb as well as leaning against walls or just plain standing as well. It looked like this was a pretty popular place.

"Let's just go eat on the beach after we get our food," I suggested. We were only a few steps away from the sand, and it would be an infinitely more romantic dining location than the crowded and noisy patio.

"We still don't know what conch fritters are, though," she laughed. "What if it's something messy? Won't it be difficult to take it all the way over there?"

"Well, I don't know what 'conch' is." I shrugged. "But fritters are little fried balls of dough, right? Seems like the perfect finger food."

"Good point," she replied as she slipped her

phone out of her pocket. I watched as she stared at it for a moment, typing something before her eyes suddenly lit up. "Aha! That's what they are."

"What?" I asked as I stepped close behind her to peer over her shoulder at her phone.

"Conch fritters," she explained triumphantly, "are made of queen conch meat. They're like little sea slugs that live inside conch shells."

"Slugs?" I deadpanned. "Awesome. I'm so glad we looked that up *after* we'd already ordered them."

"Oh, stop," she admonished me playfully as she turned around to look me in the eye. "I'm sure they'll be good. According to this blog, they're a delicacy in the Caribbean."

"I hope so," I muttered, making no move to step away from her even after she put her phone away.

"This place is so gorgeous," she hummed as she looked out along the shoreline. The sun had already dipped halfway below the horizon and was casting rays of warm pink and orange across the sand. "I wish we were here on vacation instead of to catch a bunch of sex traffickers."

"Well, we have some time to relax now," I murmured. "We should enjoy it while we can. If the rest of our time here is anything like today, I have a feeling we won't be getting a lot of downtime in the coming days."

"You're right." She nodded. "Might as well make the most of it. Let's go see if our food is ready."

We collected our dinner from the same window we'd ordered from and then headed down the beach toward the shore. The sun had completely set by now, but there was plenty of light spilling out of the restaurants behind us to illuminate us while we ate.

The beach was still full of people, but it wasn't so crowded that we weren't able to find a semi-secluded spot for the two of us to sit down on the soft sand to enjoy our dinner.

The conch fritters turned out to be a lot better than I was expecting.

"They kind of taste like scallops," Olivia remarked as she popped another one into her mouth.

The lobster, too, was delicious. It wasn't the kind of fancy seafood dish I might have found at a ritzy, upscale restaurant, but it was still good. Grilled and marinated in a rich sauce, its taste was completely unique to any lobster I'd ever had before.

After we'd finished eating, we returned to the restaurant where we'd bought our food and disposed of our trash in a large plastic bin set outside just for that purpose.

After that, at Olivia's suggestion, we began to walk along the beach.

"I'm so full," she sighed contentedly. "I wish I could taste more of this stuff, but I don't think I could handle it, to be honest."

"There's always tomorrow," I replied, hopeful that she'd be up to spend the evening together again the next night.

"You're right." She smiled up at me. "I can't imagine we'll have the entire case solved by tomorrow."

As selfish as it was, I found myself hoping that we wouldn't solve it for several days yet if it meant that Olivia and I would be able to spend more nights like this together.

"Oh, what's that?" she asked curiously as she pointed at a building a little way down the beach from us.

There was music coming from it, and as we got closer, I realized that it was a small outdoor bar set up right on the sand. It was the kind of place that was definitely marketed to tourists, with overpriced drinks and decor that was a touch on the tacky side, but it worked. The convenience of being able to have drinks right at the water's edge under the night sky was undeniable, so it wasn't surprising that the place was bustling despite the fact that they were clearly overcharging on their drinks.

Still, the atmosphere was nice enough that I didn't mind splurging a bit. After we got our drinks, we settled into a small table set just outside the bar on the sand. I had to hand it to whoever owned this place. It was an excellent idea. The ambiance was so romantic, it was no wonder people came here.

Olivia and I spent another half hour or so talking about whatever occurred to us, and it wasn't long before the topic of conversation moved on from the details of the case and into more personal matters.

"So, what are you going to do when you find it?" Olivia asked as she took a sip of her cocktail. As it tended to do around me, eventually, the conversation had circled back to the *Dragon's Rogue*.

"I don't know, actually," I replied as I thought about it. The goal had always been to find the ship. To be honest, I'd never put all that much thought into what would come after the search finally came to an end.

"What *can* you do?" she asked. "I mean, would you consider it your property if you found it? Or would it belong to the government of whichever country's waters you found it in?"

"Well, that would depend on where it is," I replied as I took a sip of my own drink. "Laws differ from place to place, and there are a lot of factors that go into deciding ownership in these kinds of situations."

"Well, shouldn't your lineage count for something?" Olivia asked with a sly smile. "I mean, it did belong to your ancestor, right? So, logically, if we were to follow the rules of inheritance, it should belong to you."

"As appealing as that sounds," I grinned, "I don't know if it actually works that way. It would be considered a historical artifact. Plus, Grendel had stolen it. If he passed it down to one of his own descendants, then that could muddy things up."

"Dang, you're right," she giggled. "Wow. If someone had told me last week that I'd be standing on a beach in Turks and Caicos discussing long-lost pirate ships with an incredibly attractive federal agent from some agency no one's ever heard of, I would have called them crazy."

My heart rate kicked up a notch at the phrase *incredibly attractive*, and I couldn't keep the goofy grin off my face. I wouldn't have thought I'd be standing on a moonlit beach next to a gorgeous woman just a few days ago, either.

Before I could say anything to that effect, though, an angry shout broke through the quiet evening air.

"I'm going to kill you!" I heard someone roar.

I turned to see what was happening. Just a few yards away, a tall, muscular man with tanned skin and curly hair was beating another man viciously into the ground.

"Hey! Stop!" I yelled as I flew into action. Even if it had nothing to do with our case, I couldn't just stand by and watch someone beat someone else to death.

"You and every last one of your little group are going to pay!" the assailant roared as he continued his assault. The man beneath him was flailing around helplessly, his face slick with blood.

"Stop!" I growled again as I grabbed the man around the shoulders to pull him off the victim.

"Get off of me!" the man yelled.

The other man wasted no time in getting up and scurrying away, leaving a trail of blood droplets behind him as he fled.

"You imbecile!" the man screamed as she shoved me away. "He got away because of you! Don't you know what he did? Who the hell do you think you are?"

"I'm a federal agent," I answered.

The man's face went blank for a moment. Then, to my surprise, it twisted into an expression of pure rage.

"You!" he sneered venomously. "You're the reason my brother is dead!"

"What?" Olivia snapped as she caught up to us, her voice laced with confusion.

"Kenny!" the man yelled at her. "Kenneth Johnson! He was my brother, and he was shot dead on this beach because of you two!"

I honestly wasn't sure how to react to his outburst. We hadn't killed him, but arguing with a grieving family member wasn't going to do me any good.

"You should have never come here!" he yelled.

He was glaring at us with so much hatred it almost gave me chills. I guessed this was the end of our date night.

15

ETHAN

"WE'RE NOT the reason your brother was killed," I replied calmly. The guy might very well be armed, and the last thing we needed was another shootout on a crowded beach.

"Like hell, you're not," he snapped back angrily. "The only reason those thugs came after him was because you were sniffing around asking questions. If you hadn't—"

"If you're that mad at them," Olivia interrupted him, "then help us find them. We'll make sure they pay for what they did to your brother."

"Ha," the man grunted humorlessly. "You really expect me to trust you?"

"You don't have any other choice," I replied. "You really think you're going to get anywhere doing what you were just doing? Going after them on your own and beating them to death one by one? You'll get yourself killed doing that, and then there will be no one left to make sure your brother gets justice."

We were still standing just outside the bar, and around us, curious onlookers were hovering around, listening in on our conversation. I wished they would just leave, honestly. We had no idea how violent this man might become, and they were putting themselves in danger by rubbernecking around.

The man's jaw was clenched, and his nostrils flared as he took ragged, uneven breaths. For a second, I was worried he was going to yell at us again and refuse our offer.

"Okay," he grumbled. "Let's talk. But not here. Too many people around."

He turned and stalked off without another word. I didn't really like the idea of blindly following this aggressive stranger to somewhere with fewer people around, but if he really was Kenneth's brother and really did know about who had attacked us, then we couldn't just let this opportunity pass us by.

I turned to look at Olivia. She glanced back at me. Her face twisted into a suspicious frown, but after a few seconds, she shrugged and began to follow the man. I followed right beside her.

He led us to a crowded bar just off the beach. No one paid us any mind as we stepped through the thick crowd and toward a table at the back of the place.

"I thought you said there were too many people on the beach," Olivia noted as we squeezed into the small booth.

"Too many people out in the open," he clarified. "In here, it doesn't matter how many people are around. It's too noisy for anyone to overhear what we say."

I didn't really agree with that logic, but I supposed if it made the guy feel comfortable enough to talk to us, it didn't really matter.

"Seems like you've thought this through quite a bit," I remarked suspiciously. "Or like you've had these kinds of clandestine meetings before."

"That's because I have," he replied simply. "I conduct drug deals often here. It's an ideal place to have quick, unnoticed transactions. My name's Raymond, by the way. Raymond Johnson."

For a moment, I just stared at him, honestly a little stunned at how casually he'd admitted to being a drug dealer.

"You don't care about that, right?" He looked at us intently. "You're not here for me. You're here for those low-lifes operating out of Grace Bay."

That was the second time we'd heard that name. Frank had also pointed us toward Grace Bay. It seemed like he'd been telling the truth.

"What makes you think they're behind what happened?" I asked him.

"People talk," he scoffed. "If you don't count all the tourists, there are less than five hundred people living in this part of the island. News travels fast, especially when it's news about a bunch of federal agents rolling into town and stirring up trouble. I know you're here asking about a prostitute. The guys over in Grace Bay are the ones who run all that."

"I see," I replied. "Do you know anything else about the girl who stole your brother's boat?"

"Hell no, man," he scoffed indignantly. "I may sell drugs, but even I'm not low enough to hang around with those types. I respect women! The kinds of things that go on in those places…"

He trailed off, shaking his head in clear disgust.

"What kinds of places do you mean?" Olivia prompted him to continue.

"Brothels." Raymond shrugged. "Back alley rooms,

dingy hotels. You name it. They don't do it out in the open, where the tourists might see, but it happens everywhere. You just need to know what to look for."

That was an unsettling thought.

"So, what do you know about these people?" I asked.

"Not much." He shrugged again. "Like I said, I'm not the type of scum that abuses women or has to pay for sex. I do know that their leader's name is Samuel."

"How do you know that?" Olivia asked. "Seems like a pretty important detail for someone who supposedly doesn't know much."

"I just told you I move drugs, didn't I?" He scoffed. "My work sometimes intersects with theirs. I couldn't tell you where he is, but I've heard the bastard's name enough times."

"Why are you telling us all this?" Olivia asked, still skeptical if the tone of her voice was anything to go by. "Aren't you worried about admitting your past crimes to a couple of federal agents?"

"I ain't worried about anything," he replied darkly. "To be honest, I don't much care what happens to me right now. All I want is to get justice for Kenny."

His voice wavered as he spoke his brother's name.

"Kenny was a good man," he muttered sadly. "He wasn't like me. Wasn't like the rest of the trash here on the island. He made an honest living fishing and taking tourists out for boat rides. It wasn't right that he was the one to die. Of all the ugly people in Turks & Caicos, there was no good reason for it to have been Kenny."

"I'm sorry about your brother." I offered him my condolences. "You're right. It wasn't fair that he died, especially not the way he did. But they did that because he was trying to help us. Trying to help a poor woman who they'd been keeping captive for nearly twenty years."

"He was a good man, my brother." Raymond sighed before looking back up at us, his gaze steely. "If you want to find them, I'd start at a bar down in Grace Bay, near the edge of the town by the high school. There's a bar by the shore there that a lot of them hang around at. You can see the girls there at night."

He pulled a pen from somewhere in his clothes and plucked a paper napkin off the dispenser on the table before quickly scribbling out a quick note.

"This is my number. Call me if you need help

with anything. You'd better get justice for my brother, Agents, or I'll be taking matters into my own hands."

I didn't even get a chance to respond before he suddenly got up and slipped his way through the crowd. He was out of sight in the blink of an eye.

"Well, that was an interesting chat," Olivia murmured.

"Yeah," I muttered as I stared into the spot where I'd last seen him standing before he'd disappeared like a shadow. "It really was."

16

ETHAN

IT WAS the morning after the tumultuous evening that Olivia and I had experienced. We'd agreed to meet in the lobby so we could head out to the antique shop. Even though we'd gotten back late, I'd still woken up at the crack of dawn. My body was just too used to its internal clock for me to sleep in. Holm had done the same, and we'd spent the early morning having coffee in the lobby while we waited for Olivia.

In the meantime, I'd caught Holm up on everything that had transpired, including the information that had been revealed to us, and he was grumpy about the fact that he'd missed out on the events that had transpired as a result.

"That's what I get for trying to be a good friend," Holm grumbled before taking a sip of coffee. "Let my buddy have a night out with the pretty FBI agent, and I end up missing out on all the action. You two were out fighting bad guys and getting leads while I was here watching some weird variety show on TV."

"You really didn't miss much," I assured him. "There wasn't much of a fight, and the guy wasn't exactly a wellspring of information. He disappeared just as suddenly as he showed up. Plus, if you had stuck around, you definitely would have been intruding on what was, up until that point, a pretty romantic evening."

"No need to brag," Holm sighed before draining the rest of his coffee. "I had quite a lovely evening to myself here in the hotel, for your information. It's not often I get to enjoy a seaside hotel view on someone else's dime. That variety show *was* pretty good, too."

We talked for a little while longer as we waited for Olivia to come down from her room.

"Sorry I'm late," Olivia apologized sheepishly as she suddenly appeared at the base of the stairs. I turned at the sound of her voice.

She was wearing a loose, sleeveless button-down

top, and her hair was down and a bit tousled, as though she hadn't had time to style it. Honestly, it didn't look bad. It was definitely different from the usual ponytail she'd been wearing it in, but I thought it framed her face nicely.

"I think the power outlet in my room is broken." She frowned as he ran a hand through her hair a few times in an attempt to smooth it out. "I put my phone on the charger, but it was dead when I woke up this morning. I never heard my alarm go off."

"It's alright." I smiled at her. "We ready to go then?"

"Let's go," Holm replied as he got up.

"Ready," Olivia replied as she started to pull her hair up into a loose ponytail. I tried not to feel disappointed at that.

I handed her the coffee I'd saved for her, and the three of us headed out of the hotel to find a cab. We had more luck this time than he had at the hospital, probably because hotels surrounded us this time.

The taxi ride from Kew to Grace Bay took about twenty minutes. I took a moment to admire the scenery as we passed. The ocean was visible from literally everywhere, and it seemed to stretch on endlessly, a clear and shining blue.

"I can't get over how pretty it is here," Olivia hummed wistfully. "I wonder what it would cost to come here again for vacation, without having a case to worry about."

"Yeah," I replied as I finished off my coffee. "It would be a nice place to get some R and R."

Everything seemed to move at an almost glacial pace here. No one seemed to be in a hurry, so it seemed like the perfect place to really slow down and relax.

Just a few minutes later, our taxi driver announced our stop, and the three of us climbed out of the car. By now, everyone had finished their coffees, so I grabbed all three cups and disposed of them in a metal trash can that was set on the corner of the street.

Even though it was still fairly early in the morning, Grace Bay was already bustling with people. The antique shop was tucked into the middle of a narrow street. It was nondescript enough that if we hadn't been looking for it, we wouldn't have even noticed it.

"I wonder who his target clientele is," I mused out loud. "Probably isn't getting a lot of tourists wandering in, and the population of the town is so small that I can't imagine they have a large pool of repeat customers."

"Unless the antiques stuff is a front." Holm shrugged. "If the guy running the place is associated with human traffickers, then it wouldn't surprise me to find out that he's dealing in something more nefarious than antiques."

"Well, there's only one way to find out," Olivia remarked. "Let's go."

We stepped toward the entrance and through the door. The inside of the store looked just as small as it did on the outside. The walls were covered floor-to-ceiling with shelves full of various odds and ends, old books and figurines, and other things I couldn't identify at a glance.

"Hello!" a deep voice boomed from the back of the small shop. "Welcome! Please come in."

I exchanged a glance with Holm and Olivia before stepping forward.

The man was short and had a head full of gray hair. He stood with a slight hunch, and his hands shook and looked frail, but his voice was loud and commanding. He was standing behind a counter, the surface of which was completely covered in random odds and ends, aside from a small space right in the middle for the cash register.

"How can I help you lovely people today?" he smiled.

There was an odd edge to his voice, not unlike what I'd heard from Captain Turner. As though he was only putting on an act of being friendly.

"We were told that you might have some information for us," I began cautiously. "Simon sent us."

For just an instant, the man's mask fell. His smile flickered, and I saw something flash across his eyes. It was gone too fast for me to gauge what it was, though.

"Ah, of course," he replied, the smile firmly back in place, though obviously more strained now. "Simon. Well, if that's the case..."

He reached slowly toward something beneath the counter, and my hand flew to the gun at my hip.

"Stop!" I warned. "Don't move!"

It was too late, though. He was already pulling a small handgun from behind the counter. I drew my own weapon just as he pulled the trigger.

I heard Olivia cry out behind me and immediately saw red. I jumped to the side and shot at the man's hand. He yelled in pain and dropped his gun as my bullet struck flesh. Holm leapt over the counter an instant later and shoved the man to the ground.

"I've got him!" he yelled over his shoulder at me. "Check on Olivia!"

I turned around and found Olivia on the ground, clutching her right arm with her left hand.

"Don't move," I cautioned her, my heart pounding anxiously as I watched the growing amount of blood streaming down her arm.

"I'm fine," she hissed through gritted teeth. "I think it was just a graze. Hurts like hell, though."

"I'll call for backup," I assured her as I looked around for something to staunch the flow of blood with. "Just keep still until then."

Since it was hot, I wasn't wearing a jacket, and I didn't really want to use anything lying around this dingy little shop on an open wound.

"Ethan," Olivia called my name firmly. "Look at me. I'm fine. I've had worse, trust me. Go help Holm with the suspect before he tries anything."

I was hesitant to leave her side, knowing that she was injured, but I knew that she was right. I turned back around and quickly vaulted over the counter. Olivia's worries were unfounded, though, as Holm didn't appear to be having any trouble subduing the old man.

"Ah!" the man cried out exaggeratedly. "You're hurting me! Someone help!"

"Oh, shut up," Holm groaned as he quickly handcuffed the man's hands together behind his back. "Save the victim act for someone who cares."

I bent down to help him pull the guy to his feet. Together, we walked him around the side of the long counter and back toward the front of the shop. I pushed him down roughly into the first chair I saw, unintentionally knocking a few things off a table as I did.

"Hey, watch it!" the old man snapped. "Those are valuable antiques!"

"Like I give a damn," I retorted as I moved to step in front of him so he'd be unable to get up. Not that he could have run or done much else. Without the gun, he was just a frail old man.

"I called for backup," Olivia informed us as she came to stand by my side. She was still clutching her arm, but at least she was up and about now. "They should be here soon."

"Good." I nodded. "In the meantime, why don't we have a little chat with our friend here?"

I turned back to the man, who was now glaring furiously up at us.

"I've got nothing to say to you," he scoffed.

"I find that hard to believe," Holm replied. "Considering you shot at us with zero provocation, I kind of suspect you might have a lot to say to us."

"That's a great point," I remarked. We hadn't even introduced ourselves as federal agents yet, so there wasn't really any explanation for why he would have reacted like that. "Why don't we start there? Why did you shoot at us?"

"You said 'Simon' sent you," he chuckled darkly. "I knew right away you was up to no good."

"Of course," I sighed. "That piece of crap Frank must have set us up."

Frank had been the one who told us to say that "Simon" had sent us. He must have known that doing so would cause the shop owner to attack us.

"Frank?" the old man cackled. "Now that's a name I know. Not surprising that he's the one who sent you here."

"So is 'Simon' some kind of code word?" I asked.

"Nah, nothing like that." The man shrugged. "Simon was an old associate of mine. He decided he was too good for us and tried to sell us out to the cops, so we had to take care of him. I knew the moment you said that name that I couldn't trust you."

"Dammit," Holm grumbled, obviously angry that we'd walked right into Frank's trap.

"Okay," I replied curtly. "Well, now that we've

gotten all that out of the way, let me tell you about the position you're in. You just assaulted three federal agents and actually managed to injure one of them."

"Did I now?" the old man grinned maliciously. He didn't seem at all concerned about the severity of what he'd just done.

"It would be in your best interest to cooperate with us," I continued.

"Or what?" he retorted. "Look at me! I know how your American court systems work, how long it takes them to do anything. I'll be dead before the trial's even over."

I clenched my jaw in frustration. It was clear that he wasn't at all worried about the consequences of his actions.

"Looks like backup's here," Holm muttered as he turned toward the front window. I turned to look, and I could see flashing lights just outside the store. "Come on, let's get Olivia patched up. We can get this one into custody and continue the interrogation later."

"I'm trembling just thinking about it," the old man sneered mockingly.

I just turned around and began to follow Olivia out of the shop to where I could already see the ambulance parked outside. The guy's cavalier attitude was pissing me off and taking a minute to collect myself would enable me to crack him later.

We were just about to walk out the door when I saw it.

I happened to glance up just in time to spot the curiously shaped object mounted on the wall. I hadn't noticed it when we'd come in because it was hung on the same wall that the door was on. There was so much crap piled up on tables and shelves in front of it that I almost didn't realize what it was at first.

"No way," I mumbled as I stepped toward the object.

"Ethan?" Olivia called. "What is it?"

"This," I replied dumbly, still too shocked to respond properly.

"This?" she repeated as she doubled back to stand beside me. "What are you talking about?"

"This," I answered as I shoved one of the tables away roughly so I could reach forward and touch the massive thing mounted on the wall. The old man was yelling something behind me, probably in protest at me throwing his stuff around, but I could barely hear him past the blood rushing through my ears.

"What is that?" Olivia asked as she leaned forward to examine the large metal object.

"An anchor," I breathed, barely able to believe what I was seeing. "It's the Dragon Rogue's anchor."

17

ETHAN

THE OLD SHOPKEEPER had been carted away, to a different police station, thankfully. At least this way, we wouldn't have to deal with the antagonistic Captain Turner. Olivia, too, had been patched up by the paramedics and cleared to continue working under the caveat that she take it easy and try not to use her right arm.

"That's not going to happen," she'd muttered skeptically.

She wouldn't be able to shoot her gun if she was unable to use her right arm, so she'd either have to sit it out the rest of the case or risk worsening her injury. Either way, it wasn't an ideal situation.

By now, the paramedics and police had all left,

aside from a single officer who had remained behind to secure the scene.

Really, we should be heading down to the station to interrogate the man who had just shot at us, but instead, I was still standing there in the tiny antique store, holding up the officer who probably just wanted to finish his job and leave, staring fixedly at an old anchor mounted on the wall.

I heard the door open, and my eyes left the anchor for just a moment to see who it was, only to resume their gazing when I saw that it was just Holm.

"Are you sure it's the anchor?" Holm asked skeptically. "Don't all anchors kind of look the same? How can you tell this one came off the *Dragon's Rogue*?"

"I'm sure," I replied firmly. "Well, mostly, anyway. I'll be able to tell without a doubt once I get a look at the other side, but I know this is it. I've seen blueprints and drawings of every part of the ship, probably a hundred times now. I knew the moment I saw it what it was."

"What's on the other side?" Holm asked.

"According to the records that exist about its construction," I explained, "Jonathan had the year it was commissioned etched into the arms. If it says sixteen-eighty-seven, then we'll know for sure. That isn't all, though. Look here. Usually, the crown of an anchor is rounded on the bottom, right? Well, the *Dragon's Rogue* anchor had a crown shaped like a letter V, instead. You can see right there that the apex is pointed instead of rounded."

"Damn." Holm whistled. "It might actually be the real deal then, huh?"

"I hope so," I replied eagerly. "It's crazy, though. What are the odds that we'd find it here?"

"Astronomically small," Holm deadpanned. "Seriously, it's kind of ridiculous how lucky you are. You keep being in the right place at the right time. Just think, if we hadn't gotten this case, we never would have come to Turks and Caicos. And even if we had, for whatever reason, what are the odds we would have ended up in this tiny little shop?"

"Maybe it's fate." I grinned. "Or the ghost of my ancestor trying to guide me to his long-lost ship."

I was so giddy I was speaking nonsense. Holm was right. The fact that we'd just happened to stumble upon the anchor was nothing short of a miracle. I was so excited that I didn't know how I should react.

"So, uh... what's your plan, then?" Holm asked me. "I mean, the shop owner just got arrested, and I doubt he's coming back anytime soon. It's not like we can just take it, either."

"I won't tell if you won't," I muttered as I admired the anchor. It was in rough condition, not surprising considering it probably hadn't been well taken care of by whoever had been in possession of it up until now. Who knew how long it had been sitting in this dusty old place, gathering rust and wearing away. Still, it was in a better state than it might have been.

"Marston." Holm admonished me gently. "Listen, brother, I know how much this means to you, but we actually can't take it with us. Even if you did manage to convince me, the thing's massive. It's not like we can smuggle it back in a suitcase."

I frowned with dismay. I knew he was right. Honestly, once the old guy was arrested, I wasn't sure who ownership of the anchor would pass to. And he was right about the logistical aspect of it as well. The anchor looked like it was around twelve feet in length, and that wasn't accounting for the arms or the key pin that jutted out of either side, making the entire thing impractically big and bulky. Even if I did somehow manage to finesse it into my possession, how exactly would I get several tons of metal back to Miami?

"I'll figure it out," I sighed, trying to convince

myself as much as Holm. "We need to focus on the case now, anyway."

"Alright." Holm clapped a hand down onto my shoulder sympathetically.

I pulled my phone out of my pocket and began to take as many photos of the anchor as I could. For now, it was all I could do, and I refused to even entertain the idea that it might be all I would manage to get.

I didn't hesitate to move the shop's furniture around so that I could get pictures from better angles. Technically, what I was doing was a huge breach of policy. I didn't really have the authority to be messing with things at a crime scene. It wasn't like I was actually searching through things, though. Surely just moving things around harmlessly wasn't too bad, right?

That was what I told myself as I maneuvered around as best I could to capture the anchor from as many different perspectives as possible. The anchor itself was far too heavy for me to move on my own, as much as I was itching for a chance to get a look at the other side.

"Don't break anything," Holm muttered as he watched me moving things around. He glanced back through the front window. I followed his gaze and saw that the officer was still outside, apparently engaged in conversation with Olivia.

After a few minutes, I put my phone away and reluctantly forced myself to look away from the anchor. As much as I wanted to stay and figure out a way to bring it with me, we were still in the middle of a case. That needed to take precedence.

I turned and walked quickly out the door before I could change my mind, Holm right behind me. The sun was almost painfully bright to my eyes after spending so long inside the tiny, dark store.

"Finally done in there?" Olivia asked me as I stepped toward where she and the officer stood on the street just in front of the shop.

"Unfortunately," I nodded. "As much as I'd like to stay, we need to get down to the station to speak to the shopkeeper. Uh, sorry to keep you waiting."

I apologized to the officer, who just waved his hand dismissively.

"Hey, don't sweat it," he replied. "It's all good."

He went into the shop then to begin closing it off as a crime scene.

"Holm told me you want to take it back to Miami." She smiled at me sympathetically. "We'll figure something out."

"Thanks." I smiled back at her. Though I didn't

feel too confident about my current chances of leaving Turks & Caicos with that anchor, her encouragement was enough to make me feel just a spark of hope that I might actually be able to get my hands on it after all.

18

ETHAN

THE STATION at Grace Bay was smaller than the one back in Kew Town. In fact, if we hadn't known that it was a police station, I would have assumed it was some kind of little boutique store.

The station was only about a five-minute walk from the antique store and was located inside a shopping plaza. The main entrance was painted a shade of bright blue, and it even had a little canopy over the front doors. The only thing that set it apart from the stores on either side of it was the little sign that read "Police Post" mounted just to the left of the entrance.

The very best part of the station, though, was the fact that we didn't have to deal with having the aggressive Captain Turner breathing down our necks.

"This is the place?" Holm asked as we stood outside the entrance.

"This is the place," Olivia confirmed with a nod. "Obviously, it's a lot smaller than the Kew Town station, but since that's a no-go, this is the next closest."

"As long as we don't have to deal with any more corrupt cops," I grumbled as I stepped through the doors.

The interior wasn't significantly different from the Kew Town station. Like that one, this station had a small desk just inside the entrance with a larger area filled with desks toward the back. The difference in atmosphere was palpable, though. Where the Kew Town station had felt cold and suffocating, the Grace Bay station felt bright and airy, in no small part due to the fresh air and sunlight that were streaming through the open windows.

"Good afternoon," the officer sitting behind the front desk greeted us. "How can I help you?"

"I'm Agent Marston," I introduced myself as I pulled my badge out of my pocket. "This is Agent Holm and Agent Hastings. We were just involved in an altercation at an antique store on Allegro Road."

"Oh! Of course." She smiled as she stood up. "The captain's waiting for you now. I can take you back to his office."

"Thanks," I replied as she led us through the small building. It was bigger than it looked on the outside but still felt cramped. After walking through a short hallway, we passed a bullpen full of desks before finally arriving at a door marked "Captain Morris." The officer knocked on the door.

"Come in!" a warm, rich voice called from inside.

"The federal agents are here," she called. She swung the door open before stepping aside to let us into the office. It was the exact opposite of Turner's, whose office had been bare and practical. Morris, on the other hand, had lined his walls with newspaper clippings, photos of what I assumed were family members, and even colorful drawings that children had clearly made.

His desk, too, was covered in picture frames and little knick-knacks that made the office seem lived in.

"Welcome to our town." He grinned widely as we stepped into his small office. "I'm Captain Everett Morris. I wish we weren't meeting under such unfortunate circumstances. I hope you will not think that all of us here on the Island are like Richard."

"Richard?" I asked.

"The man who attacked you," he clarified. "Old Richard Brown. I've always known he was up to no good in that little shop of his, but I never imagined anything like this would happen."

"What do you mean?" Olivia asked. "Why did you think he was up to no good?"

"This is a small town," Morris replied. "It's no secret that Richard had suspicious types coming and going at all hours of the day and night. I assumed it was just drugs. Something to help him make ends meet since he obviously wasn't making a living selling all that old junk."

"So you didn't know he was involved in human trafficking?" Olivia asked.

"Certainly not!" Morris replied vehemently. "Drugs are one thing. I'm not going to toss a seventy-year-old man in a cell for something so small, but if I'd known, he was tied up in all that... Listen, Agents. I won't pretend like this place is without its problems. I try my best to keep the town safe, but in a close-knit community like this, it is important to know how to choose your battles. Some drugs I might let slide, but prostitution? Abuse on women? That I will just not accept."

He seemed genuine, and I was glad that he was taking this seriously.

"We appreciate your cooperation." I nodded at him.

"Of course," he replied. "Anything I can do to keep my town safe. Now, why don't I escort you three over to where Richard is?"

He stood and led us out of the office and into a different part of the station.

"You mentioned something about the 'old junk' that he sells," I remarked as he led us to the interrogation room. "You wouldn't happen to know how he comes by it, would you?"

It was a stretch, but I would take any information I could get about the anchor. If Brown was unwilling to tell me about it, I'd have to use whatever avenues I had available.

"Not really," Morris shrugged, to my disappointment. "I know he scavenges things from off the beach. I've seen him down by the shore several times. You'd be surprised what kinds of things wash up. I once found an old ceramic teapot when I was a child, completely intact! Must have come off an old shipwreck or something."

"Really?" I asked, my interest immediately piqued. That in itself was interesting, though the more I thought about it, the less likely it seemed that Brown would have just found the anchor washed up on the beach. Anchors were heavy, and it probably wouldn't have moved much from whatever location it had sunk to on the ocean floor, and even if it had, there was no way that Brown would have been able to transport it all the way back to his shop.

"Here we are," Morris announced as he unlocked the interrogation room door with a key. "We don't have one of those two-way mirrors, but I can watch from the monitors in the room next door."

"Thanks," I replied as I stepped into the room.

The room wasn't as austere as some interrogation rooms I'd come across. The bare white walls and lack of furniture, save for a plain metal table in the center of the room, definitely gave the place an uncomfortable aura. That being said, the two large windows that were flooding the room with warm light didn't help make the room feel intimidating, despite the thick metal bars that were stretched across them.

Brown was sitting alone at the table inside. His hands were cuffed together in front of him, and there was an ugly scowl on his face.

"Ugh, you again?" He groaned as he looked up at me. "What, you didn't get enough back at the store? Just leave me alone."

"Yeah, that's not gonna happen," I replied coldly.

"We need some answers, and we're not leaving until we get them. How long that takes is up to you."

"Hah!" Brown barked out a laugh. "You can have fun waiting, then."

I regarded him carefully as I thought about how I should proceed. There was a lot I wanted to ask him, though, admittedly, some of what I was interested in knowing had nothing to do with our current case. Then again, maybe starting with something seemingly innocuous might throw him off enough to get him talking more.

"Where did you get that anchor?" I asked him casually.

"What?" He glared at me like I was crazy. "What are you talking about? What anchor?"

"The giant one mounted on the wall of your store," Olivia clarified.

"Oh, that thing?" Brown scoffed. "Hell if I can remember. I've been collecting everything in that store for my entire life, ever since I joined the British Royal Navy back in my twenties. Why do you want to know about that old hunk of junk?"

I bristled internally at the dismissive way he talked about it. This was an important historical artifact, and it was painfully obvious that he didn't see the value of it at all. Honestly, I was annoyed with

his response and more than a little disappointed that
he didn't have more information about the anchor,
but at least I'd gotten him talking, which had been
the most important goal.

"Okay, never mind about the anchor then," I
muttered. "Why don't we talk about the reason we
were at the antique store, to begin with? Tell us what
you know about the trafficking group."

"Who?" he rasped. "Oh, you mean the girls. Well,
not much, to be honest with you. It's been a while
since I went down that way myself."

He grinned lecherously, and my stomach
churned at the grotesque sight.

"I do know one of their main spots is right on the
beach up near the north edge of Kew town, off the
Millennium highway," he continued. "The boys in
charge come by every once in a while to pick up
their goods."

"And what goods are those?" Olivia jumped in.

"Drugs, mostly." Brown shrugged. "Makes the
girls easier to handle."

I could feel Olivia stiffen beside me. I knew that
hearing him talk about this so brazenly must have
been making her furious.

"Wait a minute," Holm interjected. "This place
that they operate out of, is it by a boat dock?"

"Yeah, actually, it is," Brown replied. "If I do recall correctly, it's right on the beach, just across the way from where the boats are kept."

"That explains how they knew so fast," Holm sighed before turning to look at me. "Yesterday, when we were talking to Kenneth, those guys came out of nowhere, right? They showed up, guns blazing, the moment we started speaking with him. If they were already nearby, then it would explain how they were able to get there so fast."

"You're right," I muttered. "Interesting that Frank failed to mention that little detail."

"Haha!" Brown cackled. "And here I thought you federal agent types were supposed to be smart."

"One last question," I plowed on, deliberately ignoring his obvious attempt to rile me up. "What do you know about a man named Samuel?"

"Samuel?" He parroted. "That's a pretty common name, Agent. I've known quite a few Samuels in my day, personally."

"Cut the crap," I growled at him. I was seriously losing my patience.

"Alright, settle down," Brown sighed patronizingly. "I know who you're talking about. Of course, I know about Samuel. He's the one who runs all that business."

"Do you know where we can find him?" I asked.

"Nah." He shrugged. "Like I said, I'm not too involved in all that. I only ever meet with his boys. Though from what I hear, he isn't anywhere on the Western Island."

"Thanks for your help," I replied sarcastically as I stood up from the table. "Come on. I think we need to go pay Frank another visit. Where did you say he was transferred to, Olivia?"

"I can call my director and find out," she replied as she stood up from the table after me.

I walked to the door and knocked on it loudly so that Morris could let us out.

"All done?" the captain asked us as we filed out of the interrogation room one at a time.

"Yeah, we are," I grumbled as soon as the door was closed behind us. "We didn't get much, though."

"Well, we found out that Frank was lying to us," Holm corrected me encouragingly as we began to make our way back toward the entrance of the station.

"I guess." I shrugged. "Though I wish we hadn't had to get into a gunfight with an obnoxious old man to do it."

"If we hadn't, you wouldn't have found the anchor," Olivia noted.

"Good point." I smiled. "I guess it was worth it after all."

"That's the spirit," Holm snorted.

"Anchor?" Morris asked curiously.

"Oh, it's nothing," I replied with a shrug. "Just something interesting we found while we were in the old guy's shop. Anyway, now we need to go speak to that snake, Frank."

"I'm sorry I was not able to be of more help to you," Morris apologized.

"Don't be," I replied. "You were a lot more helpful than the last police captain we had the pleasure of dealing with."

"Let me guess," he frowned, "you are talking about David Turner?"

"You know him?" Holm asked.

"I'm afraid so," Morris muttered. "I figured you must have run into him if you were in Kew before. That man is as corrupt as they come."

"No surprise there," Olivia muttered.

"What makes you say that?" I asked.

"He's an embarrassment of a police officer!" Morris growled. "Turns a blind eye to everything that goes on in that town! We were in the academy together, him and me. I knew from day one that he was a rotten egg. I'd be careful around him, Agents."

"Thanks for the warning," I replied.

"Of course." He nodded. "Please don't hesitate to seek me out if there is anything else you might need."

I thanked him again before making my way back through the bullpen and the short corridor that led to the main lobby, Olivia and Holm not far behind me.

"Well, I guess that explains why Turner was so uptight about having us snooping around," Olivia scoffed as we stepped through the doors and into the sun. "He probably has some kind of connection to the traffickers."

"That would explain how they've been able to operate for this long," I replied in agreement. "Turks & Caicos is a small place, and it's not all that densely populated. It would be almost impossible for them to carry on for this long unless they had law enforcement covering for them."

"I guess that means we'll have to be careful of who we speak to," Olivia sighed. "So far, we've managed to get more assistance from a self-confessed drug dealer than from the local authorities. Let me call my director and find out where Frank is."

She stepped away to make the call, and I took a

moment to look out over the horizon. I could see the ocean from where we were standing, which was unsurprising, considering pretty much every town and city in Turks and Caicos seemed to be situated right on the coast. The sun was already high in the sky and beating down on us, and all around us, people were going about their daily business, completely unaware of the heinous crimes that were going on right beneath their noses.

"Hell of a way to start our investigation, huh?" Holm asked me as he stretched his arms up over his head. "Feels like we've been running at full speed since the moment we landed."

"No kidding," I snorted. We'd been shot at twice in the span of just two days, and already we'd discovered that the local cops appeared to be tangled up with the traffickers. "Wouldn't have it any other way, though. It still beats sitting behind a desk at an office all day."

"I have no idea how Diane does it." Holm shook his head. "I think I'd go stir-crazy."

"You and me both," I replied.

"Okay!" Olivia announced her presence with a curt outburst. I could tell just by the tone of her voice that something was wrong. "So it turns out that there was a mix-up. Someone arranged for Frank to be transferred to one of the FBI's international branches... in Barbados."

"Barbados?!" I exclaimed, my eyes going wide with shock. "He's in Barbados?"

"No," Olivia replied. "The good news is that the FBI moves slowly, so he's still here. The bad news is that he's still back at the police station in Kew, which means that—"

"We get to deal with Turner again," Holm groaned. "I bet he's going to be thrilled to see us after the last conversation we had with him."

"Well, we're going to have to play nice," I sighed.

"To hell with that," Olivia scoffed stubbornly. "I'm not going to take any crap from that jerk."

"Listen," I sighed, "I don't like it any more than you do, but we need to be smart about this. It's clear that he doesn't like us, at best. At worst, he might even be involved somehow. The last thing we want to do is antagonize him even more."

"You're right." Olivia frowned. "As annoying as it is, so long as we're on their turf, we're at a disadvantage. We need to make sure we're ready before we do anything rash."

"Alright," Holm agreed reluctantly. "Let's go see what Frank has to say. Oh, but first, we seriously need to get a car."

19

ETHAN

IT PLEASANTLY SURPRISED me to discover that Grace Bay had an Enterprise rent-a-car location smack in the middle of the city, probably a result of seeing so many tourists year-round. I'd thought this myself, but Holm had finally suggested that we get our own car in order to facilitate ease of movement. So far, we'd done fine just walking everywhere, but if we were going to be traveling between towns more often, it only made sense to get our own form of transportation.

The inside of the building looked like a place outside of time. There was a large, old-fashioned gumball machine tucked into one corner of the lobby. Right next to it was a row of little coin-operated vending machines, the kind that would spit out small toys and stickers in exchange for a quarter.

All over the walls were a mishmash of posters and framed paintings, some that looked relatively new and some that were so yellowed and worn that it was a wonder they were still even hanging onto the wall. The walls themselves were painted a pale green color, though I could see bits of white plaster peeking through the occasional crack.

A low counter that separated the front waiting room from the rest of the small building bisected the lobby. The man standing behind the counter perked up as soon as we stepped inside.

"Welcome!" the man inside the store greeted us warmly. I'd noticed earlier how friendly everyone on the island seemed, and though it was obviously fake coming from someone like Turner, most of the people we'd encountered appeared genuinely welcoming. "What can I do for you today?"

"We need to rent a car," I replied as I approached the counter. We were the only people in the building, which wasn't that surprising, considering how few cars I'd seen on the road at all since we'd gotten here.

"Of course you do!" The man smiled as he leaned across the desk to shake my hand. "That's why you're here! My name is Monroe. Please, come this way."

He stepped out from behind the desk and led us through a door at the back of the store. It led out into a large parking lot, though I noted at once that most of the spaces were empty.

"You're in luck," he said without breaking stride. "Usually, I'm completely booked up by now. It's the busy season, you know? But I do happen to have a few cars still available."

He led us all the way to the rear end of the parking lot before coming to a stop.

"Now, what kind of car were you looking for?" he asked. "I have a few trucks available if you need the space."

"Anything's fine," Olivia replied. "We just need it to run."

"Now, hold on a minute," Holm replied. "We should at least have a look first."

"Why?" Olivia asked, sounding genuinely confused. "A car's a car, isn't it? How about that one?"

She pointed to one seemingly at random, a black sedan at the end of the lot.

"Ah, very good choice," the clerk complimented her. "Nineteen-ninety-four Chevy Impala. Very reliable car, and with plenty of horsepower, too."

"That's... not bad, actually," Holm muttered. "I mean, it's not *great*, but it's okay."

"What are you even talking about?" Olivia scoffed. "Come on, let's get the car and get back to Kew Town."

I understood where Holm was coming from. While I wouldn't say I was obsessed with car culture, Holm and I both had cars that we loved and valued, though it was clear Olivia couldn't care less.

We headed back into the shop to sign the papers and pay for the car. The clerk was kind enough to explain how people drove on the left side of the road in Turks & Caicos. He even gave us a printout explaining all the ways it was different from driving in the United States.

"Most of the cars on the island are imported from America," he explained. "So even though we drive on the left, the wheel is on the left as well. It might take some getting used to."

"Thanks." I nodded. "I think we'll manage."

"Excellent." The man smiled as he handed us the key. "Well, just bring it back here when you're done. There's also a drop-off point out by Wheeland where you can leave it instead if that is more convenient."

"Thanks," I replied as I took the key.

We headed back out into the parking lot where

the Impala was waiting. I climbed into the driver's seat without hesitation.

"I call shotgun!" Olivia spoke up immediately.

"Wait, why do you get to drive?" Holm grumbled.

"Because I got here first." I grinned at him. "You can drive next time. Come on."

Once we were all inside, I pulled my phone out of my pocket to set up the directions back to Kew. So far, we'd only been riding in taxis, so I hadn't actually paid much attention to the way there and back.

"Okay," I declared as I finished inputting the address of the police station into the GPS app. "Ready to go."

I pulled out of the parking lot and onto the road. I had to resist the urge to take my eyes off the road and look around. The island really was beautiful, everything from the greenery to the bright blue of the ocean in the distance, and even the architecture of the houses was a stunning sight to behold. So far, I'd been using the car rides as opportunities to admire the view, but that was impossible when I had to focus on driving.

"Hey, Marston?" Holm muttered as he leaned in close behind me from the backseat.

"Yes?" I asked.

"You're on the wrong side of the road," he snickered.

I flushed as I realized he was right and jerked the steering wheel sharply to the left so that the car would be in the correct lane.

"Whoa, what's going on?" Olivia flinched as the car suddenly swerved. She'd been staring down at her phone and probably hadn't even noticed that I'd been driving on the right-hand side.

"Marston was driving on the wrong side of the road," Holm laughed. "Right after the guy just got finished reminding us, too."

"I got distracted with the GPS," I smiled sheepishly, laughing in spite of myself. "Besides, he was right. It is confusing when the steering wheel's on the left side. I just went into autopilot and started driving like I usually would."

"Man, I can't believe you did that *again*," Holm chuckled.

"What do you mean 'again'?" Olivia asked, putting her phone away and sitting up straighter.

"Nothing," I snapped back at Holm.

"Come on, tell me," Olivia urged him. "I can tell there's a story here."

"There is." Holm smirked.

"Yeah." I glared back at him through the rear-view mirror. "And there are plenty of stories I could tell you about Robbie Holm, too."

We spent the next twenty minutes bickering good-naturedly, and before I knew it, we were already back at the Kew Town police station.

I felt as though I was walking into enemy territory as we stepped back into the station. We'd suspected from the beginning that there was something sketchy about Turner, but now that Morris had confirmed that the man couldn't be trusted, I felt all the more anxious being in here. Who knew just how many of these armed officers were secretly working in cahoots with the traffickers?

The same officer who'd kindly given us Frank's background information stared up at us in surprise as soon as we walked in.

"Oh, hello..." he muttered nervously before glancing back toward the corridor that led into the rest of the station. "Can I help you?"

"We need to speak to Frank Johnson," I replied sternly.

The officer's face paled at my words.

"I don't think that will be possible," he replied. He looked around again before beckoning us forward with his hand.

I exchanged a look of trepidation with Holm

before moving toward the man, my hand ready at my side to draw my weapon if necessary.

"The captain had arranged to move that inmate to a new location," he hissed at me.

"He's w*hat?!*" I snapped.

"Shhh!" He urged me to keep it down. "You did not hear this from me, okay?"

He stared at us as if waiting for confirmation that we would keep quiet about whatever he was about to say.

"Yes, fine," Olivia replied hastily. "What is it?"

"The captain had been furious ever since you left yesterday," he informed us. "I overheard him speaking on the phone. He was saying he was going to move Johnson somewhere else so you would not be able to speak with him again. He told us that he was being moved to a different police station, but I know that this is a lie."

"How do you know that?" I asked.

"The closest police station is the one in Grace Bay," he explained. "My cousin is an officer there. I asked him out of curiosity, but he claimed he did not know what I was talking about."

"Morris would have told us if that was the case," Holm remarked.

"Why are you telling us this?" Olivia asked him

warily. She must have been suspicious after what Morris had told us about Turner, and potentially his men, being corrupt.

"Officer Carson is my friend," he replied. "I know that what the captain is saying about you being responsible for his injury is a lie. There are still good police left in Kew, even if some people, like the captain, do not see it that way."

"I believe you," I assured him. He'd helped us out before, and even now, he seemed genuine. "Is Frank still here?"

As if to answer my question, the sound of several pairs of footsteps suddenly emerged from the corridor. I turned to find Frank Johnson walking toward us, escorted on either side by a police officer. Captain Turner was walking just a few steps behind them, the smug smile on his face slipping as soon as he looked up and spotted us.

"What are you doing here?" he growled angrily.

"We could ask you the same question," I retorted. "What exactly do you think you're doing with our suspect?"

"I'm having him transferred," he spat, his voice trembling slightly. "To a different station."

"Right," I bit back sarcastically. Obviously, he

intended to stick to the weak story he'd fed to the front desk officer. "On whose authority?"

"On my own authority," he snarled, squaring his shoulder and jutting out his chin. It was an aggressive, combative stance, and I knew he was on the verge of physically attacking us. "This is *my* island. I don't answer to the likes of you!"

"You don't have to," Olivia interjected calmly. "In fact, we're here to help you."

Turner and I both turned to look at her in surprise. Turner's expression was an odd mix of confusion and distrust.

"As a matter of fact," she continued, "we just got through speaking with Captain Morris down at the Grace Bay station. I'm assuming that's the station you were planning on transferring Johnson to, is that correct?"

As soon as she finished speaking, Turner's jaw fell slack in surprise.

"I... th-that's," he stuttered as he attempted to come up with some reasonable excuse. "No. That's incorrect. He's being transferred to a different station."

"Really?" I raised an eyebrow at him. "That's weird. The Grace Bay station is the closest one, isn't it? Why would you go through the trouble of sending him somewhere else?"

"That's none of your concern!" he snapped at me, spittle flying from his mouth as he spoke.

"Actually, it is," I corrected him. "Johnson is our suspect. Do you think you're slick? You're interfering in a federal investigation."

"Which is why," Olivia cut in again, "we'll be happy to transport him over to Grace Bay for you. He'll be out of your hair, and we'll have our suspect. And everyone is happy."

She was smiling, but the tone was anything but pleasant. It was obvious to everyone listening that it was closer to a threat than a request.

"I don't need your help!" he sneered.

"Well, we weren't really asking for your input," I retorted as I took a step closer to him. "And unless you want us to start spilling all of your secrets, I'd suggest you stand down."

Of course, we didn't have much in the way of dirt on him aside from some flimsy rumors, but I was willing to bet that Turner had been involved in enough shady stuff that he'd end up filling the blanks for me.

"Is that a threat?" he growled. He was scowling, but I could see a hint of fear in his eyes.

"Yes. It is," I replied simply.

We stayed that way for several tense seconds, each staring the other down until finally, Turner broke first.

"Take him," he muttered before turning to address the officers. "Hand the suspect over to the agents."

Holm moved forward immediately to take hold of Frank's arm.

"Thank you." I grinned mockingly at Turner.

"Shut up," he grumbled. "Now get the hell out of my station."

"With pleasure," Olivia responded as she took hold of Frank's other arm.

She and Holm frogmarched him out of the station, and I tossed Turner one last deprecating smirk before turning to follow after them.

"I'm being personally escorted by three federal agents?" Frank gasped in mock surprise as Holm and Olivia guided him over to the Impala. "I'm honored."

"Shut up," I grunted as I opened the door to shove him inside. "I'll ride back here and keep an eye on him. Holm can drive."

"Good," he snickered as he got into the driver's seat. "Better chance we'll survive with me behind the wheel."

"I drive on the wrong side of the road one time," I muttered.

"Technically, that's twice now," Holm replied as he started the car, "if we also count what happened back in Scotland."

"Just drive," I grumbled at him.

"What happened in Scotland?" Olivia asked as she turned around in her seat to look at me. "Is that what you guys were referencing earlier?"

"Yep." Holm grinned. "Ethan's got a track record of disregarding other country's road laws."

"I do not," I retorted. "Besides, it's especially confusing here because the steering wheel's still on the left side of the car. At least in Scotland, it was on the opposite side."

"Excuses, excuses," he sighed teasingly as he pulled out of the parking lot and back onto the road.

Frank was sitting still and quiet beside me. His hands were cuffed, so it wasn't like he'd be able to do much in a confined space with three trained federal agents, but I still made sure to keep an eye on him until we made it back to the Grace Bay station twenty minutes later.

"Come on," I growled at Frank as I pulled him roughly out of the backseat. "We need to have a word."

20

ETHAN

"Thank you again," I said to Captain Morris as Holm, Olivia, and I took a seat in his office for the second time that day, "for agreeing to help us out on such short notice."

"Don't worry yourselves," he replied. "I told you to feel free to contact me if you needed anything. I just did not think you would be coming back so soon."

"Neither did we," I remarked. "We were pretty shocked to discover that Turner was trying to smuggle him away."

"I wouldn't say 'shocked,'" Olivia scoffed. "Seems like just the kind of thing that sleazy guy would do, actually."

"I had my suspicions that he was engaging in

unsavory behavior," Morris muttered in disbelief, "But I never would have imagined he would do something so brazen."

We'd caught Captain Morris up on everything that had happened with Turner. He'd been shocked to hear that we'd caught the other man in the act of trying to hide Frank from us, and he'd agreed to keep Frank in custody until we concluded the case.

"Well, if you three are ready, I'll take you back down to the interrogation room," he announced.

I felt a sense of deja vu as the four of us got up and headed through the bullpen and into the short corridor that led to the interrogation room.

"I'll be watching from next door," Morris informed us. "Just like before. He's restrained, so he shouldn't be any trouble. I'll be on alert, though, just in case."

"Thank you," I replied before watching him step into the little monitoring room just next to the interrogation room.

For the second time that day, we found ourselves inside the interrogation room at the Grace Bay Police Station.

I pushed open the door and stepped inside, Holm and Olivia right behind me.

"Hello again, Frank," I greeted him icily as I took

a seat across from him, unable to keep the anger out of my voice. This idiot had set us up to be shot, an incident that had actually resulted in Olivia getting hurt. I was furious.

"I'm surprised to see you again, Agents," he replied bitterly.

"I'm sure you are," I snorted. "Sorry, your little plan to have us taken out didn't quite work out the way you were expecting."

"I have no idea what you're talking about," he huffed.

"Oh, cut the crap," I snapped. "We know that sending us to Brown's shop was all a ruse. He told us all about your old associate, Simon. Why don't you do us both a favor and tell us the truth this time?"

"Or what?" he sneered. "What are you going to do if I don't?"

"I'm going to make sure you rot in prison, for starters," I replied. "You've screwed yourself pretty badly here. You know that, right? Assaulting a federal agent, conspiracy to commit a murder, and let's not forget the man you shot dead on the beach."

"I didn't do that!" he protested.

"Didn't you?" I asked. "You're the only suspect we have. As far as I know, you were the one who shot the bullet that killed him. You really want to go down for everything on your own? Go off to rot in an American prison while your buddies get to keep living it up here on the island?"

His jaw was clenched so tightly that I could see a vein protruding from his neck, and his shoulders rose and fell with every heavy breath he took.

"Or we could just go find one of your buddies and have them talk instead." I shrugged nonchalantly. "Brown told us about that bar on the beach up north. I'm sure one of them will be more than willing to talk in exchange for a better deal. Come on, we're wasting our time here."

I nodded to Olivia and Holm, who both immediately understood what my plan was and stood up.

"Wait!" he finally yelled just as I was standing up in a feint at leaving. "Okay. But what's in it for me if I talk?"

"A note will be made that you cooperated with the investigation," Olivia replied as she turned around to look at him.

"What?" Frank balked. "That's it? That's not good enough!"

"It's the best you're going to get," I retorted. "At least this way, you'll control the narrative. There's no telling what kind of information your buddies might spill. It's up to you to decide whether you want to take that chance."

"Not like I have a choice, I guess," he muttered bitterly. "Fine. What do you want to know?"

"How about we start with that bar on the beach?" I replied. "You know, the one you failed to mention the last time we spoke."

"Right, that," he responded curtly. "Well, it's just as Richard said. The girls usually start working at around eight, right when the sun starts to go down."

"Give us the address," I instructed him as I pulled my phone out of my pocket to jot it down.

As he begrudgingly rattled off the address, I made a mental note to check with Morris later to make sure this was an actual address and not another trap.

"Alright, so tell us about your boss," I said after I'd finished making a note of the address and tucked my phone away.

"His name's Samuel," he mumbled. "He lives in a big house somewhere in Cockburn Town."

"Do you have that address?" I asked.

"No." He shrugged. "Why would I?"

"How do you know he lives in a big house, then?" Olivia asked.

"Because he never stops bragging about it," Frank scoffed. "Show-off."

"Do you know how to get in touch with him, then?" I asked. If he was around the guy enough to get annoyed by his boastfulness, maybe he would know how to find him.

"No," he grunted, to my dismay. "Samuel comes and goes as he pleases. Makes us all do the dirty work and shows up once in a while to collect his money and point out all the ways he thinks we're messing stuff up."

"I see." I did my best to hide my disappointment as I replied. "So, where do you usually meet with him then?"

"Down at the bar." He shrugged. "I've seen him around town a few times, too, but he won't talk to me then. Acts like he's better than the rest of us."

"So what *do* you know, then?" I asked sarcastically, irritated by the whole lot of nothing we were getting out of this guy.

"Just what I've told you," he snapped. "I don't know what else you want me to say. I go to work, I do my job, that's it. I don't have any top-secret information to give you."

"Alright," I replied calmly, despite the frustration I felt. In truth, I was a little disappointed that Frank didn't seem to have very much helpful information for us. As far as I could gather, he was just a minor cog within the greater system of the group. Ultimately, though, we wouldn't be able to squeeze blood from a stone.

"I think we're about done here, then," I said as I stood from the table. "Oh, and one last thing, Frank. These addresses had better not be another trick."

I slipped my phone from my pocket and waved it at him for emphasis.

"Or I'm personally going to make sure you get the harshest sentence a judge can conjure up."

Frank sneered at me but didn't say anything as Holm, Olivia, and I stood up and filed out of the interrogation room.

"Well, that was anticlimactic," Holm grumbled once we were all back out in the hallway. "After all the crap we went through with Brown and Turner, this seems like a big letdown."

"Don't be like that," Olivia admonished him. "We got the address, right? And now we know that Samuel's somewhere in Cockburn Town. Even if we don't know where exactly, it's a start."

The door beside us suddenly opened, and Morris stepped out to join us in the hallway.

"Do you think he was being honest?" he asked. "About not knowing anything else?"

"Yeah, unfortunately, I do," I replied with a frown. "He didn't *seem* like he was lying. Then again, he's already tricked us once, so I guess we can't be entirely sure."

"Could I see those addresses he gave you?" he asked.

"Oh, sure," I answered as I handed him the phone I still had in my hand. "I was going to ask you about them, anyway."

He took the phone from me and looked at the addresses for a moment before frowning.

"This is interesting," Morris muttered. "Both of these addresses are on Grand Turk Island, in Cockburn Town. Cockburn is the capital of Turks & Caicos and the most densely populated town. It might prove difficult to track him there."

"We'll worry about that when the time comes," I replied. "If we can track a pair of drug kingpins halfway across the planet, I'm sure we can find this guy. Meanwhile, we should focus our attention on the bar."

"Why don't we head back to my office to talk?" Morris suggested. "So we're not discussing all of this in the middle of the hall."

"Sounds good to us," Holm agreed.

We followed Morris back to his office in silence.

"Right, where were we?" Morris muttered once we were all seated in his office again. "Oh, yes, I've been wondering. What will you do now about Turner's liaison?"

"Well, working with him isn't ideal," I answered, "but our organization has extraterritorial jurisdiction in Turks & Caicos as part of our case. We prefer to have a member of local law enforcement with us—"

I faltered at the sour look Olivia tossed me.

"Well, *MBLIS* prefers to have a local liaison, though I can't speak for the FBI, to ensure we don't run into any international snags. Still, technically, we should be okay."

"That will not do." Morris shook his head disapprovingly. "I would hate for your investigation to fall apart as a result of a legal technicality. No, I will assign you one of my own officers."

"Really?" Holm asked, surprise evident in his voice.

"Of course." Morris nodded. "This is my country, and I want to keep it safe. I have just as much authority as Turner does. Just hold on for a moment, please."

He stood and stepped out of his office.

"Wow." Olivia smiled. "Total night and day difference from Captain Angry, huh?"

"Leagues," I replied. "Why couldn't we have been assigned here to begin with?"

"Because it's a tiny police box located in a strip mall?" Olivia shrugged. "I mean, don't get me wrong, small or not, it's better than having to deal with that total nut Turner, but I can see why it wouldn't be the first choice."

Captain Morris returned a few minutes later with another taller man in tow.

"Agents, this is Officer Crowley," he said as he sat back down behind his desk. "Officer Crowley, these are Agents Marston, Holm, and Hastings."

"A pleasure to meet you," the tall man said stiffly. "The captain has informed me of the situation. I'm ready to get started whenever you need me."

The man had a serious expression on his face, and he spoke in a stern, straightforward manner.

"Why don't you come back here tonight before you head to the bar this evening?" Morris suggested.

"That sounds great," I agreed before turning to look at Crowley. "We'll meet you here at eight then so we can head out together."

After thanking Captain Morris once again for his

assistance, the three of us headed back out of the police station and to the car.

"There're still a few hours until sundown," Holm noted after we settled into the rental and pulled out of the police station parking lot. "What should we do until then?"

"Oh!" Olivia exclaimed immediately. "There's a national park nearby!"

"Really?" I asked. "Here?"

"Yeah!" she replied, her eyes sparkling with excitement. "Literally right here on the Western Island. I was reading about it on the car ride down here. We can take a boat there. We'd definitely be done in time to get to the bar by eight."

"We have to take a boat to get to it?" Holm asked.

"Yeah, isn't that cool?" She grinned. "It's an island within the island. The only ways to get there are by plane or by boat, and a boat tour seems like it would be more fun anyway, right?"

She was so excited by the idea that I couldn't keep from smiling.

"I'm down for it if you are!" I called up to Holm from the backseat.

"Sure." He shrugged. "Could use a little 'R and R' before we head into the lion's den."

"Exactly." Olivia nodded. "I'll plug in the directions to the ferry port now."

Honestly, part of me felt a little bad about running off to play when we were in the middle of a case, but Olivia was so into the idea that I didn't have the heart to say no. And anyway, I'd learned a long time ago that this job could easily break a person's spirit if they didn't learn to go with the flow and have fun while they could. With all the danger and stress we dealt with, a little boat ride to blow off some steam would do us all a world of good.

21

ETHAN

Our short detour to Chalk Sound National Park turned out to be worth the time. It was known for its untouched greenery and striking turquoise-colored water, as the guide who took us out helpfully explained. Because it was a national park, large vessels like ferries weren't allowed, so we had to take a small pontoon boat out to see it.

The tour guide operating the boat also emphasized that many visitors enjoyed kayaking and paddle-boating around the park before mentioning that anyone interested could rent the necessary equipment directly from them. The idea actually sounded really fun, and had we not been busy with the case, I might have been tempted to take him up on the offer.

Because so many of the plant and animal species that inhabited the island were rigorously protected by the government, we were only allowed to step onto some of the islands in the park, and we were warned multiple times to be careful to not disturb or feed any of the animals.

The beach of the island we stopped off at had a rocky, uneven shore. As I was helping Olivia down off of the boat, she tripped on the loose rocks and fell into me. She apologized and smiled up at me sheepishly, but I noticed that she didn't make a big effort to move away from me.

The entire excursion had only taken about an hour and a half, but it was enough time for me to feel relaxed and recharged by the end of it. The grin on Olivia's face afterward had been the icing on the cake.

We'd headed back to the hotel afterward to prepare and wait for nightfall before heading over to the bar that Frank had mentioned. After we all got settled, we gathered in Holm's room, going over our plan for the night.

Since we would be the ones to go in undercover, Holm and I had changed into our most touristy-looking outfits. In my case, that meant a pair of shorts and a t-shirt I purchased from the hotel gift shop. Not my usual style, but I wanted to give off the impression of a clueless, and therefore harmless, vacationer looking for a good time.

Holm, meanwhile, had changed into a pair of jeans and a slightly oversized t-shirt with a picture of a band I'd never heard of.

"Who are they?" I asked as I sat down on the edge of the bed.

"What? Oh, the shirt?" he asked as he looked down at his own clothes. "This band a girl I once dated was into. They ended up being pretty good. I actually kept following them even after we broke up. They've been disbanded for a while, though."

"Awesome." Olivia smiled as she took a seat next to me. "Now that the two of you look like a pair of frat boys on vacation, let's go over the plan one more time."

"Holm and I will pose as prospective Johns," I reiterated. "Once we manage to convince them, we'll try to get the girl alone and see what kind of information we can get."

"What if you can't convince them to talk?" Olivia countered. "I've worked these kinds of cases before. A lot of the time, these women have spent so long being abused and brainwashed that they won't speak up against their captors even when the opportunity presents itself."

"That's a good point." Holm frowned. "But what else can we do? It'll be way more suspicious if you come in with us."

"I know," she sighed.

She hadn't been pleased when I'd suggested she stay outside as backup. On the one hand, she had a lot of experience and expertise in working with special victims. She was also a woman, which might have made it easier for her to connect with the victims. However, a woman walking into a bar looking for a prostitute would have thrown up a truckload of red flags. It would be far less conspicuous for Holm and me to go in undercover. It was a messy situation all around.

"We'll just have to play it by ear," I declared. "Worst-case scenario, Holm and I will retreat and meet you back at the meet-up point."

"One other thing, though." Olivia pursed her lips. "What if you get recognized? I mean, I know we've only been here a few days, but we have caused quite a stir, what with the whole 'shoot out in the middle of a crowded beach' thing. And one of the suspects got away. What will you do if your cover gets blown?"

"Go down swinging?" I joked.

"Very funny." She frowned at me as she crossed her arms over her chest. "Seriously, though. Shouldn't we have a backup plan?"

"That is the backup plan." I shrugged. "Obviously, I hope it doesn't come to that, but if we get made and run out of options, what else can we do? We'll try to locate one of the girls and get her alone for long enough to speak with her. If that fails, we'll confront the men directly. That being said, we've already seen that their preferred method of conflict resolution is to shoot first and ask questions never, so if it does come to that, we'll probably end up having to fight our way out."

"And you're just... okay with that?" Olivia stared at me in disbelief.

"I wouldn't say 'okay.'" Holm shrugged. "Can't say we're not used to it, though. Getting into and out of scrapes is pretty par for the course for us."

"That sounds insanely stressful," Olivia groaned. "And I thought I had it rough."

"We'll be fine," I assured her, though it did feel nice that she was worrying over me. "Holm and I have faced down a lot worse."

"Okay." Olivia nodded, though I could tell she

wasn't convinced by my reassurances. "Let's go, then."

The three of us left the hotel room and headed down to the lobby. The sun was just starting to go down as we left the hotel.

As I drove us back to the Grace Bay Police Station, I noted that the streets were still as empty as they had been earlier in the day. Though it seemed like there were always locals and tourists milling about along the boardwalks and pedestrian walkways, the actual roads seemed perpetually void of cars. It was a pleasant change from the never-ending traffic of Miami and probably explained how the air was so fresh and the skies so clear and blue.

The drive back to the Grace Bay station took no time at all, and before I knew it, we were back in Morris's office, getting ready to head to the bar with our new liaison, Officer Crowley.

Holm, Olivia, and I settled into the seats in front of Captain Morris's desk, and as ridiculous as I felt in my getup, I was buzzing with energy and ready to head out. We quickly recapped our plan that we'd discussed in the hotel, and Morris nodded agreeably as we finished.

"I'll wait outside with Agent Hastings," Crowley

declared from where he was standing by Morris's side. "The island is not very big, and there's a good chance that someone might recognize me. Our whole plan will fall apart if anyone realizes I am a cop."

"So it'll be Holm and me, then," I concluded with a nod.

"Keep this in your pocket," Morris instructed as he handed me and Holm each a small electronic device. "It's a basic one-way transmitter. Officer Crowley and Agent Hastings will be able to listen, though unfortunately, they won't be able to respond. But at least this way, they can provide aid if it seems like things are becoming dangerous."

I would have preferred something like an earpiece since putting the thing in my pocket would probably muffle sound and make it difficult for them to hear us, but wearing something so obvious would be a dead giveaway when we were trying to be discreet.

"Thank you," I replied regardless. "Let's get moving."

"Why don't we all take one car," I suggested as we left the building and stepped outside. "If we want to keep a low profile, it might make more sense to take our rental instead of a police cruiser."

"Alright." Crowley nodded after a moment of thoughtful silence.

Once the four of us were inside, I drove back to Kew, to the address Frank had given us. The place really was close to the dock, where we'd met with Kenneth a few days prior. It was a small, kind of kitschy-looking bar right on the boardwalk. As we parked out front, I could see locals and tourists alike meandering in and out. Being so close to the beach, it was probably a popular spot. I suddenly thought back to our first trip down this way and realized that we'd walked right by it. Something about the place had felt off at the time, and now I understood why.

I hadn't even stopped the car yet when I noticed a young woman standing just a few feet from the entrance, leaning against the front wall of the building. She was wearing a thin tank top and a pair of shorts, which, in and of themselves, didn't look all that out of place here by the beach.

What really stood out about her was her hunched, tense posture and the way she deliberately avoided eye contact with almost everyone passing by. She almost looked like a statue there, standing perfectly still. If I hadn't specifically been looking for her, I might have missed her entirely.

"The girl by the window," I remarked to the

others in the car. "There's something off about her, right?"

"I think so, too," Olivia replied. "I noticed as soon as we pulled up. Her body language screams discomfort."

"That might be a good place for us to start then," Holm added.

I made sure to drive past the bar before pulling the car to a stop a few buildings away. We didn't know who might be watching.

"Okay," Crowley replied. "We will wait here. The transmitter should still work from this distance, so if you need us, just give us a signal, and we'll move in."

"Got it," I replied before getting out of the car. Holm followed out after me.

I tried to put myself into the mind space of a dumb, horny tourist as I approached the girl. If she was a prostitute, then her pimp would no doubt be nearby, and playing dumb was one of the best ways to keep a suspect in the dark.

"Hey." I grinned oafishly at the young woman. She flinched and looked up at me with wide, startled eyes. "What are you doing out here all by yourself?"

"Um..." the girl muttered as she looked around, as though searching for someone.

Now that I got a closer look at her, I could see

that her hair was tangled, and she had faint cuts and bruises along her arms and legs in various stages of healing. Something was definitely up with this girl.

"Do you, uh, work here?" I asked suggestively, lowering my voice the way some sleazy guy on vacation trying to pick up a hooker might.

"Y-yes," she mumbled, still glancing around nervously.

"Cool," Holm chimed in, making an exaggerated show of looking around as though he didn't want anyone to see us. "So, how does this work, exactly?"

Before she could answer, a tall man suddenly rounded the corner of the building and stepped rapidly toward us.

"Can I help you two?" the man asked us quietly.

Got you! I thought to myself. Just as I'd suspected he would, the pimp had made an appearance right after we made initial contact.

"Oh, we were just wondering where a couple of guys could have some, uh, fun around here," I replied with a chuckle. I felt incredibly slimy, and the words I was saying tasted like bile on my tongue, but I needed to keep the act up, at least for now. I had to convince this guy that I was the type of creep who would be interested in something like this.

"Yeah," Holm added, leaning close as though sharing a secret. "You know what we mean, right?"

I tried not to flinch as I heard how awkward Holm sounded delivering that line. It was clear that he was just as uncomfortable as I was. I only hoped that the man wouldn't notice it as well.

"Yes, I think I do," the man replied, grinning darkly. "Why don't we get a drink inside? You, come on."

He called the young woman over with his finger like a dog. She followed behind him quietly with her head lowered, and I had to force myself not to react. It was infuriating having to just stand by and watch while he treated her that way, but I couldn't blow my cover.

The bar didn't seem all too different from any other one I might have found in any popular vacation spot. I could hear voices chattering happily all around us, the steady thrum only occasionally interrupted by a trill of laughter.

The smell of fried food permeated the air, and I could hear glasses clinking and silverware scraping against plates as people dug into their drinks and late dinners. The normal, cheerful atmosphere just made the entire situation we were engaged in feel that much more awful.

The man led us to a table in the rear of the bar. The four of us sat down, and the man yelled something at the bartender. A moment later, a different young woman appeared with a tray full of beers.

"Drink up," the man said after the woman had set the drinks down and walked away.

I put the bottle up to my lips but didn't actually drink any of it. The guy seemed like he was buying our act, but I wasn't going to chance being drugged.

As I pretended to drink, I glanced back at the girl out of the corner of my eye. She was still sitting completely still, her eyes cast down at the table in front of her.

"So, what exactly were you looking for?" the man asked after taking a big swig of his own beer.

"Oh, you know," Holm snickered like some frat boy as he glanced over at the young woman.

"Of course," the man replied as he eyed us warily. "And how did you hear about our services?"

"Hear about your services?" I asked innocently. "We were just looking for a place to have a few drinks when we noticed her standing outside. Wait, were we wrong? Is this not what I think it is?"

I rubbed the back of my neck and pretended to laugh nervously.

"So it was just a coincidence?" he asked, not

sounding totally convinced. "What brings you to the island?"

"Family vacation." I shrugged. "The wife decided to tuck in early. Long day at the beach and all that, you know? I told her my brother Dean and I here were going to head out for a drink, and we just happened to notice this little cutie outside. You know how it is, right? Sometimes you just need a little something different."

"Ah, I understand you perfectly well." The man smiled. He sounded more relaxed now, which was a relief because my stomach was churning after the nasty crap I'd just said, and I wasn't sure how much longer I could have kept it up.

"Well, the price is five hundred each," the man stated, getting down to business immediately. "That's for two hours. The rooms are upstairs." He gestured with his head toward a staircase behind him. "You can both go in if you'd like, or I can have another girl down here in a few minutes if you'd prefer to wait."

"I'll wait," Holm replied immediately before shooting me a look. "I'm not keen on, uh, sharing. You can go ahead. I'll just wait right out here."

"Sounds good to me." I shrugged easily. Holm had put just a little extra emphasis on that last sentence, and I realized immediately that it was his way of telling me that he'd keep watch while I went in to speak with the girl. I dug my wallet out of my pants pocket and pulled out the bills. I made a show of looking around before discreetly passing the money over.

"Get up." He sneered at the girl as he stood up from the table himself.

She obeyed without protest and immediately got up.

"Follow me," he said before turning and heading toward the stairs. I felt just a little trepidation about splitting up from my partner, but I trusted him and knew that he was perfectly capable of taking care of himself, and this way, he could give me a heads up if it seemed like something was wrong.

The staircase led up to a dimly lit hallway, lined on either side with two doors each. I could easily imagine what was going on behind those doors, and it was disgusting to think of what was happening here just above the bar, where tourists were happily enjoying drinks and having a good time.

"In here," the man directed us toward the first door on the right. The girl stepped inside first, and I stepped in behind her.

"I'll be back in two hours," was all the man said before shutting the door behind us.

I turned around to look at the girl. She had moved to sit on the bed, one of the few pieces of furniture in the sparsely decorated room. In fact, aside from the bed, the only thing inside the room was a cheap-looking table and a wooden chair. The walls, which had once probably been white, were stained a dingy yellow and covered in suspicious-looking dark stains.

The girl hadn't moved since she'd sat down. She was completely still, the same way she'd been outside, and her eyes were glazed over as she stared at something far away.

"Hello," I murmured softly as I moved to crouch in front of her. I reached into my pocket to pull out my badge. "My name is Ethan Marston. I'm a federal agent with an American agency called MBLIS. I'm here to help you."

"What?" the girl yelped, the blank look in her eyes gone in an instant as she stared down at me.

"I'm a federal agent," I repeated. "The man I came here with is my partner. I'm sorry about what we said before. We just needed to get that man's trust so we could speak with you."

"No," she whimpered as she looked around the room wildly. She looked terrified, which really wasn't the reaction I'd been expecting. "You need to leave. I don't want any trouble."

"You won't get in trouble," I tried to reassure her. She was beginning to raise her voice, and I needed her to calm down before the man got suspicious and returned. "We're here to help you. Just please calm down—"

"No!" she suddenly screamed. "No! Help! Help!"

"What the hell?" I hissed. Why was she reacting like this? Had I made some massive error in judgment? No, there was no way. It was evident from her body language and how she'd been behaving the entire time we'd been here that she was being abused and manipulated, so why was she panicking at my offer of help?

I tried to plead with her to stop yelling, but the door burst open with a bang just moments later. The man from before was standing there, a gun clutched in his hand.

"What's going on here?" he yelled, his eyes bugging out as he looked between the girl and me.

"H-he's a cop!" she shrieked as she pointed an accusing finger at me.

The man lifted his gun, and I jumped out of the way just as he pulled the trigger. The girl screamed as the bullet tore through the mattress just a foot away from where she was sitting. I reached for my own gun but couldn't quite get to it from my current position on the ground.

The man turned his gun toward me again, and for one terrifying moment, I was staring straight down the barrel of it.

Before he could pull the trigger, though, I heard a dull thump, and the man collapsed to the ground with a groan. As he fell, I realized that Holm was standing just behind him, his own gun held aloft in his hand. He'd pistol-whipped him just a moment before he'd gotten the chance to shoot.

"Thanks, brother," I breathed as I got back onto my feet.

"No problem," he replied as he crouched down to handcuff the unconscious man. "What the hell happened, though? We heard screams."

I turned to look expectantly at the girl sitting on the bed. I was honestly wondering what that was about, too.

"I-I'm sorry," she stuttered, her eyes welling up with tears. "I didn't mean to—I mean, I was just scared that..."

She kept cutting herself off as she gasped for breath between sobs. Despite the mess she'd caused by screaming, I couldn't help but feel sorry for her. It was obvious that the poor girl had been through a lot.

Before doing anything else, I reached into my pocket to pull out the listening device, ready to give Olivia and Crowley an update as to what had just happened. Before I could, though, someone else burst into the room.

"What the hell is this?" the newcomer asked as his eyes flitted between me, the girl, and Holm, who was still on the ground, getting the fallen man's hands cuffed. He seemed familiar, and it took me a second to realize that it was the same man we'd seen on the beach a few days earlier—the one who had shot our first police liaison, Walter, before escaping.

It seemed he recognized me at the exact moment because his eyes suddenly lit up, and his face twisted into an angry snarl.

"You!" he roared as he reached behind his back.

I lifted my own gun just as he was drawing his, and I managed to pull the trigger a fraction of a second before he could. He cried out in pain as my bullet struck him, and he fell to the ground with a loud thump.

Holm leapt up from his position on the floor and quickly rushed to the newcomer's side to retrieve his fallen gun.

I let out a shaky breath as I looked around for the listening device. It wasn't in my hand anymore, which meant that I must have dropped at some point while I was focused on the new suspect.

"We're here," Olivia's voice suddenly called, to my surprise.

I looked up and found her rushing into the room, her own gun drawn.

"We heard the gunshots over the transmitter," Crowley explained. "We thought we did, anyway. Once everyone started rushing out, it became obvious that something bad was going on. We came as soon as we heard, but it was a struggle to make our way through the crowd. Everyone was rushing out the same door."

"He's dead," Holm declared as he took the pulse of the man I'd just shot before nodding toward the other man who was still unconscious. "We could call for an ambulance for that one."

"I'll do it," Crowley volunteered as he reached for the radio at his hip.

I re-holstered my gun and took a deep breath. Things had gone from zero to a hundred really fast there, and my mind was still reeling.

While Crowley called for an ambulance, Olivia

stepped further into the room and passed me until she was standing right in front of the girl.

"Hello," she greeted softly as she knelt down in front of her. "My name's Olivia. Can you tell me yours?"

"Jenny," she mumbled faintly. "It's Jenny."

"Hi, Jenny." Olivia smiled warmly at her before pulling her badge out of her pocket, just like I had done earlier. "I'm an agent with the FBI. My job is to help women and children who are in bad situations, like you. What do you say we get out of here? You can get cleaned up and have something to eat, and then we can talk. How does that sound?"

"Good," she replied softly.

"Okay." Olivia nodded. "As soon as the ambulance gets here, we can go, okay?"

"Okay." The girl, Jenny, nodded tersely.

Olivia gave her one last smile before standing back up straight and turning to look at me. There was a pained expression in her eyes, but I was impressed by how she had handled that. Considering how the girl had reacted to me, I wasn't sure what would have happened if she hadn't been here with us.

Once again, I found myself feeling glad that we were working this case together.

22

ETHAN

IT WAS LATE at night by the time we'd finished dealing with the aftermath of the shoot-out at the bar. Since someone had died, there was, of course, a long list of procedures that needed to be followed to document everything that had happened. Then we'd needed to deal with making sure that the surviving suspect was placed under surveillance even while at the hospital. Holm had gotten him good, and though he had woken up and was responding normally, the doctor had advised us to wait at least until the next day to interrogate him to ensure that he didn't have any severe head injury that might affect his judgment or memory.

While Holm, Crowley, and I handled all that, Olivia had decided to head back with the victim,

Jenny. Considering how Jenny had acted around us, it seemed like a better option for Olivia to go alone with her, anyway. After all, she had more experience in this, and it would probably give her a chance to build a rapport and get the girl to open up.

I was beat by the time we made it back to the Grace Bay station, where Olivia was waiting with Jenny. It was fully dark out now as we got out of the car, and with so little light pollution, I could see the stars in the sky in stunning clarity. It was a discordant sensation to look at something so pretty up above while such heinous things were happening there on the ground.

Captain Morris met us inside as soon as we entered.

"I'm glad to see you're all okay." He smiled. "I heard that you ran into a bit of trouble. I was relieved to learn that none of you had been injured."

"Well, it was pretty close," I replied. "Luckily, we all made it out okay."

"Good." He nodded. "Agent Hastings is waiting for you now. I'll take you back there."

He led us down a long hallway, past the few empty holding cells, and toward a room at the very end of the hall. Even before he'd opened the door, I could hear Olivia's familiar voice coming from inside.

The door opened with a creak, and the talking stopped as Holm, Crowley, and I stepped inside.

"Hey, guys," Olivia greeted us, her tone light and friendly. She and Jenny were sitting closely together, side by side on the couch against the wall. Olivia turned away from us to look back at Jenny before speaking again. "Are you still okay with what we talked about?"

The girl nodded stiffly before looking up at us.

I noted at once that her hair wasn't tangled anymore. It had clearly been washed and brushed, and even her skin had a healthier tint to it now.

"Jenny has agreed to speak with us for a while." Olivia turned to look at us. "Which was very kind and brave of her. Of course, if you want to stop at any point, just tell me, okay?"

"Okay." Jenny nodded again before peering up at us nervously.

I moved to sit down on the couch opposite them. We were in some kind of break room. There was a table and a small fridge at one end of the room, and even a vending machine tucked in the corner. It had definitely been a smarter choice than sticking her in some tiny interview room.

"Thank you for agreeing to talk with us," I told her slowly as Holm and Crowley also sat down. "And I'm sorry if I scared you earlier. That wasn't my intention."

"No." She suddenly shook her head furiously. "You didn't. I mean, you did. But it's okay. I was just —I'm sorry."

"It's okay, Jenny." Olivia reached out to take her hand. "He isn't mad. None of us are upset with you at all."

Jenny's shoulders were hunched up almost to her ears, and she looked like she didn't totally believe us. I clenched my jaw in frustration. What kind of awful things had those monsters done to get this woman to react like this to an apology, of all things?

"She's right," I replied. "I'm not mad. You seemed scared, so I was just worried I might have upset you."

"I'm sorry," she apologized again before smiling bitterly. "I don't know why I did that. I've dreamed of having someone swoop in and offer to take me away. It's just... the first thing that popped into my mind was how much trouble I would be in if Antonio found out what was happening. Girls have tried to run away before, and it never ends well for them. Sometimes they don't even come back... I didn't want him to be mad, so I just started screaming. I'm really, really sorry."

She was starting to cry again, and Olivia reached a hand out to rub her back comfortingly.

"It's okay, Jenny," she insisted firmly. "We all understand that you were just scared. What's important is that you're here now, safe with us."

"Thank you." She smiled weakly at Olivia before turning to look at me again. "Um... Olivia said you want to ask me some things."

"That's right," I replied. "To start with, can you tell me if you know a woman named Allison? She was about your height, with curly blond hair and blue eyes."

"No." Jenny frowned. "I've never met anyone named Allison. But there was a girl here once who looked like that. Her name was Cat, though. At least, that's what we called her."

"Did she have a child?" Olivia interjected. "A little boy about five years old, named Eddy?"

Jenny's eyes went wide, and her jaw dropped at the name.

"Yeah, that's Cat," she gasped. "Do you know where she is? She disappeared one day a few weeks ago. There were rumors that she'd run away, been sold off, killed. No one knew for sure. Is she okay? Where is she?"

She was hitting us with questions rapid-fire, her small hands clenched into fists as she spoke.

"Jenny, I'm sorry," Olivia began delicately.

She didn't have to finish her sentence for Jenny to deflate, her eyes reddening as fresh tears threatened to spill.

"No," she whimpered as she dropped her head into her hands. "But... why? She never did anything wrong. She always did just as she was told, so they wouldn't hurt Eddy."

She gasped again and snapped her head up to look at us.

"What about Eddy? Is he okay? Don't tell me—"

"He's fine," I hurried to assure her. "He's with his grandmother now, and his aunt. Allison, er, Cat made sure that he made it to the US safely."

"He's with his grandma?" She smiled with disbelief. "So she did run away. I can't believe it... I'm so glad."

"Was she a friend of yours?" Olivia prompted.

"Yeah." Jenny sniffed. "She was really nice to everyone. She'd been here for a really long time too. A lot longer than I have. When they first brought me here, she was the first one to be kind to me."

"It sounds like she was a good person." Olivia smiled sadly.

"Yeah," Jenny sighed before suddenly frowning. "But wait, if the men didn't kill her, and she made it to the US, then what happened?"

"We think she died of exposure," I replied honestly. Her face fell as I spoke, and I felt a pang of sympathy for them. It must have been painful to hear that she had managed to make it so far only to die in the end, after all.

"A combination of that and dehydration, most likely. She took off on a fishing boat and managed to make it all the way to Miami. Eddy survived the trip, but unfortunately, she didn't."

"That's Cat." She nodded as she wiped her eyes clear. "She did everything for that little boy. Danny told me that she had run away, but I just wasn't sure what to believe."

"Danny?" I repeated, the name ringing familiar in my mind.

"She's one of the girls," Jenny clarified, her voice suddenly a few degrees colder. "Though sometimes it seems like she's more on the men's side than ours. She's kind of like the mother hen, you know? Keeps an eye on everyone and everything when the men aren't around. Sometimes, I'm not sure how much I can trust her, so I didn't know what to think when she'd told me that Cat had run away."

That was when it hit me. Eddy had talked about a "Danny" as well. He'd said that she was a friend of his and his mother's, the same one who had taught him the names of the dinosaurs.

He'd made her sound like a friendly and caring person, but the way that Jenny was now sitting hunched and stiff just at the mention of her appeared to indicate otherwise. I'd need to keep that in mind going forward.

"Can you tell us more about the men?" I asked. I noticed that she kept referring to them with that phrase.

"They're the ones keeping us here." She shrugged. She looked down and shifted uncomfortably on the couch as she replied. "I don't know all their names. I only know Antonio since he's the one who brings us over from Cockburn Town. He stays with us most of the time."

"Cockburn Town?" Olivia asked. "Is that where you live?"

"Most of the time." She nodded. "Sometimes we stay out for a few days at a time, though. There's a house there where they keep all the girls until we get assigned to a bar or hotel."

"Do you know where the house is?" I asked.

"Not exactly," she mumbled, her voice cracking as her eyes filled with tears again. "I could recognize it, but I'm not really sure about how to get there. They make us wear blindfolds while we're in the car. We can't take them off until we're on the boat."

"A boat?" Crowley suddenly chimed in. Jenny jumped a little at the deep timbre of his voice. Honestly, even I was a bit surprised to hear him speak for the first time during the conversation. "There aren't any ferries from Cockburn to the Western Island."

"It must be a privately owned vessel, then," I concluded before turning to look at Holm. "We should look into boat owners here on the Island."

"That's going to be a long list," Crowley remarked before turning to address Jenny. "Do you know exactly what kind of boat it is?"

"N-no," she stuttered. "I'm sorry. It's usually dark when we get on it. Um... it's pretty big? And white? I'm sorry, I'm not being helpful."

"It's okay, Jenny," Olivia assured her as she began to cry again. She rubbed a soothing hand along the girl's back and waited until she'd calmed down before speaking again. "You're doing amazing. This is plenty for us to go off of. You've already given us a ton of useful information."

"Really?" she muttered through tears. "Okay... I'm fine. I can keep going."

"Thank you, Jenny." I smiled at her. "We've heard that the name of the leader of the group who was holding you is named Samuel. Do you know anything about that?"

"I've heard that name." She nodded slowly. "I've never met him before. I don't think so, anyway, but I've heard the men talking about him."

"I see," I replied, a little disappointed that she didn't know more. I couldn't show that, though. The poor girl kept breaking into tears every time she thought she did something wrong, so I definitely couldn't look like I was displeased by her answer.

"I know you said you're not sure where the main house is," I continued. "But do you know the addresses of the other locations? You mentioned that there were several bars and hotels that you've been sent to, right?"

"Yes, I do," she replied. "I know one for sure because it's the only bar in the whole town."

"Where is it?" I asked eagerly.

"We're in Grace Bay right now, right?" she asked as she looked around the room, as though she'd be able to recognize the town just from the inside of the police station.

"Yes, we are," I replied, my brows furrowed in confusion. "Why?"

"It's right here," she replied.

23

ETHAN

As soon as Jenny revealed that one of the bars where the women were being forced to work was here in Grace Bay, all the weariness I'd felt before evaporated. I'd been ready to head back to the hotel and call it a night after finishing our interview with Jenny, but there was no way I'd be able to sleep now, knowing how close we were.

After wrapping up the interview, Holm, Crowley, and I headed over to Morris's office to relay everything we had learned. Olivia had stayed behind to make sure that Jenny wouldn't feel scared being alone in the police station by herself. Morris had been aghast to discover that one of the prostitution hot spots was right here in his own town.

"This is unbelievable," Captain Morris growled

as he paced back and forth in front of his desk. "It must be the Oasis Lounge. That's the biggest bar in all of Grace Bay. Right on the beach and a magnet for tourists."

"She did say that it was the biggest bar in town," I replied from where I was leaning against the wall beside the door.

"There aren't very many bars here as it is," Crowley added. "I think three in total. The Oasis definitely gets the most foot traffic."

"Which means it would be the most ideal for moving around undetected," I concluded. "When it comes to human trafficking, it's easier to hide in plain sight."

"So, what do we do now?" Olivia asked before turning to look at Holm and me. "Will you go in undercover again? Pose as prospective clients?"

"I don't know if that will work again," Holm argued. "We just caused a pretty big stir back at the bar in Kew Town, didn't we? You don't think they'll have their guard up now?"

Holm did have a point. It had been a few hours since the shootout in the bar already, and there was a good chance that word about what had happened in Kew had already made its way over to Grace Bay. If that were the case, then the traffickers would be on the lookout for us anyway, so there was no point in trying to be sneaky.

"He's right," Morris replied as he came to an abrupt stop from his pacing. His face was scrunched into a scowl, and his fists were clenched. "It's possible they're already aware that you're investigating. I think it would be best if we approached this more officially."

"What do you mean?" I asked.

"I mean, we should forego the idea of being covert," he grumbled, "and simply strike directly. Last time, Officer Crowley waited outside to not tip them off. I think this time, you should all go in and make it clear that they're being investigated. I will not stand to have this going on right beneath my nose."

It was clear that he was taking this very personally. I supposed it was one thing to have a crime going on in the next town over, but another to have it be happening right down the street. Still, I couldn't help but worry that he was being a little too rash right now.

"Officer Crowley will go in and request to speak with the owner," Morris declared. "If he refuses to cooperate, arrest him under suspicion of prostitution."

"Okay," I replied. "Let's go and let Olivia know about our plan."

After finishing our meeting in Morris's office, Holm, Crowley, and I went back down to the break room where the two women were waiting.

"I can't say I'm thrilled by the idea of you just barging in headfirst," she muttered after we'd explained the plan to her. She and I had stepped away from the rest of the group to talk. Jenny had immediately curled in on herself when Olivia had left her side, and she kept glancing anxiously toward where we were standing. "But I didn't like the idea of you sneaking around pretending to be a John, either, so I guess it's as good a plan as any."

"That's kind of what I was thinking, too," I replied. "What about you? Will you stay here with Jenny?"

"Yeah, I think I will." She nodded. "She's still pretty shaken up. I've spoken with my director and arranged for a hotel room for her, so I'll help her settle in and make sure there's a patrol nearby to make sure nothing happens. Kenneth Johnson mentioned that one of the men shot at Allison while she was trying to escape. I wouldn't put it past them to try to kill Jenny to keep her silent about everything."

"That's a good call," I replied as I looked over to where Jenny was sitting on the couch just a few feet away, out of earshot of our conversation. She didn't look nearly as terrified as before, though her posture was still stiff and hunched, and I could tell she was tense.

"I'll see you when you get back, then." Olivia offered me a small smile as she reached up to stroke my arm. Her touch lingered for just a moment too long to be considered strictly friendly, and my arm felt oddly cold and bereft the moment she pulled her hand away.

"Yeah, you will." I smiled back at her.

Her face turned a shade redder. I wanted to tease her, but she turned and walked back to Jenny's side before I could say anything. It was obvious how much she cared about making her feel safe. I thought it was admirable how devoted she was to her job of helping special victims.

"You know," Holm hummed once Olivia had stepped away to go speak to Jenny, "Some people might call it unprofessional to fraternize with every woman you meet while on the job."

"I have no idea what you're talking about," I replied dismissively.

"Wait, what?" Crowley blinked at me in apparent

confusion. "She's not your girlfriend? This whole time, that's the impression I've had."

"Ha!" Holm laughed. "Even people we've just met can tell! You're a lot of things, Marston, but subtle is not one of them."

"Sounds like someone's just jealous because he doesn't have any game," I retorted playfully.

"That's a low blow," Holm replied as he crossed his arms across his chest. "And I'll have you know that I have plenty of game. I'm just not a walking cliche like you are. Honestly, the two of you looked like something out of a movie just then, staring into each other's eyes like that."

"Like I said," I teased smugly. "*Jealous.*"

We spent a bit longer trading barbs back and forth while Olivia got Jenny ready to go. Five minutes later, all of us were standing in the parking lot. Olivia was about to head off to the hotel with Jenny and another officer, who would be keeping watch for the time being, and Holm, Crowley, and I were about to head to the Oasis Lounge. We would be taking separate cars this time since Morris wanted to make it clear that this was a police investigation.

The bar was close enough to have walked, but since we might make arrests or need to make a speedy exit, we opted to drive instead. After only about five minutes, I knew we'd made it to the correct spot before Crowley had even pulled in.

A single building stood out among the rest, easily twice as big and lit up like a firework. Even from the outside, I could see colorful lights streaming through the windows, and the closer we got, the more I could hear the music emanating from inside.

"No wonder Jenny said she was sure which one it was," I remarked as we pulled into the parking lot. "I couldn't miss this place if I tried."

I parked the car next to Crowley's cruiser before getting out. He was already waiting for us, his lips set into a thin, angry line. It seemed he was just as upset about what was going on as Morris was.

"Let's go," he said before taking off at a steady pace toward the massive bar.

Holm and I followed closely behind him, the music getting increasingly louder the closer we got to the front doors. As we stepped inside, I realized just how many people there were in here. The parking lot hadn't had that many cars in it, so I was surprised to find that the place was absolutely packed. Grace Bay wasn't very large, though, so it was reasonable to assume all of these people had just walked here from their homes and hotels.

The place was surprisingly big, to the point that it seemed a little out of place in the otherwise scenic and peaceful town. It looked more like a club than a typical bar, with a large dance floor in the center surrounded by several sitting areas.

Women in tight, short dresses moved languidly around the floor, trays of expensive drinks in their hands. My eyes were drawn to them first, but it didn't seem like they were in distress. Unlike Jenny, who had stood stock still and kept her gaze fixed unwaveringly on the ground, these women were wearing forced, plastic smiles as they flirted with the patrons around the bar, coaxing them into spending more money. It didn't look sincere, but it didn't look like they were in danger, either.

Crowley strode confidently through the bar and toward the first bartender he spotted. I still felt displeased about this plan. It would completely kill any element of surprise we had, and nothing was stopping the traffickers from fleeing the moment they realized we were in here poking around. I didn't want to go against Morris's wishes, though. He'd been extremely helpful to us so far, and clashing with local law enforcement was never a good idea in any case if we could help it.

"Hello," Crowley greeted the man behind the bar.

"Good evening," the man replied warily. His eyes immediately flitted down to Crowley's police uniform, and I could tell that his guard was up. "How can I help you gentlemen?"

"We need to speak to the owner of this establishment," Crowley declared.

"I'm sorry," the bartender replied slowly, "he's not here tonight."

"Well, call him," Crowley retorted angrily. "We need to speak with him right now."

"I'm afraid that's not going to be possible," the man replied.

I was about to chime in when I noticed something out of the corner of my eye. A woman was standing on the other side of the bar, but she was staring directly at us. She was standing just behind a circle of couches where several other women were sitting. The first thing that jumped out to me about them was how similar they all seemed to Jenny. All of them were done up with makeup and were wearing short, revealing dresses, but unlike the servers, they were all sitting unnaturally still, their eyes downcast.

I turned to look at the standing woman, and the moment our eyes met, something akin to fear flashed across her face. I watched as she leaned down to whisper something to one of the women sitting in front of her. The woman snapped her head around to look at me, her eyes wide with shock. She turned back around just as quickly.

"Hey." I nudged Holm in the side with my elbow. "Something's weird over there."

I gestured in their direction with a short nod. The first woman I'd noticed kept tossing surreptitious glances in our direction while the rest of the girls slowly started to get up from the couches.

I turned back to Crowley. He and the bartender were still arguing, and both seemed entirely focused on their own conversation.

"Come on," I hissed at Holm before quickly taking off toward where the girls were now standing. Something was definitely up, and this might be a good chance to get some info while Crowley inadvertently distracted the bartender.

Holm and I set off quickly toward the group of women.

The woman standing above the group flinched

as she caught our rapid approach, and I watched as she leaned forward to say something to the girls. We were far enough away that I couldn't catch what she said over the noise of the crowd. Whatever she said lit a fire beneath them because all of a sudden, they were all scrambling away from the sitting area.

One of them, in her haste, accidentally moved directly into our path before realizing her error. She looked up at me with large, terrified eyes before suddenly spinning on her heel and attempting to walk in the other direction.

"Wait," I called as I walked briskly forward and took hold of her arm.

"Don't touch her," the first woman snapped at me as she shoved my arm away from the girl.

"We don't mean any harm," Holm tried to reassure her.

"Linda, go," the woman said to the younger girl curtly.

The girl nodded and scampered off, and the woman turned back to me.

"You should leave," she sneered. Now that I was standing closer to her, I was able to get a better look at her features. She looked like she was in her early to mid-forties. She had deeply tanned skin, and her dark hair was flecked with streaks of gray. Her hazel eyes were fixed into a steely, unyielding glare.

"We only want to help," I replied. "We know about what's going on here."

"Get out, *now,*" she growled at me through gritted teeth. "Or I'll start screaming. I can have ten armed men on you in an instant."

"Please don't do that," Holm replied as he looked around, ready to react the moment the threat materialized.

"Then get out of here," she countered before looking past us. "And take that cop friend of yours with you. Before he does something that gets us all in trouble."

I could hear Crowley's raised voice from here, and I knew that he must be causing a scene.

"Please, just listen," I pleaded as the woman began to walk away. "We're federal agents. We're here to investigate the death of Allison Newark—I mean, Cat. You probably knew her as Cat."

She immediately froze at the name and turned around slowly to look at us, her eyebrows furrowed in suspicion.

"What did you say?" she rasped.

"We spoke with Jenny," I explained. "We have

her. She's safe right now with another agent. She's the one who gave us that name."

She blinked several times as she processed the information I'd just given her. Then she suddenly looked around quickly before beckoning us to come toward her with a flick of her hand.

"This way," she whispered before turning and walking off.

Holm and I both did as we were asked. She led us into a small sitting area separated from the rest of the bar by a large, thick curtain. It looked like some kind of VIP section. The moment we were out of sight from the rest of the people in the bar, she spun around to look at us.

"You said that Jenny was with you. Is that true?" she demanded to know.

"Yes," I replied. "She's at the police station now."

"Police?" the woman exclaimed. "Why? She's been arrested?"

"No," Holm interjected. "She got caught up in a scuffle we had with one of the men at a bar in Kew Town. We brought her with us for her own safety."

"I see," the woman replied, the earlier tension easing out of her shoulders. "I'm glad to hear that."

She laced her fingers together and bit her lip

nervously. I could tell she was thinking deeply about something, though I couldn't be sure what.

"You reacted pretty strongly when I mentioned we were investigating Cat's death," I muttered. "Why is that?"

A look of pain flashed across her face for just a moment. It was gone soon after, her face smoothed into a look of restrained calm, but it was there for long enough for me to take notice. This woman was obviously used to controlling her emotions.

"So she is dead," she sighed, her eyes downcast. "I had hoped..."

She trailed off, the careful mask slipping once more as she frowned.

"Are you Danny?" I asked on a hunch as I recalled what Jenny and Eddy had told us.

"You can call me Daniela." She frowned at me. "But yes, that's generally what the girls call me."

"Eddy mentioned you," I informed her. "He said that you taught him about dinosaurs."

"He's alive?" she gasped. "But, how?"

"They managed to make it to the United States," I explained. "Unfortunately, only Eddy survived the trip. From what we could gather, they were out on the water for several days with very little to eat or drink. Eddy had bad sunburns all over his body by the time they finally made it to shore."

"Thank goodness," she breathed, her clasped hands trembling. "The day that she suddenly took off like that, I didn't know what to think. I had no idea if she even had a plan. It breaks my heart to hear that she's... that she's dead. But at least little Eddy is okay."

"He is." I nodded. "And we want to get justice for his mother. That's why we're here."

All at once, she stopped shaking and looked up at me with a hard gaze.

"Are you serious about that?" she asked me coldly. "Do you really know what it is you're up against?"

"Honestly? No," I answered. "That's the reason we came here, to see what we could find out. If you have information that could help us, you need to share it."

She bit her lip again and looked away from me. I wanted to groan in frustration. We didn't have time for this. We needed to act as quickly as possible to get ahead of the traffickers. I remembered what Jenny had said, though, about panicking because she didn't know if she could really trust us. Daniela was probably thinking the same thing.

"Okay." She finally nodded after what felt like an eternity of silence. "I'll speak with you. But not here, and not until I'm sure my girls are safe. We've already spent too long talking. We need to hurry, or the men will realize what's going on."

"Okay, then when?" I asked, my heart racing with urgency.

"Tomorrow," she replied. "Around midday. The men will still be asleep then, except for one guard. Normally, the girls would be too, but I'll speak to them tonight and make sure they're ready."

"Ready for what?" Holm interrupted, his voice laced with concern.

"Ready to leave, of course," she replied as though the answer were obvious. "I told you, I won't speak with you unless I'm certain my girls are safe. Get us out, and I'll tell you whatever you want to know. There will be five men in total. They have guns, but with you on our side, we'll be able to overpower them."

There were so many things that could go wrong with this plan, but with the clock ticking on our time to speak, I couldn't find many other options.

"Okay," I agreed. "I'll speak to the police captain and figure out a plan. But I—"

"You need to go," she suddenly interrupted me,

her eyes going wide as she looked at something over my shoulder. "Now. We're out of time."

She didn't offer any further explanation before striding confidently out of the small sectioned-off area and back onto the main floor.

"Let's go," I murmured to Holm as I walked casually back toward the bar where we'd left Crowley. He wasn't there anymore, and it took me a moment to spot him standing by the entrance, scanning over the crowd with an annoyed look on his face.

"There you are!" He scowled as I approached him. "Where did you go? I turned around, and you were both gone!"

"Not here," I muttered out of the corner of my mouth, barely slowing down as I walked past him and toward the door. "We need to go."

His expression instantly became more serious, but he didn't question me as he trailed Holm and me out of the bar. I didn't stop until we had made it back to the car.

"What happened?" he asked me seriously.

"We met with Danny," I replied. "Come on, I'll explain everything back at the station."

"What?" He balked. "We're just leaving?"

"For now, yeah." I nodded. "Look, just trust me, okay? We might have a solid plan of attack here, but it's all going to come crumbling down if we get caught right now. I'll take the blame if Captain Morris gets upset."

He shot me a look of clear displeasure.

"Fine," he sighed after a moment of hesitation. "Let's get back, then."

I watched him climb into his patrol car before getting into the driver's seat of the Impala. Once Holm was inside, I started the ignition and pulled out of the parking lot.

As we drove back, my mind raced with all the ways this could go wrong. We hadn't had any time to finalize any of the details of the plan with Daniela, and I hated going in blind like that. I could only hope that things would go well tomorrow afternoon.

24

OLIVIA

OLIVIA SIGHED as she sank into the brown leather couch back at the Grace Bay Police Station. She'd just finished getting Jenny settled into her hotel room. The girl had seemed totally fine with everything until it was actually time for Olivia to leave. Then all of a sudden, she'd started to panic.

It was obvious that she'd latched onto Olivia as a kind of security blanket. It was understandable, considering everything the poor girl had gone through. She saw the agent as a beacon of safety, so of course, she felt groundless when the time had come for Olivia to leave.

She'd felt awful about it and had even been tempted to stay for longer, but she couldn't postpone it indefinitely. She needed to continue this investigation, so after staying just a little longer to help her relax, she'd finally managed to leave and make her way back to the station.

Olivia felt drained. It was always so emotionally taxing interacting with victims of abuse. She loved her job, but having to stay strong in the face of such an awful reality and be someone's pillar of support took a toll on her. Sometimes she just wanted to break down and cry hearing some of these victim's stories, but of course, she couldn't do that. She needed to be the one they looked to for support, not the one making them feel worse by turning into a blubbering mess.

She wondered vaguely how long it would be until Ethan got back. It hadn't been all that long, so she knew that it was unreasonable to start worrying. Still, her mind kept drifting back to him. She wasn't sure when it had started. Maybe it had been when she'd watched the delicate way he'd handled Eddy's interview. Lately, she had found herself more and more drawn to him, and she worried every time he and Holm did something stupid. Which was pretty much every time they did anything since it seemed like they couldn't go more than a few hours without getting involved in some sort of brawl or gunfight.

She glanced at the time on her phone again and

frowned when she realized it had only been two minutes since she'd last checked.

"Get a grip," she muttered to herself.

Was she really getting all worked up over some guy she had met, what, less than a week ago? Sure, he had those unbelievable baby blue eyes and that obnoxiously cute smirk, and he knew his way around a gun, which she'd never realized until now was actually a pretty attractive feature, and...

She groaned as she realized she was doing it again, letting her mind be consumed by this man. One romantic evening on the beach and suddenly she was acting like a lovesick teenager.

She stood up and walked to the vending machine, determined to keep her mind occupied when the break room door suddenly creaked open.

She snapped her head around to see who it was and felt a wave of relief wash over her when she saw it was Ethan and Holm, both unscathed as far as she could tell.

"How did it go?" she asked as she rushed toward them, vending machine completely forgotten.

"Well, we met Danny," Ethan replied a little sourly as he stepped into the room and headed straight for the couch.

"Why do you not sound happy about that?" she asked as she took a seat next to him.

"Because she's kind of blackmailing us into busting her and the rest of the girls out of the bar tomorrow," Holm replied flatly as he fell backward onto the couch.

"I'm sorry, what?" Olivia asked in surprise.

"Exactly what he just said." Ethan shrugged as he placed his hands on his hips. "She was just as sketchy as Jenny made her sound. She agreed to tell us what she knows about the traffickers, but only if we help get her and the other girls out tomorrow. Which, of course, we want to do, but she didn't exactly give us much time to plan."

"So, what did you say?" she asked as she sat back down on the couch.

"Didn't have time to say much," Ethan scoffed. "She dropped her conditions on us and then ushered us out so we wouldn't get caught by the traffickers. Of course, Morris was a little ticked off that we left without arresting anyone."

"She told us to come back at noon tomorrow," Holm added as he sank into one of the empty chairs near the couch. "Apparently, the men will still be asleep around then, aside from one guard. Aside from that, we don't have much as far as a plan goes."

"I see," Olivia muttered as she thought over everything they had just told her. On the one hand, she could understand Danny's desire to make sure the girls were safe before she did anything. Heck, the thought of leaving the girls there even one more night made her stomach churn, so she could understand why Danny would use their rescue as a bargaining chip. On the other hand, there were so many ways this could go badly for both the women and the agents. If any of the traffickers caught wind of the plan, they might end up walking straight into a trap. If the mission failed, the men might retaliate against the women and kill them.

Olivia looked up, ready to express her concerns to the MBLIS agents, when she noticed just how tired they both looked. It was almost ten now, and the day had been both physically and mentally draining, so it wasn't surprising that they both looked like they were ready to collapse.

"Why don't we head back to the hotel?" she suggested instead. "It's been a long day. We might end up making mistakes if we keep trying to run on fumes like this. We can get up early tomorrow and figure everything out before we have to head down to the bar again at noon."

"That sounds like a good idea," Holm replied as he stood up from the couch.

"Okay," Ethan replied with a short nod. "Let's head back."

The three of them walked back out of the police station and to the car. Olivia offered to drive this time since both men seemed like they could use a break. It wasn't the first time she'd driven on the left-hand side of the road. She'd worked on a few international cases before, so she had some experience with it, but Ethan had been right when he'd commented that it felt weird to be on the left side when the steering wheel was also on the left side of the car. The space to her right seemed far too big, and she had a little trouble gauging how close she was to the lines on the road.

She was so concentrated on driving that she didn't say a single word the entire drive. It wasn't until they pulled into the parking lot that she even glanced over at Ethan, who was sitting beside her in the front passenger seat. He was staring intently at his phone, typing away with his fingers.

He stayed that way even as the three agents got out of the car and headed into the hotel. By the time they'd made it to the elevator, she couldn't take the curiosity anymore.

"What are you looking at?" she asked him as they made our way up to the floor all three of them were staying on.

"Oh, it's nothing, really," he replied, though the grin on his face indicated otherwise.

His eyes were lit up at whatever he was looking at, and her curiosity only grew stronger as she watched him.

"Alright," Holm sighed as we made it to his door. "Good night, guys. I'll see you tomorrow."

He opened his door wearily, and Olivia waited until it was shut before she turned her attention back to Ethan, secretly glad that Holm's room was the first one they had passed.

"Come on," she pestered him once more. "What's got you in such a good mood all of a sudden? You were acting all worn out back at the station, and now you're all smiles."

"It's just *Dragon's Rogue* stuff," he replied, his smile widening as he showed me his phone. It was opened to a text conversation that he had uploaded several pictures of the anchor to. With all the commotion lately, Olivia had almost forgotten about the big discovery he'd made back in the antique shop.

"Who's Tessa?" Olivia asked as her eyes roved up to the name of the recipient.

"Oh, she's a friend of mine," Ethan replied easily. "She's been helping me with my search for a while now. I always share everything I find with her. She's probably the only person who gets as excited about this stuff as I do."

"*A friend, huh?*" The thought came to Olivia's mind unbidden. She had no reason to believe otherwise, but something about the way Ethan was smiling down at his phone while texting this woman was filling her with an uncomfortable sensation that she absolutely refused to recognize as jealousy.

"Hey, what do you say we have a couple of drinks before we turn in?" she asked him before she could think twice about it. "I know we said we should just go to sleep and get an early start tomorrow, but you seem pretty awake right now."

He blinked at her with a look of mild surprise before smiling at her and slipping his phone back into his pocket.

"Sure," he replied as she changed direction toward her room.

She felt a smug feeling of satisfaction at having pulled his attention away from the phone. She felt a little silly over how jealous she'd gotten over a name in his contact list, but was she really wrong to want his attention to herself tonight? She wasn't an idiot. She was perfectly aware of the way they'd been flirting with each other over the last few days. The anxiety she'd felt tonight as he and Holm had gone off to the bar had only cemented her desire to do something about it all the more quickly.

She quickly unlocked her hotel room door, and the pair stepped inside.

"I wonder if they have anything good in that little mini-fridge," Ethan remarked as he stooped down to peer into the small refrigerator tucked beneath the TV stand.

"Forget that," Olivia scoffed as she walked over to the suitcase at the foot of her bed. "Overpriced beers and tiny bottles of cheap wine? I've got something way better."

She rummaged through her suitcase for a moment before she finally found what she was looking for, a bottle of her favorite whiskey.

"Here it is." She smiled triumphantly as she pulled the bottle from where it was tucked beneath a stack of clothes.

"Wow," Ethan chuckled behind her as he moved to sit on the only chair in the small hotel room. "You came prepared."

"I always make sure I have a bottle of the good stuff when I travel," she replied as she set the bottle on the table before walking over to where the coffee maker was and grabbing two glasses. "Special victims cases can get pretty... taxing. Rape, child abuse, vulnerable people with no one to stick up for them. I try not to rely on it too much, but sometimes, a nice hard drink is exactly what I need after a long day of work."

"Hey, I'm not judging," Ethan replied as he took one of the glasses from her. "Not everyone can do what you do. There's nothing wrong with taking the edge off once in a while."

"Oh, shoot," she huffed after crouching down to get some ice out of the refrigerator. "There's no ice in here."

"I think I saw a sign for an ice machine down at the end of the hall," Ethan replied as he stood up. "I'll go get us some."

Olivia sat down on the edge of the bed and watched as he grabbed another glass off of the stand where the coffee maker was before heading out the door. They hadn't even started drinking yet, and she already felt wired, as though every nerve in her body was on fire. Truthfully, it had been a while since she'd experienced any kind of romantic encounter.

Sure, she went on dates here and there, but most days, it was the last thing on her mind after spending all day dealing with distraught victims.

It was different with Ethan, though. Even though they were in the middle of an intense case, she still couldn't keep her mind from wandering back to thoughts of him. Hell, maybe the intensity of the case was actually exacerbating it. She honestly wasn't used to being caught in the middle of so many exhilarating, life-or-death situations, and there was something kind of exciting about it, especially when there was an extremely attractive man by her side the entire time.

"Sorry that took so long." Ethan apologized once he returned a few minutes later. "I could have sworn I saw something that looked like an ice machine at the end of the hall, but there was nothing there when I checked. Anyway, I did find some on the next floor down."

"No problem." Olivia smiled as she took the ice from him to prepare their drinks. "Now, tell me more about that anchor we found. You seemed really excited about it when you were texting your friend. What's so special about it?"

Ethan launched into an explanation about why he suspected that the anchor once belonged to the ship he was so determined to find. Olivia couldn't hold back a smile as she watched how animated he became when he talked about the pirate ship, and she spent the next half hour listening intently as he gave her a full rundown of the ship's history.

"So, this Grendel guy was bad because he stole the ship?" she asked as she lifted the bottle to pour herself another glass. "But he was also kind of a good guy because he shared his riches with the poor?"

"Something like that," Ethan replied with a small nod. "Though 'good' is kind of a relative term."

"Well, people aren't black and white." Olivia shrugged as she leaned forward to pour Ethan another glass as well. The heavy bottle wobbled in her hand as she poured, and she inadvertently spilled some over the table and onto Ethan as well.

"Damn, sorry," she hissed as she placed the bottle back onto the table.

"It's fine," Ethan assured her as he quickly stood up. As he did, his face came within inches of Olivia's, who was still leaning toward him.

For a moment, they just looked at each other. Olivia couldn't tell who moved first, but an instant later, their lips were pressed together, and she was winding her arms around his neck. She stumbled slightly as he gently pushed her backward toward the bed.

They were supposed to be waking up early tomorrow. She knew that, but at that moment, she really didn't care.

25

ETHAN

I DRAINED the last of my coffee and did one final check to make sure I had everything I would need before heading out. Olivia and I had spent the previous evening awake well into the night, so when my alarm had gone off at seven the following day, I'd needed to force myself out of bed and back into my own room to get changed and ready. I'd enjoyed one cup of coffee in Olivia's room with her and then another in my own room after taking a shower. I was finally starting to feel a little less groggy, which was good because we still needed to figure out exactly what our plan for the day was.

I made my way down to the lobby to wait for Holm and Olivia, but to my surprise, they were both already down there.

"Nice of you to join us," Holm teased as I walked over to where they were both sitting on one of the couches. "I just got a call from Morris."

"Did he sound angry?" I asked, recalling how annoyed he'd been the previous day that we'd returned from the bar without arresting anyone.

"Nah." Holm shook his head. "He sounded as chill as he did before, so I think he's cooled off. Anyway, he called to tell us that the guy we arrested in Kew yesterday is ready for us to interrogate."

"Really?" I asked. "The hospital cleared him?"

"I guess so." Holm shrugged. "Morris said that he was there at the station and that we could stop by as soon as we were ready."

"That's perfect," I replied enthusiastically. "We still have four hours until noon. We can go speak to him and see if we can pull any information from him that might help us today during the raid."

"That's exactly what I was thinking." Olivia smiled at me.

I smiled back at her before turning back to Holm.

"Well, what are we waiting for then?" I asked.

The three of us made our way out of the hotel and into the car. As I drove down to the Grace Bay station, I couldn't help but glance over at Olivia sitting in the passenger seat next to me. We hadn't had a lot of time to talk that morning since I'd needed to rush off after that first cup of coffee to shower and get dressed. I'd been a little surprised by her sudden offer of drinks the previous night, though pleasantly so. After she'd suggested we head to bed early, I hadn't expected us to end up spending the night together. Not that I was complaining, of course.

"How do you think we should approach the interrogation?" Holm asked as I parked the car outside of the station. "You have a plan in mind?"

"Well, we should focus on seeing what he knows about the Oasis," I replied as I turned off the ignition and got out. "Daniela said that there would only be one guard awake on duty, but we should make sure that's accurate. Regardless of her status, she's still one of the victims. There may be things she's kept in the dark about."

The three of us headed into the station. The officer sitting behind the desk greeted us as soon as we entered.

"Good morning," he announced. "Are you the federal agents?"

"That's us," I confirmed as I pulled my badge out of my pocket out of habit.

"The captain is expecting you," he replied after taking a close look at my badge. He pointed down the hallway with his pen. "Do you know the way to his office?"

"We do," Olivia replied with a smile. "Thank you."

We headed back off through the familiar bullpen and short corridor that we'd walked through so many times over the past few days. We had made it about halfway to Morris's office when we were intercepted by Crowley. He stepped out of a room just as we were passing by, and he jumped in surprise when he looked up and found us standing in front of him.

"Oh, you scared me," he breathed as his shoulders relaxed. "I was just getting the information off the suspect's fingerprints." He held up the bundle of papers he was holding for emphasis. "You came at the perfect time. Come on, the suspect is down this way."

We followed him down another corridor and into a short hallway lined with holding cells. I recognized it from the previous night when we'd walked through there on our way to speak with Jenny. The cells had all been empty then, but today one of them had clearly been occupied recently. The door was open, and the sheets on the bed were rumpled.

We walked past the cell and toward a room just a few feet away. There was no two-way mirror like I was used to, but I could see the man from the night before through the small, rectangular window set into the door. His face was twisted into a scowl, and even from here, I could see how furious he was.

"His name is Antonio Roberts," Crowley informed us as he glanced down at a tablet he was holding in his arms. "He has a few prior arrests on his record for public drunkenness, as well as one for domestic violence against an ex-girlfriend."

"Sounds like a great guy," Olivia muttered darkly.

"Oh, there's more," Crowley scoffed. "We looked into his employment history, assuming that he must work at the bar where he was arrested. Curiously, though, we were unable to obtain employment records for the last four months."

"What do you mean?" I turned to look at him.

"Well, he *was* employed there," Crowley explained. "He was a manager there for about a year. However, when we went to the bar, we could not find any official records for him beginning four months ago. No pay stubs, no tax paperwork. We also learned from a different employee that the owner of the bar suddenly stopped making his weekly visits approximately four months ago."

"What?" Olivia gasped. "That's a hell of a coincidence."

"Indeed." Crowley nodded gravely. "Apparently, Roberts told the other employees, most of whom are part-timers, that the owner had gone on vacation. None of them thought to question it until what happened last night."

"Murder's a pretty big step up from the petty crimes he's been arrested for before," I muttered as I turned to peer at him through the window. "Though I guess I shouldn't be surprised, considering he did shoot at *us* and in a bar full of people no less."

"Maybe the owner found out what he was up to," Holm suggested. "If he wasn't in on it himself, Roberts would have to shut him up before he went to the police."

"Let's find out," I replied as I pushed the door open.

Roberts looked up at us as we entered, the scowl on his face growing even more menacing as he recognized us.

"I'll kill you," he snarled, his teeth bared like a rabid dog.

"I'm sure you will," I replied sarcastically as I sat down in front of him. His face turned a shade redder at the casual way in which I'd dismissed him. That was good. The more I poked his buttons, the easier it would be to get him to talk.

"You have quite the little operation going on down at that bar in Kew Town, huh?"

He snorted at me derisively before looking away, clearly intending not to talk. Why did they always have to do this the hard way?

"Tell me, just how long have you been doing this?" I asked, unable to keep the disgust I felt out of my voice. "It must be quite a while now, considering one of your victims was kidnapped nearly twenty years ago. You know who I'm talking about, don't you?"

His gaze slid over to meet mine. He had an unreadable expression on his face. I couldn't tell what he was thinking, but I did know that my words had at least caught his attention.

"Allison Newark," Olivia suddenly chimed in. "I believe you knew her as Cat. Does that ring any bells?"

That definitely stirred a reaction. Roberts leaned across the table to sneer at her.

"What the hell is it to you?" he snapped at her.

"So you do know her," I surmised. "Then you must have been there the day she escaped, too. Were you the one who shot at her?"

"Of course I did!" he roared, catching me by surprise. There was so much fury in his voice, more than seemed normal even for a piece of criminal scum like him. "She thought she could just leave! Run off and take the kid with her! Who the hell did she think she was?"

"Why wouldn't she take her child with her?" Olivia asked, obviously confused by the man's phrasing.

"Because she belongs to me!" he hissed back. "All of those girls do! She had no right doing *anything* without my permission!"

"Yeah, I don't think so," I replied. Olivia's eyes were burning with untempered hatred, and as repulsed as the guy made me as well, I needed to keep this interrogation on track. "Unfortunately for you, she managed to make it all the way to Miami. That's why we're here, and that's how we know about everything you and your little group have been up to."

I deliberately decided to leave out the fact that she had ultimately died. There was no reason to give this jerk the satisfaction.

"She made it?" he gaped at me, his face draining of color. "She actually survived?"

"Eddy's been reunited with his grandmother." I

dodged his last question. "He's safe and sound, far away from your reach. So why don't you start telling us what we want to know?"

"Why should I?" he scoffed in a show of indifference. I could hear the tremor in his voice, though, and I knew that his nerves were starting to wear thin.

"Maybe because we know what you did to the owner of the bar," Olivia bluffed.

Robert's eyes went wide at her words, and his mouth clamped shut with an audible click.

"A murder charge on top of everything we already have on you?" she continued. "That's a pretty rough situation to be in. Of course, the FBI has pull all over the world. Maybe, if you cooperate with us, I can see about putting in a good word for you."

He narrowed his eyes at her as though he was trying to gauge just from her face whether she was lying, which I was almost certain she was. While it was true that the FBI had the power to cut deals, I seriously doubted that Olivia would extend such an offer to a man as despicable as him. There was no reason for him to know that, though.

"Fine," he finally spat after a moment of consideration. "What do you want to know?"

"First off," I started, "what do you know about your boss, Samuel?"

"What do you mean, 'what do I know?'" He scowled at me. "I know he runs things. I know that I do what he says, and I get paid to do it."

"Do you know the address of the house he lives in?" I asked.

"The one in Cockburn?" he asked. "Yeah, I know it."

"Good," I replied as I pulled my phone out of my pocket. "What about the house that all the women are kept in? Do you know where that is?"

"Yeah, I do," he grumbled.

"Great," I replied as calmly as I could, though inside, I was thrilled. "We're going to need both of those."

I listened as he rattled off the addresses, recording them in my own phone as he did.

"I'll let the captain know as soon as we're done," Crowley said to me. "We can run a search and make sure he isn't lying to us."

"Why would I lie?" he scoffed, sounding almost indignant at the accusation.

"Why would a human trafficker who isn't afraid to shoot at a federal agent lie?" Olivia deadpanned mockingly. "Gee, I can't imagine why."

He bared his teeth at her in a snarl. A vein throbbed in his neck, and I could tell that he was itching to snap at her. It was probably driving him insane to be spoken to like that by a woman.

"One last thing," I said as I slipped my phone back into my pocket. "I'm going to need you to tell me everything you know about the Oasis Lounge. How many men are there currently, how many women, and what is the security like?"

"And don't get any funny ideas about pulling anything," Crowley threatened. "Give us false information, and I'll personally make sure you regret it. I don't care what kind of deal the FBI wants to give you."

He was absolutely seething, and for a moment, Roberts seemed to shrink away from Crowley's tall, hulking form.

"Okay," he grumbled. "I'll tell you everything."

I listened intently as he gave me all the information I wanted to know. As he did, I began to formulate a plan in my head. It would still be risky attempting to free all those women, but at least now we knew what we would be up against. I was going to make sure we succeeded and rescued all the victims trapped inside of that bar.

26

ETHAN

WE SPRANG into action as soon as the interrogation was finished. The first thing we needed to do was to build a team big enough to handle such a big rescue mission.

"Agents," Captain Morris had said once we were all back in his office, "this is Officer Emerson Davis, Officer Gloria Thompson, Officer Mike Grayson, and Officer William Hanks. They'll be accompanying you on your mission today."

"Good to meet you," I replied as I reached forward to shake each of their hands. Since the mission involved several victims, we needed to ensure we had enough manpower to get them all out safely.

"We're happy to help," Officer Grayson replied.

"It's hard to believe something like this is even happening. These kinds of things just don't happen here, you know?"

No one ever thought that awful things could happen in their calm, peaceful town until they did. Nevertheless, it was comforting to know how determined these officers were to help us put a stop to this.

We spent the next hour or so going over the details of what we'd learned from the interview. Then, all we could do was wait until the appointed time.

It was now only ten minutes until noon, and we were about to put our plan into action. Antonio had confirmed what Daniela had told us about the traffickers still being asleep at this hour. According to him, the bar stayed open until about five in the morning, and there were rooms on the second floor of the Oasis Lounge, just like in the other bar in Kew Town. Aside from one or two men to keep watch, everyone would still be asleep for another few hours.

We were being accompanied by two other pairs of officers, aside from Crowley, to make sure we had plenty of backup. Assuming Daniela had done her part to make sure the women were ready to move ASAP, our current plan was to storm straight in and catch them unawares. Since we needed to make sure we had the element of surprise on our side, we had waited until just before twelve to arrive, just in case we happened to get spotted.

As we pulled into the parking lot, I was immediately alarmed to find someone standing outside the building, just beside the door. My anxiety eased somewhat as we got closer and I realized it was only Daniela.

As I got out of the car, I noticed that her posture was rigid. She looked tense as she surveyed everyone as they all got out of their vehicles, distrust bright and clear in her stern expression.

"Part of me didn't believe you'd actually come," she muttered as I approached her. "I'm so used to disappointment. I don't believe a thing until I see it with my own eyes."

"Well, we're here now," I replied. "And we're ready to move. How many men are inside right now?"

"Six in total," she replied quietly as everyone gathered around to listen. "Two of them are awake. They're supposed to be keeping watch, but I managed to distract them. They're both sitting at the bar right now."

"Good." I nodded. "And the women?"

"Upstairs," she replied. "I've gathered them all into one room, the one immediately to the right as soon as you get upstairs. They're ready to go as soon as we get your signal."

"What about the rest of the men?" I asked urgently, nervous about wasting time out here.

"They're upstairs as well." She frowned. "Though I'm not exactly sure which rooms they're in."

"Okay," I replied as I turned to address the group. "Once we're inside, Holm, Crowley, and I will deal with the two men at the bar. Officers Davis, Thompson, Grayson, and Hanks, you head upstairs and secure the remaining men. In the meantime, Agent Hastings and Daniela can get to the girls and get them out of the bar as quickly as possible."

The officers who had been sent to work with us all nodded in agreement.

"Okay," Holm replied. "Let's go."

Daniela opened the door quietly. I drew my gun from my holster, and all around me, everyone else did the same. As soon as it was open wide enough for us to step through, we all rushed forward.

"Federal Agents!" I yelled as Holm, Crowley, and I moved quickly forward, straight toward the bar at the center of the floor. Two men were sitting there, just as Daniela had said, tall pints of beer clutched in their hands.

"What the hell is this?!" one of the men roared as he jumped to his feet.

"Don't move another inch!" Crowley yelled as he stepped forward, his gun pointed straight at the men.

The man halted in his motions, his hand frozen halfway toward his back.

Out of the corner of my eyes, I spotted the rest of our group running toward the back of the bar to make their way upstairs.

One of the men must have noticed them, too, because an instant later, he disregarded Crowley's order and pulled something from behind his back.

"Stop!" Crowley yelled just as I pointed my gun at the man and pulled the trigger.

I was just a fraction of a second too late, though. The man had already managed to shoot. Luckily, the bullet didn't hit any of our comrades, instead striking a table by the window.

The man fell with a groan as my own bullet hit him. His buddy yelled with fury and reached behind his back.

"Don't even think about it!" I yelled as I pointed

my gun at him. "Unless you want to end up like your friend there."

The man gritted his teeth and glared at me but didn't otherwise move.

"Put your hands up," Crowley commanded. "And step away from him, slowly."

The man did as he was told and continued to follow Crowley's instructions. I waited until he had the man on the ground before moving forward to check on the one I had shot.

The first thing I did was retrieve the gun he'd dropped when I'd shot him. The second was to check his pulse. It was extremely faint, and he wasn't at all responsive.

"I'll call an ambulance," I muttered as I looked over to Crowley and Holm, who were getting the other suspect into a set of handcuffs. Honestly, it probably wouldn't do much good. I'd shot the guy square in the chest at pretty close range. It would be a miracle if he survived, not that I would be all that broken up about it.

Before I could call, an ear-splitting bang rang out from the second floor.

"Dammit," I hissed as I shoved my phone back into my pocket and took off. Something must have gone wrong. Holm was beside me in an instant, though I didn't see Crowley. He must have stayed behind to watch the suspect.

We ran toward the back of the bar where I'd seen the rest of our group headed. There was a wide door tucked into the back corner of the bar marked "stairs." I pushed the door open just as another round of gunshots went off.

My heart was pounding almost painfully as we raced up the stairs. I had no idea what was waiting for us at the top. I didn't even know who it was that was shooting.

I got my answer as we made it to the top of the stairs and burst through the door that led to the second floor. The door opened into the end of a long hall lined with doors on either side. Just a few feet away, two of the officers that had accompanied us, Davis and Thompson, were down on the ground. I couldn't see any blood, likely due to their bullet-proof vests, but it looked like they were out cold. One other man I didn't recognize was down as well. He must have been one of the other traffickers.

Standing further down the hallway, a few feet away from the strewn bodies and in front of an open doorway, were Olivia and Daniela. Behind them, several women were cowering in fear, and in front of them were two other men, their guns drawn and pointed directly at them. The other two officers were further down at the far end of the hall, their weapons pointed at the two suspects. They were all locked in a tense standoff.

One of the suspects turned at the sound of the door being opened as Holm and I burst in. The moment he did, one of the other officers, Grayson, took advantage of the distraction and fired his gun at him.

Unfortunately, it missed the man and struck the wall just behind him. He roared with anger and spun on the man as he fired his own weapon. His aim was more accurate, and Grayson was knocked backward as the bullet hit him.

I lifted my own gun and rushed forward, but just as I did, Daniela began to usher the women toward the stairs. In their panic, some of them ran directly into my path, inadvertently blocking my shot.

The other suspect realized what was going on and quickly lifted his gun toward the fleeing women.

"No!" Olivia screamed. She ran forward just as the man pulled the trigger, only barely managing to push Daniela out of the way. Unfortunately, in doing so, she put herself directly in the bullet's path instead.

She let out a short, strangled cry of pain as the

bullet tore through her arm. I saw red as I watched her fall to the ground and lifted my gun again, firing it three times directly at the man who had just shot her.

He groaned with pain as he fell back against the wall behind him. He struck the back of his head before crumpling to the ground. The other suspect turned around at the sound of his friend's yell. He tried to lift his gun again, but before he could, he was tackled to the ground by Hanks, the only other officer still left standing.

Daniela had turned around in horror when Olivia had pushed her out of harm's way, but as soon as the suspect was down, she'd focused her attention on getting the girls down the stairs and to safety.

I rushed to check on Olivia. As I ran to her, I kept telling myself that the bullet had only hit her arm, that she'd be okay. I pointedly ignored the nagging voice in the back of my head that reminded me that even a bullet to the arm could be fatal if she was unlucky enough to have been hit in an artery.

To my relief, she was completely conscious when I reached her.

"Are you okay?" I asked as I gently helped her sit up.

"That stupid little—" she hissed as she pressed

her hand to her injured arm. It came away slick and red with blood. "Ugh. He got me good. So much for not straining my arm."

I realized only then that he'd managed to shoot her almost in the exact same spot that the antique shop owner had a few days earlier. Seeing the injury made my blood boil all over again, and if the guy wasn't already bleeding out on the ground, I might have been tempted to shoot him again.

"How are Daniela and the rest of the girls?" she asked me through gritted teeth. Of course, even with a bullet in her arm, they would be her priority.

"I'll go check on them now," I replied as I got back to my feet. I was reluctant to leave her, but getting the victims to safety was most important right now.

As soon as I stood up, I heard Hanks shout behind me. I turned around and found him on the ground, out cold. The suspect that he had tackled had somehow managed to get the upper hand and was now standing over the officer, his gun drawn and ready to fire.

"No!" I yelled to distract the man as I pulled my own gun.

Just as I'd hoped, the suspect turned his attention from Hanks and onto me. I fired my gun, but the man dodged, and my shot missed. He lifted his own gun and pulled the trigger, but the gun just clicked uselessly. The man stared down at the weapon in disbelief, pulling the trigger again and again to no avail.

I saw my chance and rushed forward. He was so distracted by his gun that he didn't see me coming until I was already upon him.

I punched him hard across the face. Usually, a blow like that to the head would have been enough to render most men unconscious. The suspect, however, bounced back surprisingly quickly and answered my punch with one of his own.

I lifted my arms just in time to block his strike. The man was tougher than he looked, and faster.

He tried to punch me again, but I sidestepped the blow, causing him to lose his balance as he thrust forward. I took advantage of this to kick him hard in the stomach, his own forward momentum working against him.

He wheezed as the kick knocked the wind out of him, and, not wanting to give him the chance to recover, I reeled back to punch him in the face again. I felt a satisfying crunch as my fist collided with his nose.

However, I was shocked when the man regained

his footing and let out a guttural roar at me, despite the blood now gushing from his nose. He lunged toward me, but it was clear by the way he stumbled that his injuries were starting to affect his performance.

He grabbed my arm, but I shook him off and delivered another punch to his face, this time hitting him directly in the eye.

Finally, he let out a short, pained grunt before falling to the ground in a daze.

I fell to a crouch and pulled his wrists together to get them cuffed. By now, I was huffing for breath. The fight had been tougher than I'd expected from some goon like him.

"You okay?" Holm asked as he knelt down beside me to assist. "It looked like things were handled up here, so I went down to help Daniela and the girls. What happened?"

"He overpowered Hanks," I replied as I looked back at the officer. He was just starting to sit up now, clearly dazed but otherwise alright. "At least we got them all, though."

"Wait!" Holm suddenly exclaimed as he got to his feet and looked around frantically. "I count five suspects, including the two downstairs. Daniela said there were six men in total. Where's the other one?"

Horror dawned on me as I realized that he was right. We were missing a suspect.

"Right here," an unfamiliar voice rasped as a man suddenly stepped out of one of the rooms between us and the stairwell. He had scraggly dark hair, and a scar shaped like an X over one of his cheeks. Standing just in front of him was a young woman wearing a tank top and a pair of loose shorts. He had her in a chokehold and was pressing a gun to her head.

"Stop!" Olivia croaked as she attempted to get to her feet.

"Don't move!" the man snarled as he pressed the barrel of the gun harder into the girl's temple. She started crying as he did so. "None of you move, or I'll blow her brains out!"

"Just take it easy," I replied calmly. This wasn't good. Most of our officers were down. Olivia was injured and clearly unsteady on her feet right now. It was possible that Grayson, Holm, and I might have been able to take him on, but doing anything right now might cause him to pull the trigger. We just couldn't risk the hostage's life like that.

"Don't move," the man growled again as he began to move back toward the stairs. I watched helplessly as he disappeared through the door. It had all happened too fast for me to think of any other solution than to just let him leave. Still, I couldn't just do nothing.

"Call for an ambulance!" I yelled to Grayson before taking off after the man. Holm followed right behind me.

I could hear screaming as we moved into the stairwell. A few steps down, the girl was struggling to break out of the man's hold. He was still clutching the gun, but it wasn't pointed at her anymore.

"Let her go!" I yelled as I pointed my gun at him. I wanted to shoot, but the girl was still standing too close to him. The stairs also created an awkward angle, so it was too risky for me to fire just yet.

He glared up at me before shoving the girl away from him forcefully. She screamed as she fell backward, hitting her head on the concrete steps as she fell. Once the shot was clear, I fired, but the bullet missed and embedded itself into the wall behind him.

He continued his way down the steps, and Holm and I rushed to the girl's side. She was unconscious, and there was a spot of blood beneath her head.

"Go!" Holm yelled as he crouched over her. "I've got her. You get him!"

I nodded and rushed after the man. Neither of us

was a doctor, so there wasn't much point in both of us staying here with her. I could hear screaming as I made it to the base of the stairs. I shoved the door leading to the main floor open just in time to see the man disappear through the front door of the bar. Some of the girls were still screaming, cowering at one corner of the main floor. They'd probably panicked when the suspect had come rushing through.

I cursed as I raced after him, through the bar, and out the door into the bright Caribbean sun. I looked around frantically as soon as I was outside, but I couldn't find any sign of him. Tourists and locals alike were milling around, going about their day, but there weren't nearly enough of them that he could have disappeared into the crowd.

Suddenly, I heard the sound of tires screeching, and a second later, a black car came tearing around the side of the building, directly toward me. I managed to leap out of the way just as it sped over the spot where I'd just been standing. I watched from the ground as it jumped the sidewalk and almost took out a pair of women wearing wide-brimmed hats before speeding off down the road.

One of the women screamed and stumbled back-ward onto the ground as the car narrowly avoided hitting her. She scrambled back to her feet before dragging her friend away from the scene. A few people on the other side of the road were staring wide-eyed at me as well.

"Damn," I grunted as I got back onto my feet, bits of dust and gravel stuck to my clothes where I'd hit the ground. My heart was racing, and I could feel adrenaline still coursing through my body as I yanked my phone from my pocket to call Captain Morris.

"Hello?" he answered right away. "Is everything okay?"

"No," I replied hastily. "One of the suspects got away. He's fleeing in a black car, some kind of two-door sedan, I think. I didn't get a great look. I was too busy trying not to get hit."

"I'm on it," Morris replied. "Which way did it go?"

"Left?" I muttered as I tried to find a road sign in this unfamiliar area. "I think that would be south, then. On Bonaventure Crescent."

"I'll send a car out," Morris replied. "Do you need anything else?"

"Yeah, a few ambulances," I answered. "It's a mess here."

"Okay," Morris grumbled, his voice laced with concern. "I'll dispatch them right away."

"Thanks." I sighed. "I'm going to go see how everyone's doing. Bye."

I ended the call and walked back into the bar. The women were all huddled at one end of the main floor. Crowley and Daniela were standing over them as though guarding them. I was just about to go back into the stairwell when the door leading to it suddenly popped open, and Olivia stepped through. Just behind her was the girl that had hit her head on the edge of the stairs, being supported by Holm.

"I tried to tell her not to move," he explained. "She insisted. Said she wanted to see Daniela."

"Danny!" the girl yelled as soon as she spotted the woman.

Daniela turned at her nickname and stretched her arms out to the girl. The girl's eyes welled up with fresh tears as she pulled away from Holm and went running to her.

As I watched them embrace, some of the earlier fury I'd felt after watching the suspect get away ebbed. Things hadn't gone exactly as planned, and we'd incurred a lot of injuries in the process, but the women were safe now. Ultimately, that was what mattered.

27

ETHAN

A FEW HOURS had passed since the mission to rescue the women from the Oasis Lounge. Holm, Olivia, and I were in the hospital, getting ready to head back to the Grace Bay Police Station to speak with the victims.

We hadn't had a chance to speak with any of the girls up until now because we'd been too busy dealing with the aftermath of the fight. Three of the officers who had been assigned to assist us had been hurt. Luckily, they'd all been wearing standard bulletproof vests, so although they'd sustained injuries, none of them were life-threatening. On top of that, three of the suspects had died during the battle, and one had managed to escape. Even though

Morris had sent officers out to look for the car, by the time they'd arrived, he was already long gone.

However, my main concern had been Olivia, who'd been shot in the arm in nearly the same place that the antique shop owner had shot her a few days prior. As a result, the stitches on her old wound had opened up. This time, the doctor had told her that it was imperative that she not use her arm to give herself a chance to recover fully and had even recommended that she stay in the hospital for a few days. Olivia wouldn't hear a word of it.

"Are you sure you don't want to stay?" I asked her once again. I was genuinely worried about her. She'd taken two bullets to the arm in less than a week, and this injury had been significantly worse than the last one, enough so that she was now confined to a sling.

"It's not that I don't *want* to," she sighed as she looked down at the bandages on her arm. "It's that I can't. Look, it's not that I don't trust you and Robbie to be able to handle this, but the fact is that things will probably be a lot smoother if I'm there. These women have spent years being victimized by men, possibly for their whole lives if any of them have been here for as long as Allison was. I know that you and Robbie are good, decent people, but they don't. All they'll see is that they're suddenly in a police station, surrounded by more men that they don't know. On top of that, I've already built a rapport with Jenny. That'll really help when it comes to connecting with the other victims."

I knew she was right. After all, she was the expert in this field, but I still wasn't all that happy about it. I could tell from the way her lip would suddenly twitch and her voice would catch as she spoke that she was in pain. She should be taking it easy for the moment, but she was too focused on the victims to think of herself.

"Yeah, you're right," I muttered as the three of us made our way out of the hospital and into the parking lot. "Just, don't do anything too crazy, alright?"

"Aww, are you worried about me, Ethan?" She smirked as she bumped her uninjured shoulder against mine.

"Of course I am," I retorted. "Seems like you can't go a day without getting shot."

"Funny," she chuckled. "I was just thinking the same thing about you yesterday."

"Oh, were you worried about me, then?" I grinned at her.

"Eh, maybe," she mumbled with a slight shrug, her cheeks reddening as she spoke.

"Guys, I am *right here,*" Holm groaned good-naturedly. "Not that this whole exchange wasn't adorable, but could you maybe not make eyes at each other when I'm standing two feet away?"

Olivia cleared her throat with embarrassment as I reached over to swat at Holm, who ducked out of the way of my attack smoothly. Now that we'd accomplished our mission and gotten the victimized women to safety, we felt a little more at ease, enough to joke around like this at least.

We couldn't get too complacent, though. We still needed to find the leader of the group, Samuel, and though we'd rescued several women, Jenny had told us about a house in Cockburn Town where they stayed while they weren't out working. We still didn't know how many other victims there were out there, still waiting for our help.

That was what weighed on my mind as we made the drive back to the Grace Bay Police Station.

"Remember," Olivia cautioned us as we parked and made our way inside. "These women have been through a lot. They might react with fear or hostility, just like Jenny did. If that happens, just back off. We won't get anywhere by pressuring them."

This actually wasn't the first time we'd dealt with something of this nature. I could distinctly recall a similar case we'd handled involving a group of trafficked women who'd hijacked the boat they were being transported on. Several of them had reacted to the presence of law enforcement with aggression as well. Fight or flight was a natural survival response, after all. Some people chose to fight.

"I wish I'd been able to stay here with them," Olivia muttered anxiously. "Stupid gunshot wound. I hope none of the cops did anything to upset them."

I was surprised to find two officers stationed outside the main entrance door as we pulled into the parking lot.

"Tight security," I noted as the three of us got out of the car. It made sense, considering one of the suspects had managed to escape. He would most likely report back to his superiors, so we couldn't be too careful about the women's safety.

One of the officers blocked our path as we approached.

"Can I help you?" he asked sternly. He was a very tall man, a few inches taller than I was, and broad-shouldered. With his imposing stature and unwavering gaze, he made for a good guard.

Before I could reply, the door opened, and Officer Crowley stepped outside.

"Agents, you're here," he greeted us before

turning to the two men on guard. "It's okay. We're expecting them."

The officer who had blocked my path nodded and stepped aside to let us through. As we walked inside, I noticed that there was an unusually tense atmosphere.

"Everyone's on high alert," Crowley informed me, as though reading my thoughts. "I know it sounds cliche, but none of us ever thought anything like this could happen in our town. It's the kind of thing that only happens in movies. Most days, the most exciting thing I do is collect the drunks and bring them in to sober up. But this? And right under our noses... Everyone's in a bad mood right now."

That much I could tell as we made our way down the hall. All the officers we passed had grim, almost pained expressions on their faces. It must have come as quite a shock to them to discover that their peaceful slice of Caribbean paradise was hiding such a dark secret.

"We gave the women the main conference room," he explained as we came to a stop outside a closed door, also guarded by an officer. "It's the largest room we have in the station. We offered to call a doctor, but none wanted anything aside from some food and water. I think they were waiting for you, actually."

"Me?" Olivia asked as he nodded at her.

"That girl from earlier," he replied. "Jenny. We brought her here a little while ago. When she heard that the other women were here, she asked to come. We thought it would be safer to have them all together, anyway. I'm not sure what all they talked about, but I think she spoke well of you."

"Well, I'm glad to hear that." Olivia smiled at him. "We'll go in now if that's okay?"

"Of course." Crowley nodded as he took a seat in a chair just outside the door. "I'll be out here if you need me. I've noticed that they tend to get nervous when the other officers or I linger around too much. We've been trying to give them space."

So Olivia's assumption had been correct. They had developed such a negative association with men that even the police officers were causing them to be wary.

I could hear the faint sounds of chatter from beyond the door, but it died down as soon as Olivia cracked it open.

Several pairs of eyes turned to look at us as we stepped inside. I could count about a dozen women at first glance. Most of them had pulled the chairs away from the large conference table and sat together at one end of the room. I spotted Daniela almost immediately, standing just behind the group, as though watching over them.

"Olivia!" one of the women exclaimed. It took me a moment to realize that it was Jenny. The first time I'd seen her, her skin had been a sallow gray color, and she'd barely been able to lift her head. She looked much healthier just a day and a half later, her cheeks rosy and her sleek brown hair pulled into a loose ponytail.

"Hi, Jenny," Olivia smiled at her as Jenny came to greet her. "I'm so happy to see you again. How are you feeling?"

"Good." She nodded enthusiastically before turning back to look at the other women. "Much better now that I know everyone else is okay."

"I'm glad," Olivia replied before turning to look at the other women as well. They were watching the interaction with curious, albeit wary, eyes. "I was hoping we might be able to talk a bit. We think maybe some of you might know information that could help us catch the rest of the men responsible for this."

"We already know that," Daniela replied curtly. "We've talked it over. We agree that it's fair after what you did to help us. On one condition, though."

"And what is that?" Olivia asked cautiously.

"We stay together," she replied with finality. "None of us are going anywhere with anyone alone. We stay together."

Behind her, the women muttered amongst themselves, some of them nodding along in agreement. It was clear that Daniela was acting as the spokesperson for the group.

"We can work with that." Olivia nodded slowly as she stepped toward the group. Holm and I followed behind her. Olivia and Holm pulled the remaining chairs to sit in, while I opted to just sit on the table itself.

"So, what do you want to know?" Daniela asked as she crossed her arms over her chest.

"First," Olivia started, "I'd like to know what you all knew about Cat. Did any of you see her the day she fled?"

"Cat?" one of the women immediately piped up. She looked young and had dark skin and thick black hair. "Why? Do you guys know what happened to her? Is she okay?"

I watched as Daniela's lips set into a hard line. She'd learned the truth of Allison's demise yesterday, but obviously, she hadn't gotten around to sharing the information with the rest of the women.

"No, I'm afraid she's not okay," Olivia replied gently after a moment of hesitation. "She didn't survive the trip to the United States. Only Eddy did."

"No," the girl gasped as she pressed her hands to her mouth, her eyes immediately welling up with tears. "Don't say that. Don't tell me that."

"I'm sorry," Olivia replied as the girl started to cry. "Were you and her close?"

"Yeah," the girl sniffled. "She was really nice. I used to watch Eddy for her sometimes when she was gone with Antonio. You said he's okay, right?"

"Yes, he's fine," Olivia replied hastily. "You just mentioned Antonio. Where would Cat go with him?"

"Oh, I... you don't know?" The girl looked at her in confusion. "Antonio is Eddy's dad."

I felt like a lead weight had fallen into my gut at that bit of information. That piece of remorseless trash was the kid's father?

"You're certain about that?" Olivia asked.

"Well, yeah," the girl scoffed through angry tears. "Why do you think Eddy was allowed to stay around? Cat wasn't the first to get pregnant, you know. Just usually, we ain't allowed to keep them. Pregnant girls and babies ain't good for business."

It occurred to me suddenly that Antonio's earlier outburst about her running off with Eddy made more sense now. He wasn't just angry because she was escaping. He was angry because she was taking off with *his kid*.

"Ever since Cat got pregnant, she didn't take no Johns anymore," the girl continued, her mouth twisted into a disgusted scowl. "Antonio didn't like sharing. Mostly she just stuck around the house with Eddy until Antonio called for her. Then we'd take turns watching him. We all loved that little boy."

Several of the other women nodded at her statement. I noticed that a few of them had started crying at some point as well.

"His full name is Edward Jefferson, you know." She smiled tearfully. "Cat said she wanted him to have a powerful name, the kind of name that important people have. She said 'Edward' was the fanciest name for a boy she'd ever heard, and since she didn't know what her last name was, she chose 'Jefferson' for him. Like Thomas Jefferson. She always said that she wanted him to grow up to be somebody. The day she ran off... I knew it was for him. I knew she was just trying to do right by little Eddy."

"Did you see her the day that she fled?" Olivia asked as the girl started to cry in earnest again.

"Yeah." The girl nodded as she wiped her eyes dry with the back of her hand. "She almost never left the main house, but Antonio was on guard duty that day, and he wanted her to come, so she came. I didn't even notice when she left, though. All of a sudden, I just heard Antonio yelling. He was stomping around the bar, screaming her name. Then he ran out the door. We were all so shocked."

"And that was the last you saw of her?" Olivia asked.

The girl nodded sadly without saying anything.

"Okay," Olivia replied softly. "We actually spoke with Antonio just yesterday. We have him in custody right now."

"Jenny told us," the girl replied. "Thank you for that."

"It's my pleasure, believe me," Olivia scoffed as she slipped her phone out of her pocket. "But I bring it up because he gave us a couple of addresses. I just wanted to confirm with you that he wasn't lying before we head there. Jenny told us that she wasn't sure because the men would blindfold you any time you moved, but maybe one of you knows something."

The girl took the phone from her and stared down at it.

"I'm sorry." She shook her head slowly. "I'm not sure."

"Let me see," Daniela said as she took the phone from the girl. She examined the addresses for just a moment before handing the phone back to Olivia. "They're correct. At least the one for the house I'm almost certain is right. I know that it's pretty far toward the southern tip, just off of Lighthouse Road. I've been here long enough to know that much. The other address, I'm not sure, though it wouldn't surprise me. I've heard that old bastard Samuel lives in a big, expensive house. The Bajari Beach Club is an expensive tourist area. It would make sense for his house to be there."

"Thank you," Olivia replied as she tucked her phone back into her pocket. "One last thing. We'll likely be executing another mission like the one today. We need to know how many more women are still in the main house, as well as how many men."

"There are five other girls," Daniela answered. "They stay behind when they're on their cycle. They'll be on the second floor of the house. As for how many men, I'm not sure how many might be there when you arrive."

"That's fine," Olivia replied. "That information is good enough. You've all been a huge help, so thank you, everyone. In just a moment, I'm going to make a call to my director and make arrangements so that you all get to wherever you want to be from here. For now, we'll work something out with the police to get you set up in the same hotel that Jenny was staying in. How does that sound?"

A ripple of chatter broke out among the women at Olivia's words.

"That will be fine," Daniela replied for the group. "Thank you, Agent Olivia. And you two, as well."

I felt a little surprised when she turned to speak to us as well. Olivia had been doing such a good job communicating with them that Holm and I had just decided to keep our mouths shut.

"You don't have to thank us," I replied earnestly. "What happened to you should have never happened to begin with. We're going to do our best to see that you get justice."

Daniela gave me a small, somber smile in response.

"I'll come back as soon as I get some news," Olivia told them as she got up. Holm and I followed her out of the room. I could hear the women talking among themselves as the door closed quietly behind us.

"How did it go?" Officer Crowley stood up from his chair once the door was completely shut.

"Good," I replied. "Well, relatively speaking, I guess. There's really nothing 'good' about any of this."

"That is true," Crowley sighed bitterly. "So, what are we doing now?"

"We need to head to Cockburn Town," I replied. "That's where Samuel is, and according to Daniela, there are still five other victims there."

"Cockburn is all the way on the southern island." Crowley frowned. "We'll need to take a boat or a plane there. It might take us hours to procure either."

"Not necessarily." I smirked. "I happen to know a guy who owns a boat. And it just so happens that he really, really hates the traffickers."

28

ETHAN

After we finished speaking with the women, I suggested that we call Raymond and take him up on his offer of help. He'd given us vital information at the beginning of our investigation here. He'd been so furious about the death of his brother at the hands of the traffickers that he'd offered to do whatever he could to assist us in catching them. I called him using the number he had left us, and I found him extremely enthusiastic about the idea.

"Are you certain that this man can be trusted?" Crowley muttered apprehensively as we made our way down the beach toward the boat docks.

"Honestly? I'm not sure," I replied. "I barely know the guy. But I do know that he offered to lend us his boat, and considering he knows the traffickers and what we're getting into, he probably won't be surprised if his boat gets destroyed in the process."

I flashed back to our previous mission in Scotland. We'd inadvertently damaged not one but two boats, both belonging to the same man. Raymond Johnson was so incensed by his need for vengeance that he probably wouldn't care as much as the other guy had.

"After everything that has happened," Hanks added, "I'm not sure who to trust anymore."

Hanks, the only officer who had remained uninjured during the fight at the Oasis Lounge, was accompanying us instead of Olivia. She'd chosen to stay behind to figure things out as far as relocating the women. She'd also said that she wouldn't be of much help, considering she was injured and down an arm. It felt odd not to have her around, but at the same time, I was a bit relieved. If she had come, I would have spent the entire time worrying about her.

"There you are!" Raymond called from the deck of his boat as he spotted us approaching. "Hurry up! We haven't got all day."

"He seems just a little too eager, I think," Holm muttered uneasily.

"Can you blame the guy?" I replied. "Jerks shot his baby brother dead in cold blood."

"Yeah, I guess I get that," Holm mumbled. "I'd probably react the same way if it was my sister."

That being said, Raymond did seem a bit too giddy as we boarded the fishing boat.

"Sorry space is so cramped," he said as he stepped over to the helm. "I have bigger ones, but this one here is the fastest. Speed is what we need right now, right?"

"That's right," I answered as I sat on one of the seats behind the helm.

"Well, then hold on." He grinned as he turned around and moved something at the helm. A moment later, the boat took off at a fast pace, causing the surrounding water to splash and spray up into the boat.

The trip from Kew to Cockburn would take about an hour by boat. It was a bit of a ride, but faster than taking a plane. Though a flight would have only been about half an hour, we'd have lost time going through the airport, not to mention actually driving to the location after landing. With a boat, we'd be able to go directly to where the main house was.

"We'll hit the main house first." I went over the

plan one more time as we made our way there. "Our priority is getting the victims to safety. If Samuel isn't there, then we'll hit his house after."

"You think they're waiting for us?" Holm called over the sound of the boat motor and splashing water. "It's been a few hours since the fight at the Oasis Lounge. The suspect that got away had plenty of time to warn them."

"That's possible," I called back. "We'll just have to assume they know we're coming and go for a direct attack."

Our faces had already been seen, so there was no point in trying to go for a covert approach. We needed to just move in as quickly as possible and secure the remaining women.

"A police escort will be waiting for us when we arrive!" Crowley yelled. "They'll be waiting by the docks to take us straight to the house. I'll call ahead and have them keep eyes on the building!"

"Good plan!" I yelled back.

We fell silent then, the anticipation growing more intense with every second that passed.

As we tore across the water, I couldn't help but think about how pretty the sea looked against the setting sun. Right now, the sky looked orange, and the part of the sea that met the horizon looked pink.

We were far away enough from Western Caicos now that it just looked like a dark blotch in the distance. All around us were nothing but multicolored ocean waves.

It was admittedly kind of a strange thought to have when we were in the middle of a risky mission, but in a way, these were the kinds of things that helped me stay sane. Drugs, murder, trafficking, missing kids, the list of things we dealt with on a daily basis could go on and on. If I couldn't take some time to appreciate something as simple as a sunset over the ocean, I would lose my mind.

The sky was beginning to darken when the dock finally came into view. It had been such a busy day that I'd barely noticed how quickly time had passed. I realized suddenly that I'd barely had anything to eat that day, and I made a mental note to have dinner with Olivia that night as soon as we got back. Maybe we could hit up one of those restaurants along the beach again.

There was a large black police van waiting for us on the dock, and I saw two men get out as Raymond pulled the boat in.

"Here we are," he announced as he brought the boat to a stop. I climbed out immediately, eager to stretch my legs after sitting for over an hour.

"Hello," one of the uniformed officers greeted us as we got off of the boat. "I'm Officer Stevens, and this is my partner, Officer Anderson."

"Nice to meet you," I stepped forward to shake their hands. "I'm Agent Marston with MBLIS. This is my partner, Agent Holm, and this is Officer Crowley and Officer Hanks."

"We spoke on the phone," Crowley said as he stepped forward. "Has there been any movement at the house?"

"None so far," Stevens replied. "A pair of officers are stationed there now, but so far, it's been totally quiet."

"We should get down there ASAP and see for ourselves," I replied.

Stevens nodded and began to lead us back to where the van was parked.

"I'll uh... wait right here," Raymond called after us as we began to walk away.

I turned around to look at him. There was something off about the way he'd said that, but I needed to focus on the mission first. I put the thought aside for the moment and followed Stevens over to the van.

The drive from the docks to the address that Antonio had given us was scarcely five minutes. It was an ordinary-looking building if a little rundown. There was nothing about it that stood out in particular from among the rest of the houses in the area. We drove a little ways past it and parked on the side of the street next to a police cruiser. From here, the house was still visible, though the cars were obscured enough by trees and other foliage that someone looking out from a window probably wouldn't spot them at first glance.

Two different officers stepped out of the patrol car just as we got out of the van.

"Anything?" Stevens asked.

"Nothing." One of the officers shook his head. "No movement since we got here."

"Isn't that a little strange?" I wondered out loud. I was sure that word would have gotten back by this point, so why wasn't anything happening?

"Maybe it's a trap," Holm suggested.

"That may be the case." Crowley nodded thoughtfully. "Regardless, we knew that was a possibility from the beginning. I think we should stick to the plan. Direct attack."

"I think so too," I agreed as I pulled my gun out of its holster. "No point in standing around here."

Holm and the other officers drew their weapons as well. Then we moved in.

"Remember," I warned as we stepped quickly toward the front of the house. "Daniela said the women would most likely be upstairs, but we can't be sure. Their safety is the priority, do not shoot unless you're sure they're not in the crossfire."

My heart beat faster the closer we got to the house. Once he was just a few yards away, Crowley broke into a run and headed straight for the door, kicking it in with an intense blow.

"Everyone freeze!" he roared as he stormed into the house, his gun held aloft. "This is the police!"

Holm and I raced in after him, followed by the other officers. As we spilled into the main foyer of the house, our weapons drawn and adrenaline pumping through our veins, one thing became abundantly clear.

The house was empty.

"Stay alert," Crowley cautioned us before looking at the other officers. "They might still be here. Hanks and I will take the right if you two will clear the left."

They took off to clear the few rooms on the main floor of the house, but I had a feeling that they wouldn't find anything. Years of trusting my instincts to survive had taught me how to hone in on signs of life. The house just felt devoid of that.

Aside from a few couches and chairs, there was

so little furniture that the place didn't seem anything like a home. The walls were bare, with no photos or decorations of any kind. The floors were covered in a dingy brown carpet that looked like it hadn't been vacuumed or washed in a long time. The walls might have been white, but in the darkness, without any interior lights on, they were a sinister blue shade.

I could see into the small kitchen from the main entryway. It was just as sparsely furnished and just as empty as the rest of the house. Really, the house was so open and devoid of furnishings that it would have been impossible for anyone to hide anywhere on the main floor. If someone *was* here, then they had to be on the second floor.

"Let's head upstairs," I suggested to Holm as the officers finished clearing the first floor.

"Okay," he replied as he followed close behind me.

I stayed on high alert as we ascended the stairs. Though the house seemed empty, it was always possible that my hunch was wrong.

The upstairs seemed just as quiet as the first floor, though.

I turned to look at Holm before slowly placing my hand over the doorknob of the door nearest to us. After confirming that he was ready with a silent nod, I threw the door open and rushed inside, my gun at the ready.

"Empty," I muttered as I took a quick look around the room. There wasn't much to see, only a set of beds and a worn-out-looking chair in one corner.

I moved to the other side of the hall to the room just opposite this one. This time, Holm was the one to open the door, only for us to be met with the same result.

"Everything good up here?" Crowley asked as he and the other officers came running up the stairs.

"So far," I replied. "It's looking like the place is totally empty."

"They might have fled when they realized we were coming," Crowley replied as the other officers went on to search the rest of the rooms on the second floor. "Dammit. What do we do now?"

"There's someone in here!" Hank suddenly yelled.

I spun around at the sound of his voice. One of the doors at the very end of the hall was open, and I rushed toward it, Holm, Crowley, and the other officers right behind me.

Hanks was leaning over one of the beds as I burst

into the room, and I realized the "someone" he had found wasn't one of the traffickers but rather one of the victims.

The woman lying on the bed looked deathly pale. The thin tank top she was wearing was damp with sweat, and her eyes were half-lidded, as though she wasn't completely conscious.

"She's in rough shape," Hanks muttered as I came to stand beside him. "Looks like she might be on something. Or coming down from something."

It looked to me like he was right. The girl was shaking so much that her teeth were chattering, and her skin was covered in a thin sheen of sweat. Her eyes were unfocused, and her breathing was shallow and labored, as well. She was either extremely sick or going through some kind of withdrawal.

"The rest of the house is empty," one of the local officers noted as he came to stand beside me. "I can't believe they just left her here alone like this."

"You can't?" I scoffed. "They don't exactly seem like upstanding people. They view these women as property rather than human beings. They probably cleared out as quickly as they could and decided to just ditch her here rather than deal with the dead weight."

"They must have left before we got here," the

officer replied. "We've been stationed right outside ever since we got the call from Captain Morris. No one entered or left this house in that time."

"There's no telling how far they might have gotten by now, then," I replied angrily before turning to Crowley. "We need eyes on the water. The women mentioned that they were always transported from Cockburn to Western Caicos on a private boat. Unless they're hiding somewhere on the island, it's possible they fled that way."

"Alright," Crowley replied. "I'll get on it as soon as we secure medical attention for this woman."

"Good," I replied before turning to Holm and the other officers. "We need to head straight to the address we have for Samuel's place now. That's where they're most likely to be."

I waited impatiently as Crowley called for an ambulance. I knew that making sure the woman got medical attention was important, but I was starting to get anxious now that we'd discovered that the men weren't here. Every second that passed was another that Samuel and the traffickers might be using to get that much further away.

I was jarred out of my thoughts by the sound of my phone ringing. I pulled it out of my pocket and frowned at the name on the screen.

"What's up?" Holm asked.

"It's Raymond," I muttered back before answering and putting the phone to my ear. The moment I did, I jumped as the bang of a gunshot rang through the line.

"What the hell is happening?" I yelled into my phone's speaker.

"Agent Marston," Raymond's pained voice groaned. "I have a bit of a problem."

"Yeah, no kidding," I snapped back as I heard more gunshots. "What did you do?"

"I found the men," he rasped. His voice sounded airy, as though he were struggling to draw breath. "I came to the house. I overheard you talking about it when you were discussing your plans on the way over. I'm sorry, but I couldn't just wait around while the people that killed my baby brother walked free."

"Dammit, Raymond!" I yelled.

"What's going on?" Holm stared at me in confusion. Crowley and the other officers were also staring at me with similar looks of horror and bewilderment.

"Hold on," I said as I pulled the phone away from my ear and put it on speaker so they could hear the chaos as well. "Raymond, where are you now?"

"Right outside the house," he coughed. "I caught

them as they were getting ready to leave. I managed to shoot a few of them, but there were too many. They're getting on the boat now."

"The address we had for Samuel's house was right on the beach!" Holm exclaimed. "You were right, Ethan. They're trying to flee by water."

"You go," one of the local officers suddenly spoke up as he tossed Crowley the keys to the police van. "We'll stay here with the girl until the ambulance arrives."

"Okay, let's go," I said to Holm and Crowley before turning on my heel and quickly leaving the room. It wasn't ideal to split up like this, but we didn't have time to spare right now.

"Raymond!" I yelled through the phone. "How many men are still there? I can hear the gunshots."

"Ah... two, I think," he gasped. His voice was getting more strained every time he spoke. "I'm inside the house now, taking cover. I'm not too sure."

"Okay, just hold tight," I called as I raced down the stairs and through the front door of the house, Holm and Crowley hot on my trail. "We're coming to you now."

"I'll try not to die before then," he laughed brokenly before hanging up.

"How long until we get to the address?" I asked Crowley as we piled into the police van.

"About four minutes by car," he replied as he turned the ignition.

"I hope Raymond can hold out for that long," I muttered bitterly in response as the car took off. Outside, the sky was beginning to darken with foreboding storm clouds. I hoped the sudden unexpected storm wasn't an omen of things to come.

29

ETHAN

EVEN THOUGH THE drive to Samuel's house only took a few minutes, it felt like an eternity had passed when Crowley finally pulled the car to a stop with a loud screech. The house we'd arrived at was larger than most of the ones I'd seen around Turks & Caicos before. It was a little bigger than the one we'd just left but significantly more well-maintained. The exterior walls were coated with a crisp, fresh coat of paint, and the windows were decorated with fancy, brightly colored wooden shutters. At least, the ones that hadn't been shot to bits were.

The three of us got out of the car and immediately rushed forward. We were almost to the front door when it suddenly burst open. A man wearing a dark blue bandana over his head stepped out. He looked extremely shocked to see us.

"Freeze!" I shouted, but the man was already lifting the gun he was holding in his hand.

I jumped to the side and unholstered my own gun in one swift moment. The man fired, but his bullet missed and struck the side of the police van. I fired my own pistol, and the man fell backward as he was hit in the arm.

Holm and I both rushed forward to restrain him before he could get back up. As we did, I noticed a blur of movement from around the corner of the house. I snapped my head up and found a second man quickly coming around from the side of the house, his gun pointed right toward us.

"Holm, get down!" I yelled as I lifted my gun.

He dropped to the ground immediately. Before the man could fire, both Crowley and I shot at him, and he fell over with a short cry of pain.

"Go find Raymond," Crowley huffed as he bent down to handcuff the man that Holm was restraining. "I've got this one."

I nodded before rushing into the house. I was wary about the possibility that there might be even more men inside, but I didn't want to take too long clearing the house when I knew that Raymond was somewhere in here, very obviously injured.

Several pieces of furniture were overturned, and a few things had clear bullet holes through them. It was evident that Raymond hadn't gone down without a fight.

"Raymond?" I yelled as I ran toward the rear of the first floor. As soon as I called his name, I heard what sounded like a banging noise somewhere to my left. I tried the door nearest to me and found that it was locked.

"What was that?" Holm asked as he ran up to me, having obviously heard the banging noise as well.

"Raymond?" I called again. "Are you in there?"

There was a shuffling sound from inside, and I braced myself, gun ready to shoot just in case it *wasn't* actually him in there. A second later, the door handle wiggled and unlocked with a click before the door finally opened.

"I was worried I'd be a dead man before you got here," Raymond wheezed as he pushed the door open wider. He was hunched over and pressing one of his hands to his bloodied side. His nose was crooked and swollen, and he had a black eye as well.

I glanced behind him and realized we were

inside a bathroom. He must have taken cover there once the men started gaining the upper hand.

"How badly are you injured?" I asked as I slung his arm over my shoulders so I could help him walk.

"They got me good," he replied with a mirthless chuckle as he glanced down at the wound on his side. "Starting to feel a little dizzy, actually."

"Just take it easy," I replied as Holm and I helped him out of the house.

"I've got the suspect in the car," Crowley informed us as he came jogging up to assist. "And I've got another ambulance heading this way. How bad is it?"

"Something like this isn't gonna take me out," Raymond slurred weakly. He said that, but his eyes were becoming unfocused, and he was wobbling more with every step he took.

"Here, sit down for a minute," I suggested as I helped him down onto the grass in front of the house. "Try not to move too much until help arrives."

"Not sure I could if I wanted to," he wheezed as he reached into his pocket. His hand emerged clutching the boat key, which he held out to me. "You need to go after them. Don't let the bastard who murdered my brother get away."

"I'll stay here with him," Crowley spoke up immediately. "The suspect is handcuffed and secured inside the back of the van. We'll lose too much time if we all wait."

"Alright," I replied as I took the key from Raymond. "Which way to the beach?"

"Just there," he said as he lifted his arm shakily to point toward a throng of trees that bisected one half of the neighborhood from the other. "The beach is only a few hundred meters from here. Just keep going straight. I docked the boat there. I saw them heading in that direction with the girls."

"Okay." I nodded before getting to my feet. "Come on, Holm, we don't have any time to lose."

Together, we took off toward the trees. The moment we cleared them, I could see the beach in the distance. The buildings here were all on the larger side, brightly colored in shades of turquoise, green, and pale yellow. Just like Western Caicos, there weren't a lot of cars on the road, though there were plenty of locals and tourists alike, even despite the unpleasant weather.

Some people tossed us curious expressions as we ran by. Everyone was moving at such a relaxed, leisurely pace that we must have looked extremely out-of-place booking it through the street like this.

"Do you see it?!" Holm yelled as we raced onto the sandy beach. The rain had finally started to come down, and it was difficult to see. I scanned my eyes across the shoreline until they finally landed on something white in the distance.

"There!" I shouted back before taking off in that direction. It was definitely Raymond's boat. I recognized the distinctive blue stripe across the right side. It was also the only boat docked next to what was more of a small pier than a proper docking area. Raymond must have just chosen the first place he could find to leave his boat on his quest to find Samuel and the other traffickers.

"How did he even climb up here?" Holm grumbled as we ducked beneath the railing of the pier and down onto the boat. It was a good question since the floor of the pier was a good four feet above the deck of the boat.

"Never underestimate a man intent on revenge," I muttered as I moved quickly to the helm. It was a familiar system. I'd driven countless boats in my life, many more complicated than his simple fishing vessel.

"I see something out there." Holm tapped me on the shoulder to get my attention. He pointed at something through the glass window at the front of the helm.

Sure enough, I could see another boat in the distance. It was difficult to tell just how large it was from so far away, but it was definitely bigger than ours.

"Think that's them?" I muttered as I rummaged through the shelves and drawers beneath the helm. Maybe Raymond had a set of binoculars or a spyglass somewhere in here.

"I don't see anyone else on the water," Holm replied as he stepped toward the side of the boat to undo the line.

"We'll assume it is, then," I decided as I pushed the throttle to get the boat going.

It had only been a few minutes since Raymond had called us to let us know that the men were escaping from Samuel's house. If that were the case, then it was possible they hadn't made it very far yet. I only hoped we weren't chasing after the wrong boat and wasting even more time.

I hadn't noticed it before because I'd been so focused on going over the details of the mission, but now that I was actually at the helm, I realized just how fast Raymond's boat was. The thing was tiny, but it was practically bouncing across the water at an alarming speed. We were catching up to the much larger vessel in no time.

"Aha!" Holm exclaimed when we were about a hundred yards away from it. "I found some binoculars back here."

I glanced back at him and saw him holding the small, portable set of binoculars in one hand.

"Alright, tell me what you see!" I called over the sound of rushing water as I turned my focus back to steering. At the speed we were going, I didn't want to lose control or crash into anything.

"It's still kind of hard to tell through the rain!" he yelled back. "Oh, wait, no, I see men. And I see *guns.* I think these are our guys."

"How many men?!" I called over my shoulder as the boat got ever closer. They were bound to notice us any moment now if they hadn't already.

"I count three!" he shouted as he came to stand next to me at the helm. "But that doesn't include whoever's driving or anyone that might be below deck. See for yourself."

He took over the steering so I could peer through the binoculars. The boat looked like it was about three times as big as the one Holm and I were on. It was a small yacht, and I could see three men wandering around on the main deck. They all had guns at their hips, and one even had a rifle slung over his shoulder. A second after I'd fixed the binoculars on him, he turned to look directly at me.

"Crap!" I yelled as the man whipped the rifle off his shoulder. "Holm, get down!"

He swore as he ducked down below the helm as far as he could without letting go of the wheel. We were still a few yards away from the boat, but we were close enough that we might crash directly into it in a matter of seconds if he lost control, especially with the storm making the water so rough and choppy.

I flattened myself onto the deck of the boat as bullets tore through. I flinched as part of the seat above me suddenly exploded into a cloud of vinyl and stuffing. As bits of dust and fluff rained down over my head, it dawned on me just how close I had just been to being shot.

"I can't see where I'm going!" Holm shouted over the barrage of bullets.

"Hang on!" I yelled back as I crawled on my elbows to get better cover behind the seat. I peaked out over the edge to the deck of the larger boat. The man with the rifle was leaning over the gunwale of the boat as he shot at us. One of the other men was at his side, firing his pistol as well. I couldn't see the third man anymore.

I lifted my gun and fired toward where they were standing. It was difficult to aim while the boat was moving so quickly and so erratically, but I still managed to hit the one holding the pistol, though I couldn't tell where. I only saw him fall backward suddenly.

The man with the rifle stopped firing for just a moment to check on his buddy. I seized the opportunity and fired two more shots. The man screamed and dropped his gun directly off the side of the boat, though he didn't fall as his friend did.

"Move closer now!" I yelled at Holm. "He's lost the gun. Bring the boat in as close as you can."

"Got it!" Holm shouted back as he stood up and began to steer properly again.

I got to my feet and climbed up onto one of the chairs before jumping up to grab onto the hardtop of the helm. Up there, I'd be at just the right height to jump onto the deck of the yacht.

I was just getting to my feet when a bullet tore through the metal just in front of where I was standing.

"Whoa!" Holm yelled from below. The bullet

must have sailed clean through the roof and into the helm below.

I looked up and found the same man who'd been holding the rifle pointing a pistol at me. I lifted my own gun and shot back at him just as he fired again. His shot missed me, and this time, he did fall backward as my bullet hit him square in the chest.

I allowed myself to breathe a sigh of relief now that both of the hostiles were down. However, it was short-lived as I realized an instant later that we were only feet away from the other boat now.

I swore as I got shoved my gun back into its holster and got ready to jump. I only had seconds until we made impact.

I leapt forward just as the fishing boat crashed into the side of the yacht. I barely managed to land on the deck of the larger vessel, and I stumbled to the ground as I lost my footing on the slippery, rain-soaked deck.

"Are you okay?!" Holm yelled. "Damn, sorry, I lost control when that bullet whizzed by my head. Are you alive? Ethan, say something!"

"I'm fine!" I yelled as I peered down over the edge of the boat. "Quit yelling and get up here. We're not out of the woods yet."

He climbed onto the hardtop in the same way I

had earlier, though he had a much harder time since the boat was now quickly taking on water and trying its best to float away now that Holm had left the helm. I reached down to help him up onto the deck.

"Hope Raymond's not too mad," he remarked as we turned to look down at the sinking vessel.

"As long as we grab Samuel, I doubt he's going to care," I replied as I turned around. I couldn't see the cockpit for the entrance to the lower cabin from where we were standing.

"Careful," I cautioned Holm as he made our way carefully to the other side of the boat. There was still at least one man left unaccounted for, not to mention whoever was driving the boat.

I paused for just a moment before we made it to the cockpit where the helm was. I lifted my gun and then quickly rushed toward the stern of the vessel. To my surprise, no one was at the wheel.

"He must have gone below deck after the fighting started," Holm guessed as we took a look around the helm. "Damn. Okay, let's go."

Together, we made our way down the steps and into the darkened cabin below. We'd just made it to the end of the staircase when I heard screams from a room at the end of the hall. I rushed forward instinctively, only realizing my error when it was too late.

I failed to notice an open doorway to my left until I'd already run past. I caught a flash of movement out of the corner of my eye, but before I could turn around, something blunt hit me on the back of the head.

Stars burst in front of my eyes as I stumbled forward, almost falling to my knees as my vision swam and made it hard to stay upright. I spun around to face my attacker, but the movement only caused my dizziness to worsen.

The man had a crazed look in his eye as he lifted whatever he'd used to hit me above his head. Before he could strike again, though, Holm tackled him to the ground from behind, the two of them falling into a heap together on the floor.

"I'm going to kill you!" the man screamed as he thrashed around in Holm's grip. I crouched down and punched the man in the face twice. The second blow caused him to hit the back of his head on the hard metal ground, and he groaned as his eyes drifted in and out of focus before finally shutting.

He dropped his weapon as he finally fell unconscious.

"What is that?" Holm huffed for breath as he reached for the thing he'd dropped. "A wrench!?

How are you still standing after taking a blow from this to the back of the head?"

"He didn't hit me that hard," I hissed as I gingerly touched the back of my head. My hand came away wet with blood. "Still hurts, though. Guess I'm lucky it's so dark down here. He probably couldn't see."

"Are you good?" he asked as he leaned down to cuff the guy to the stair railing. "You were looking a little out of it there for a second."

"I'm fine," I grumbled, though my head was throbbing. "Come on, we need to find the women."

We continued our way down the short hallway again, more carefully this time. There wasn't anywhere else for anyone to hide, though. All that was left was the door to the main cabin.

I pressed myself as close to the wall beside the door as I could before turning to look at Holm.

"Ready?" I whispered as I slowly put my hand on the door handle.

"Ready." He nodded, his gun gripped tightly in both hands.

I pushed the door open and ran inside, my gun held out in front of me.

"Freeze!" I yelled as I stepped into the room, Holm right beside me. The room was dark. The storm was in full force outside by this point, blocking out any chance of moonlight, so it was difficult to see in the small room. Several women were huddled on the ground at the rear corner of the cabin, their faces streaked with tears. They screamed as Holm and I burst into the room.

Standing in the center of the room, just in front of a desk, were two men. I instantly recognized one of them as the man who had managed to escape from the Oasis Lounge earlier in the day. The scar on his cheek was too distinctive for me to forget it.

Standing just beside him was a hunched man with graying hair who looked like he was about the same age as Richard, the antique store owner who had shot at us earlier in the week. This time, he was the one holding one of the women hostage while the man with the scar pointed a gun at us.

"Don't come any closer," the old man warned as he pressed a knife to the girl's neck.

"Don't be stupid," I snapped at him. "What do you think is going to happen here, huh? We're in the middle of the ocean, on a boat. You can't run anywhere."

"You're right," the man with the scar sneered as he took a step forward. "Which is why we're going to kill you right here."

For a few painstaking moments, nobody moved. We were at a complete standoff. Holm and I couldn't shoot while the girl was still in danger, and the man with the scar knew that the moment he shot at either of us, the other one would take him out.

I gritted my teeth as I thought about what to do when I noticed one of the women slowly getting to her feet at the back of the room. I tried not to make it obvious that I had noticed her so I wouldn't alert the two men.

For just a second, the woman made eye contact with me, and I watched as she silently raised a finger to her lips. She crept soundlessly across the carpeted floor behind the desk the two men were standing in front of. I wasn't sure what she was doing, but I needed to keep their focus on me before they noticed her.

"There's still a way out of this," I blurted out the first thing that came to mind as the woman reached forward to pick up a heavy binder that was sitting on the top of the desk. "No one has to get hurt."

"Shut up!" the man with the scar roared.

The old man said something too, but I was too focused on the woman behind him to pay attention to what it was. She held the binder over her head, a mixture of fury and fear and hatred burning in her eyes.

She suddenly let out a scream of anger as she brought the heavy thing down over the old man's head.

Then several things happened at once. The old man let out a cry of pain as he fell forward, the girl shrieked as the knife he was holding cut into her neck, and the man with the scar spun around at the unexpected scream.

"Samuel!" the man snarled as he watched the old man crumple to the ground. He turned his fury onto the girl and spun around to point his gun at her instead of us.

I moved the moment the opportunity presented itself.

"Hey!" I yelled to distract him from shooting at her. He spun around to look at me, his face colliding directly with my fist as he did.

He roared in a mixture of pain and anger as he swung his own fist at me. I blocked him with my arm and punched him again. This time he fell backward onto the desk.

As he did, I turned around to check on the girl he'd cut. Holm was with her now, so I turned back to the suspect. He'd recovered more quickly than I'd expected, and I was just a split second too slow to block his next blow.

I hissed with pain as his fist struck the side of my chin. He grinned, clearly pleased that he'd managed to land a punch, and pulled his fist back to hit me again.

As he did, I swung around to punch him in the stomach. His eyes bugged out as he coughed and sputtered from the strength of the blow. I followed that hit up with another directly to his face. He fell backward again, this time slamming his elbow against the edge of the desk as he fell onto the ground.

He growled at me as he attempted to kick me from his position on the floor, but I returned his efforts with my own kick to his side. He groaned with pain, but I didn't let up. I crouched down to deliver one final punch to his face, rendering him unconscious.

"Hey," I called to Holm as I slowly regained my breath. "You got any more handcuffs? I used my last set on that idiot in the hallway."

"Yeah," he replied. "I'll be right there. She's bleeding a lot."

I looked up and saw him still kneeling next to the girl. She was kneeling on the ground, rocking back and forth and clutching at her neck as blood trickled down from the wound.

I got up and walked over to where they were.

"Let me see," I said gently as I tried to examine the wound without scaring or jostling her too much. It didn't look very deep. The knife must have just nicked her as she fell. She might need stitches, but her life wasn't in danger.

I looked around for something I could use to staunch the blood flow before settling on a thin curtain slung over one of the windows. A dirty old curtain wasn't ideal, but it would have to do. I tore it off of the rod and shook it out to clear it of as much dirt as dust as possible before returning to the girl's side.

"Press this against your neck, okay?" I instructed her as I placed the wad of fabric into her hand. "We're going to get you all back to shore as quickly as possible."

I looked up at the woman who had bashed the old man over the head. She was still standing in the exact same spot, her eyes wide and blank, as though she couldn't believe what she'd just done.

The man in question groaned as he began to regain consciousness.

"Oh, no, you don't," I snarled as I quickly moved to restrain his arms behind his back.

"Ah!" he cried out as I forced his wrists roughly together. "You're hurting me!"

"Good," I sneered, unable to keep the venom out of my voice as I pulled a set of handcuffs from my belt. "After everything you've done, it's the least you deserve, *Samuel.*"

I'd heard the man with the scar yell that name as the old man went down. Finally, we'd managed to track down the man we'd been looking for all this time. Finally, we'd be able to get justice for Allison Newark and her son, Eddy.

30

ETHAN

I BREATHED a sigh of relief as we finally made it back to Cockburn Town. A line of police cars was parked along the beach, as well as a few ambulances. Their flashing lights were a welcome beacon after the storm we'd just endured. The sky had even started clearing up, and the heavy downpour from earlier was now a light drizzle.

I looked down at the three men we had hand-cuffed to the railing at the front of the boat. Holm and I had decided to move Samuel, the man with the scar, and the man who'd hit me with the wrench up here, both so we could keep an eye on them and so that the girls wouldn't have to be stuck down there with them.

"Not much longer now," I muttered smugly to myself as I turned back to the beach. I waited anxiously as Holm brought the massive vessel into the dock. No sooner had he stopped than several police officers began to climb on board to collect the men we'd apprehended. Several pairs of paramedics carrying stretchers climbed on board as well to retrieve the bodies of the men we'd shot.

"One of the victims was injured," I informed them as they began to board. "She's below in the main cabin. One of the suspects cut her throat with a knife."

"We'll see to it," one of them responded before heading downstairs. I was glad. It only made sense, in my opinion, to focus first on the injured victim rather than the dead criminals.

"Ethan!"

A welcome and familiar voice called my name. I turned around and found Olivia climbing onto the boat. I barely had time to react before she was throwing her uninjured arm around my neck in a one-armed hug. "I'm so glad you're okay."

"Of course I am." I smiled at her. "You didn't have to come all this way, though. How's your arm?"

"It's fine." She waved her hand dismissively. "Besides, I've been up and about since you left, so it's not a big deal. I had just finished getting everything with the women's living accommodations handled when I heard that something had gone wrong and Raymond had been shot. I called Crowley, and he said that you and Holm had run off *by yourselves* to chase down Samuel. I got a flight down here as soon as I heard that."

She swatted me on the arm admonishingly.

"Well, we couldn't just let him get away," I countered. "They were taking the rest of the women who-knows-where. We needed to take the risk."

"I know, I know," she sighed as she fiddled with one of the buttons on my shirt. "Just... don't make doing reckless things a habit, alright?"

"Too late for that," Holm suddenly scoffed from somewhere behind me. "Ethan can't even go on *vacation* without getting into trouble."

"That was one time," I grumbled as I turned around to glare at him.

"Okay, I want to hear that story," Olivia snickered.

"Later." I turned around to look back at her. "First, let's get back to dry land and maybe into some dry clothes. Holm and I are soaked."

"Fine," she replied as she stepped away from me. I felt colder immediately, especially with how cold and wet my shirt was. "But I'm holding you to it."

"I'll keep that in mind." I grinned as the three of us got off the boat and onto the dock. A nice hot shower sounded amazing right about then, but I'd have to settle for a quick change of clothes. Though my body felt fatigued, my mind was still racing, and I didn't want to put off Samuel's interrogation any longer than I had to. As soon as everything was ready, I would finish this case, once and for all.

Three hours, a fresh change of clothes, and a strong cup of coffee later, Holm, Olivia, and I were standing outside of the Grace Bay Police Station interrogation room. A medical examination had confirmed that, though he might have a mild concussion, he didn't need any further medical treatment and could be interrogated right away.

It was nearly midnight by that point, and though I'd felt a little tired earlier, I was now buzzing with energy.

"Are you ready to go in?" Captain Morris asked us. He'd accompanied us down to the interrogation room personally, eager to see the man who had committed unspeakable crimes in his town get his comeuppance.

"Yeah, we're ready," I replied.

He opened the door to let us in, and Holm, Olivia, and I stepped inside.

Samuel was sitting in front of the large table in the room, his shoulders slumped forward and an angry scowl on his face.

"Hello, Samuel," I greeted him acerbically as I sat down across from him. Holm and Olivia both sat down on either side of me.

"What do you want?" he grumbled.

"We need to have a talk," I answered him curtly.

"What?" he scoffed. "You caught me red-handed. You won, Agents. What the hell else do you want from me?"

"You're right." Olivia glared at him. "We did catch you, and you're going to rot in a prison cell for the rest of your life, but before you do, I need you to tell me about them."

He pulled two photos out of her bag. One was of Eddy, and the other was a picture of Allison's body from the morgue. She slammed them down on the table in front of him.

"What is *that*?" Samuel sneered as she reached for the photo of Allison.

"*She* is Allison Newark," Olivia corrected him with a snarl. "She was one of the women you and your men were keeping captive. You knew her as Cat."

"Oh, her," he huffed with a shrug. "I barely recognized her. She looks like hell."

Even though she was sitting a foot away from me, I could practically feel Olivia tensing with anger at his rude response.

"Yeah, well, if she hadn't sailed from here to Miami in a tiny fishing boat, maybe she wouldn't be in that state," I retorted.

"Right, right," he muttered. "She's the one that took off a few weeks back with Antonio's kid. I told that idiot keeping them around was a stupid idea. Looks like I was right."

He was smirking as though he found all of this funny. It pissed me off.

"Allison was kidnapped from her parents nearly twenty years ago," Olivia continued calmly, though I could tell she was annoyed. "Do you know anything about that?"

"Of course," the man grinned, exposing his gnarled and yellowed teeth. "I'm the one who grabbed her."

"You what?!" Olivia exclaimed.

"Just what I said," Samuel cackled. "I was just a grunt worker back then. I had a part-time job as a custodian at the hotel she and her parents were staying at. I still remember that day. I knew the moment I saw her that she'd fetch a huge price. Blond hair and blue eyes, and milky white skin, too. You don't find girls like that here, aside from the tourists. Clients will pay a lot more for a girl with her looks."

"She was a child!" Olivia gasped as she stood up, her chair dragging across the floor with a scrape.

"So?" Samuel shrugged. "She was going to grow up eventually, and boy, did she grow up fine, eh?"

I literally shuddered at the way he chuckled at his own disgusting thoughts. I glanced over at Olivia. She was glaring at Samuel with a look of unbridled hatred, and for a moment, I was genuinely concerned that she was about to attack him. After a few seconds, though, she slowly sat back down.

"I was right, too," Samuel continued. "She was a big money-maker. At least until Antonio went and knocked her up. I told him to arrange for her to get rid of it, but he insisted that he wanted her to have it. We had other girls by then, younger ones, so it wasn't a big deal."

"You're a monster," I uttered, unable to hold back any longer.

"Ha!" he scoffed at my insult. "You think I haven't

heard it all? I'm no monster, boy. I'm a businessman. I'll bet you make a pittance doing that little government job of yours. You go out, risk your life, spend all day getting shot at, and for what? Meanwhile, I'm here, basking in paradise and getting rich off the backs of others."

"You're sitting in a police station," I deadpanned in response. "And you won't ever be a free man again, I can assure you of that. Say whatever you want, but you're going to pay for everything you've done."

Samuel's face scrunched up like he'd just smelled something rotten.

"Whatever," he replied petulantly.

"Captain Turner," Olivia suddenly spoke up. "From the Kew Town police station. Is he working with you?"

"Turner?" Samuel raised an eyebrow at her. "Why do you want to know? What's in it for me if I talk?"

"You're in no position to be making bargains," Olivia snapped angrily at him. "Answer the damned question."

"Alright, alright." Samuel shrugged. "I guess if I'm going down, I might as well take him with me! Yeah, he is, in a way. He uh... looks the other way, if you know what I mean. And In return, I give him a small cut of our monthly earnings."

"That explains why he kept trying to hinder our investigation," Holm muttered.

"What a shock," Olivia scoffed bitterly.

"One more question before we go, Samuel." I kept my voice as even as I could. My skin was crawling just being near this unimaginable monster, and I wanted to get out of there as soon as possible. "You said that you were the one who grabbed Allison all those years ago. How long has this group been operating?"

"Oh, hell if I know," he shrugged. "I've been working for them practically my whole life. Worked my way up, right to the tippy top."

He smirked proudly as he spoke, and it made me sick.

"Yeah, well, it's all going to end here," I told him as I stood up. "You're going to be extradited to the United States, and you're going to spend the rest of your miserable life locked in a tiny box. Everything you dedicated your life to has come crashing down, and I hope you die angry about it."

He glared at me as I turned to leave the room, Holm and Olivia following closely behind me.

As soon as the door closed behind us, Olivia

buried her face in her hands and let out a long, anguished groan.

"You cannot imagine how close I was to doing something I would have regretted," she said as she ran a hand through her hair.

"Oh, I think I can," I scoffed.

"How can someone be so cruel?" Holm grimaced. "I mean, being a jerk is one thing, but he seemed almost *proud* while he was talking about everything he did."

"He was proud," Olivia huffed. "That's the whole reason he talked to us so easily. It gave him a chance to brag about everything he'd done."

"I need a shower," Holm grumbled. "Or maybe two, after that interrogation."

"I hear you," I sighed. "But what's important is that we caught him. According to what Samuel said, we put a stop to a group that had been operating for *decades*. He's going to spend the rest of his life rotting in prison. Let him brag all he wants in there."

"You're right," Olivia replied. "At least now, we can give the Newark family some closure, too. We were able to get justice for Allison."

I smiled as I thought about how we'd managed to pull a twenty-year-old case to a close. It was unfortunate that Allison hadn't survived, but Eddy and all the other women were now safe because of her.

"Okay," I declared. "Let's head back to Captain Morris's office. We need to sort out all the extradition details."

"Great," Holm sighed as we made our way down the hall. "My favorite part of any case. Paperwork."

31

ETHAN

I TRIPLE-CHECKED TO make sure I had everything on my list before heading to the checkout. It had been a few weeks since we'd gotten back home from Turks & Caicos, and I'd invited Olivia over to celebrate both the conclusion of the case and the fact that she'd been released from her arm sling. We were both so busy that it had taken a few days for us to both find a day when we were free to meet up. We'd finally managed to sort it out, and I'd decided to run to the store to pick up some ingredients to make dinner. Olivia had sounded really enthusiastic about the idea of me cooking.

As I scanned my purchases, I thought back to everything that had happened since that final inter-view with Samuel. He'd been extradited, of course, and was currently awaiting trial. Captain Turner, too, had been taken into custody by local authorities in Turks & Caicos for the part he'd played in helping the traffickers get away with their crimes. Olivia had been giving me updates about the women we'd rescued as well. Apparently, the FBI was making sure that they were all receiving the help and support they needed and helping those kidnapped, like Allison, return to their homes.

I felt content as I loaded the groceries into my car. Ultimately, the case had turned out as well as we could have hoped.

I parked my car at the entrance to the dock where my boat was and retrieved the bags from the trunk. As I did, I noticed two men carting a massive crate on a dolly between them. I wondered vaguely what it could be and who might have bought it. I peered around the lid of my trunk to watch them, and my curiosity quickly turned to confusion as I realized they were heading straight for *my* boat.

I was about to call out to them to ask what they thought they were doing, but another voice beat me to it.

"Over here!" Olivia called from the deck of my boat as she waved to the two men.

I was surprised to see her there already, though

honestly no less confused. I decided to forget about the groceries for the moment and closed the trunk before walking briskly toward where my boat was docked on the water.

"How am I supposed to get it in here, though?" I heard her say to herself.

"What even is it?!" I called out to her.

"Ethan!" She jumped in surprise at my voice. "I didn't realize you were back already. Dang, you couldn't have taken a little longer at the store?"

"What?" I chuckled as I watched the two men set the crate down in front of my boat. "What is this?"

"It was *supposed* to be a surprise." She pouted as she climbed down off the boat before turning to address the two men. "It's fine right there. We'll figure it out from here."

"We will?" I stared at her in disbelief. "You think you could clue me in a little?"

"I pulled some strings." She shrugged demurely before smirking at me. "Remember Richard? The antique store owner? Well, the FBI needed to do an investigation on him as part of the case, and wouldn't you know it, most of the stuff in his store was stolen, or otherwise illegal for him to own in some way."

"Okay..." I replied nervously, afraid to even dream that this was going where I thought it was.

"So, naturally, we had to confiscate all of it," Olivia continued with a sly smile. "You wouldn't believe some of the stuff that we found in there. Apparently, they found some rare piece of Polynesian pottery in there, hundreds of years old and worth thousands. How did he even come across something like that?"

"Is there an ancient Polynesian vase in that crate?" I asked her.

"Nope." She grinned. "Something even better. See, I knew that with so much rare and priceless evidence to go through, it was unlikely that anyone was going to miss some grubby old anchor."

"You're kidding," I breathed, unable to keep the smile off my face.

"Do I look like I'm kidding?" She smirked as she leaned back against the crate. "I'd say you owe me one hell of a dinner for this one, Marston."

I reached out to pull her to me and crashed my lips against hers, unable to contain myself anymore. She wrapped her arms around my neck and kissed me back.

"Maybe we should take this inside," she

murmured. "Unless you want to give all of your neighbors a free show."

I took her hand and led her onto the boat, groceries entirely forgotten at that point. Frankly, I wasn't sure I'd ever received a gift this amazing, and right now, I wanted to shower Olivia with as much gratitude as I could.

We spent the rest of the day together, and it wasn't until much later, after we'd finally had that dinner, that I finally noticed the missed call on my phone. I'd been so preoccupied that it wasn't until late at night when I was in bed that I even looked at my phone for the first time since Olivia had arrived.

I was surprised to see that Tessa had called me earlier that day, around the same time that Olivia had gotten there. She hadn't left a voice message, but she had texted me. As soon as I opened the message, my eyes went wide, and I nearly dropped my phone.

Ethan, call me back ASAP. They opened the chest!

I was so stunned that I read the message twice just to make sure I'd gotten it right. She was, of course, talking about the old treasure chest I'd found inside a sunken pirate ship a few weeks earlier. I couldn't believe that, on top of the anchor, I was about to find out what was inside that old chest.

I got out of bed immediately, all thoughts of sleep instantly gone at Tessa's message. As I crept my way out of the room and up onto the deck to call her back, my head was filled with thoughts of how I was getting closer and closer to finally finding the *Dragon's Rogue*.

EPILOGUE

"Wow," Jeff muttered solemnly as I pulled the story to a close. "Man, that was a rough one."

"Yeah." Charlie frowned. "I got shivers just hearing you talk about the way Samuel acted. I can't imagine how bad it must have been to be there."

"It was unsettling." I nodded. "You could tell that he really felt no remorse about the things he'd done."

The kids were all quiet and serious. Even Ty, who was usually the most boisterous of the bunch, was staring thoughtfully ahead.

"But he did end up paying for it, right?" Jeff asked. "What happened at the trial?"

"Oh, the judge threw the book at him," I replied.

"He died in his prison cell, just like I told him he would."

"Good," Mac replied with a firm nod. "Although it doesn't make up for what those poor women had to go through."

"Yeah," Charlie chimed in. "What happened to all the women?"

"Olivia made sure they were all well taken care of." I smiled fondly. "She was absolutely devoted to her job and the victims she helped. She made sure that the ones who wanted to go back home got there and that the ones who just wanted a new start, like Daniela, got that too."

"So, Daniela wasn't with the traffickers?" Jeff asked as he leaned his elbows onto the bar top. "I mean, she acted kind of sketchy, and even that one girl, Jenny, said she didn't really trust her."

"Daniela was a victim just as much as any of them," I replied as I took a sip of my drink. It was always a little hard to recall the details of some of these more brutal cases, and a nice shot of liquor helped dull the sting. "It turned out that she'd been there for a really long time, about as long as Allison had, though she was much older when she was kidnapped. Working as a sort of warden for the traffickers was just a survival mechanism. She did what she had to do to survive, and in the end, it was beneficial to us since the men trusted her enough that she was able to help us with our plan."

"Man, that's sad." Ty shook his head. "Having to work with the enemy just to survive? That must mess with your head."

"I think so too." I nodded. "Maybe that's why she wanted to have a clean start. Last I heard, she took off to someplace in Europe, as far away from Turks & Caicos as she could get."

"I don't blame her," Mac snorted before taking a sip of her beer. "Oh, and what happened to Eddy? Did he get to stay with his Grandma?"

"Of course." I smiled in response. "There were a few issues with social services and such. He was severely malnourished, developmentally delayed, and just in a very bad state when he was found. They needed to make sure they did right by him, but Olivia was there every step of the way to make sure that he got back to his grandmother and aunt as soon as possible."

"That's good," Charlie replied. "I'm glad the little dude got a happy ending. I can't imagine being, what, five years old? Going through all the stuff he did? Little man's a fighter."

"He is," I agreed. "He's doing well, too. His aunt,

Christina, kept us updated for a few years. From what I heard, he made it into a pretty prestigious university a few years back."

"What about Olivia?" Jeff suddenly changed the subject with a sly smirk. "Seems like she was competing with Tessa there at the end with the *Dragon's Rogue* stuff."

"Answering texts from a woman while you're in bed with another one," Mac shook her head in mock disapproval. "For shame, Ethan."

"Hey, it was an important text!" I replied with a chuckle. "I needed to answer it. And Olivia did stick around for a while."

"Oh, really?" Charlie asked. "I wanna hear more about that."

"What?" Jeff scoffed at him before turning to look at me. "Man, forget that. I want to hear about the *Dragon's Rogue*. Come on, you can't leave us hanging. What was inside the chest?"

"Oh, would you look at the time?" I teased them as I pretended to glance at the clock on the wall. "It's getting pretty late. I think we should call it a night."

"What? No!" Ty groaned. "You always do this!"

"Then you should be used to it by now." I smirked. "Another time, kids. If I keep going, we'll be here all night."

"Okay," Jeff sighed as he finished his drink and hopped off the stool. "But I'm holding you to that. The next time we come back, you better tell us what was in there."

"I promise," I laughed as the kids all got up and made their way out of the bar. As usual, they were my last customers. Even Nadia had gone home already. Though she usually stayed for my stories, she'd said something about having a prior engagement.

As I got up to lock up for the night, I glanced up at the massive sheet of parchment that was mounted on the wall above the bar. It had been in several pieces once. It had taken me quite a long time to find someone who was able to get it put back together and framed so I could hang it up like this.

It was an 18th-century map of the world, worn and yellowed with age, so faded in some spots that it was difficult to tell where the X's were marked unless you looked up close.

I smirked to myself as I remembered the story of that map. The kids were just going to have to wait.

AUTHOR'S NOTE

Hey, if you got here, I just want you to know that you're awesome! I wrote this book just for someone like you, and if you want another one, it is super important that you leave a review.

The more reviews this book gets, the more likely it is there will be a sequel to it. After all, I'm only human, and you have no idea how far a simple "your book was great!" goes to brighten my day.

Also, if you want to know when the sequel comes out, you absolutely must join my Facebook group and follow me on Amazon. Doing one won't be enough because it relies on either Facebook or Amazon telling you the book is out, and they might not do it.

You might miss out on all my books forever, if you only do one!

Here's the link to follow me through e-mail.

Here's the link to my Facebook Group.

Made in the USA
Columbia, SC
31 March 2025